'One of the sexiest, most compelling debuts I've come across this year, it cries out to become a TV drama. But I recommend you read it first.'
Daily Mail

'Gripping, tragic, and sometimes insane, Guilt is an intense exploration of love, sibling relationships, obsession, drug abuse, secrets, and rape.'
Seattle Book Review

'Fast moving. Compulsive reading.'
Jane Corry, author of *The Dead Ex*

'An addictive, compelling read, full of tension.'
Karen Hamilton, author of *The Perfect Girlfriend*

'Absolutely powered through Guilt. Totally addictive and unputdownable.'
Roz Watkins, author of *The Devil's Dice*

'I read Guilt over one weekend, completely enthralled. This twisty and complex tale of twin sisters and the dangerous, damaged man who comes between them kept me guessing.'
Emma Curtis, author of *When I Find You*

'Robson's writing is sharp and emotive; the plot so tense and engaging. A fantastic read.'
Elisabeth Carpenter, author of *99 Red Balloons*

'Packed with shocking twists, Guilt is a gritty, page-turning read that is not to be missed.'
Petrina Banfield, author of *Letters from Alice*

'I absolutely loved it and raced through it. Thrilling,
unputdownable a fabulous ~~...~~ ~~...~~ ~~roaster~~ of a read –
I was obsessed by this book.'
B.A. Paris, bestselling author of
Behind Closed Doors* and *Bring Me Back

'*Obsession* is a welcome addition to the domestic
noir bookshelf. Robson explores marriage, jealousy
and lust with brutal clarity, making for a taut thriller
full of page-turning suspense.'
Emma Flint, author of *Little Deaths*

'What a page turner! Desperately flawed characters.
Bad behaviour. Drugs. Sex. Murder. It's all in there, on every
page, pulling you to the next chapter until you find out
where it will all end. I was compelled not only to see what
every one of them would do, but also how they would
describe their actions – they are brutally honest and stripped
bare. This is one highly addictive novel!'
Wendy Walker, author of *All Is Not Forgotten*

'A compelling page-turner on the dark underbelly
of marriage, friendship & lust. (If you're considering
an affair, you might want a rethink.)'
Fiona Cummins, author of *Rattle*

'Very pacy and twisted – a seemingly harmless conversation
between husband and wife spins out into a twisted web of
lies and deceit with devastating consequences.'
Colette McBeth, author of *The Life I Left Behind*

ENVY

After graduating, Amanda Robson worked in medical research at The London School of Hygiene and Tropical Medicine, and at the Poisons Unit at Guy's Hospital where she became a co-author of a book on cyanide poisoning. Amanda attended the Faber novel writing course and writes full-time. Her debut novel, *Obsession*, became a bestseller in 2017 and has received widespread acclaim from authors and press alike. Her second novel, *Guilt*, was a *Sunday Times* bestseller. *Envy* is her third book.

By the same author:

Obsession
Guilt

AMANDA ROBSON

ENVY

avon.

Published by AVON
A division of HarperCollins*Publishers* Ltd
1 London Bridge Street
London SE1 9GF

www.harpercollins.co.uk

A Paperback Original 2019

1

A catalogue copy of this book is available from the British Library.

ISBN: 978-0-00-829187-7

Typeset in Bembo by Palimpsest Book Production Ltd, Falkirk, Stirlingshire
Printed and bound in UK by CPI Group (UK) Ltd, Croydon CR0 4YY

MIX
Paper from
responsible sources
FSC™ C007454

To my family.

1

Erica

I watch you every day, walking past my flat on the way to the school drop-off, holding your older daughter's hand, pushing the younger one along in the buggy. Sometimes strolling and chatting. Sometimes rushing. Usually wearing your gym kit. Judging by your body shape, your commitment to exercise is worth it. I wish I had a figure like yours.

Your older daughter has gappy teeth and straggly hair. Nowhere near as pretty as you. Your husband must have diluted the gene pool. The younger one, the toddler, is always asleep in the buggy. She looks to have stronger hair, and a chubbier face. I would have loved to have children, but I've never been in the right relationship.

I envy you, and have from the first moment I saw you scurry past. A moment I recall so well. I was bored. I had nothing to do but look out of my front window, and watch the world go by. Three p.m. Parents rushing to the primary school at pickup time. Parents, nannies, and then you. The woman I would look like if I could, moving past me. The image of my mother from my only remaining photograph. So similar you made me hold my breath.

A few days ago, when you dropped your gym card, I finally found out that your name is Faye Baker. You didn't notice it fall from the back pocket of your jeans as you tightened your laces, did you? As you turned in to the school gates I left my flat, and crossed the road to pick it up. Later that day I handed it in to the school reception. Were you grateful, Faye?

2

Faye

We move towards the school gates through air intertwined with drizzle. The drizzle tightens and turns to icy drops of rain, which spit into my face and make me wince a little. I squeeze my elder daughter Tamsin's hand more tightly.

'Let's hurry up, otherwise we'll be drenched,' I tell her.

Together, we push the buggy and run laughing into the school playground. Breathless now, Tamsin and I hug and part. My five-year-old disappears into the classroom. Into its light and warmth. Its quirky smell of woodchip and Play-Doh.

Free for a while from the responsibility of looking after her, my body lightens. But the rain is thickening. I fasten the rain hood more tightly across the buggy and navigate our way back across the playground, sighing inside, dodging puddles. Later on I'll have to do my hair again. I always have to do my hair again when it rains.

As I walk along the side of Twickenham Green, past the bistro restaurant that used to be the public toilets, towards the gym – trainers squelching across dark grey paving stones, the rain begins to fall in sheets. Through the town centre, rain intensifying. I arrive at the Anytime Leisure Club looking as if I've been for a swim, and use my card to check through reception. Some kind soul handed it in to the school office when I dropped it last week. Georgia is still fast asleep in her buggy as I deposit her in the crèche.

At last, still rather damp, I make it into class. Legs, bums and tums today. Anastasia, our instructor, stands beaming at the front. She is about ten years older than me. Her healthy glow contains a whiff of Botox and facial fillers. An attractive hint of plasticity that so many people have these days. I'll have to start before too long, when my husband Phillip gets his next major pay rise. The sooner you start the greater the effects. I've read about it on the internet.

Anastasia begins. We copy. Stretching out on our floor mats, progressing through our usual early positions. Back stretch first, then gentle stomach crunches. My body is my asset. I was academic at school. I have good GCSEs. Good A levels. But lots of people have good A levels, and not many people have a body like mine. My face and body are what differentiate me. I need to work hard to maintain them. My exercise class is my everyday routine; essential for my career.

'Lift your right elbow to your left knee,' Anastasia instructs in her bell-like voice.

My mind starts to drift back to the evening I became Miss Surrey. Eighteen years old, standing on stage decked in a ribbon and a crown, listening to the clapping of the audience. So beautiful. So special. Nothing else mattered but the moment. My stomach tightens in pain. That moment didn't last. I never became Miss England. The higher echelons of beauty pageants were denied to me.

'Lie back and stretch. Arms above your head,' Anastasia bellows from the front.

But age has brought a maturity to my beauty that has improved my looks. And several modelling jobs: M&S Foods, Accessorize, and the Littlewoods magazine. Not much to shout about, but give me time.

'Lower the right arm. Keep the left arm raised. Back flat against the floor. Flat as you can. Don't forget to breathe.'

I'll get my break, one day. Slowly, slowly, I breathe in. Slowly, slowly, I exhale. Until that day I must look after my body, and never give up.

3

Erica

I watch you walk past, faster than usual because of the sudden heavy rain, which has really caught you out. You are not even wearing a raincoat. Your normally bouffant hair is wet and flat. Why don't you wear a hat, just in case? Are you too cool for that, Faye?

After you have gone, the cold of my flat begins to sink into my bones and I find myself shivering. I have been living here for two years, surrounded by fingers of mould, which creep up the tile grouting and form a black mist on the walls. The central heating doesn't work. I have tried contacting the landlord, but he never replies. Sometimes I use a fan heater, but it doesn't really help. It just circulates overheated air making me feel so claustrophobic that after about twenty minutes I turn it off. So most of the time in winter I walk around my flat wrapped in a scratchy old blanket. Mouse says I look like a tramp in it, so I try not to wear it when he is around. Not that he comes here very often. His flat is so much more comfortable than mine; I usually visit him there.

I sit, feeling empty inside. Coping with each day has, for many years, been a struggle. A plethora of temporary jobs. No focus. But it's become easier in the last six months. Since I started to follow you. Since I started spending time with Mouse. It's raining today, so I cannot follow you. When it rains I need to check on Mouse.

Mouse lives in the flat directly above mine. I pad up the communal staircase.

'It's Erica,' I shout through his letter box.

Slowly, slowly, the door opens. I step straight into his living room. He stands in front of me, agitated.

'Wotcha.'

'Wotcha, Erica,' he replies.

I high-five him. He high-fives me back. A ritual between us, the result of watching too many American films together. I cast my eye around his flat and feel a tremor of envy. His father bought it for him, and helped him decorate it. It has central heating that works, and is beautifully appointed. IKEA furniture. Copious kitchen equipment. But then Mouse is vulnerable and he really needs his father's help. I must not resent the good fortune of a friend.

He walks into the sitting area of his living room. I follow him. He stalks up and down in front of the window, wringing his hands and glowering at the rain. I walk over to him and put my hand on his arm.

'The rain isn't going to hurt you.' I pause and look into his anxious face.

Grey-brown eyes stiffen. 'It wants to.'

'It can't, remember? As long as you stay inside.'

His eyes soften. He frowns. He sighs and flops down into the middle of the sofa. I sink into the easy chair opposite him.

Mouse. Thirty years old. Nicknamed Mouse because of his timid personality and grey-brown hair.

'What's up?' he asks.

'Been busy.'

'Because of Faye?'

'Yep.'

He leans across and takes my hands in his, face pressed towards mine. 'But you're here today.'

I squeeze his hands. Mouse has difficulty reading emotions

and suffers from phobias. I have confidence issues because of my upbringing. Perhaps one day I will be able to overcome them. But Mouse won't recover from his issues. He just has to learn to live in this world despite them. That's why Mouse's father has done so much to support him. Mouse's father is my hero. I wish I had a father like that. But I do not have a father. My mother never knew who my father was.

We sit in silence for a while.

'I've bought something at the charity shop,' Mouse eventually announces as he pads across the room. 'I'll show you.'

Rain forgotten now that I'm here, he opens his living room cupboard and pulls out a large cardboard box. He places it in the middle of the sitting area, lifts out a silver and bronze chess set, the pieces finely etched, and puts it on the floor. He stands up, shoulders back in pride.

'That looks fantastic,' I tell him.

He smiles at me. A broad, effervescent smile. When he smiles, despite his rough-hewn features, Mouse is good-looking.

'Do you want to play chess with me?'

'You'll have to teach me.'

'That's fine. I bought it for both of us so that we could play together.'

My heart lurches. What would I do if I didn't have Mouse?

I close my eyes and feel again my mother's heat as I lay clamped against her, waiting for her to wake up. I feel her breath steady and even, not the agonising rasping I heard when I first called the ambulance. Eleven years old. A man stepping towards me, to prise me away. A man who smells of nicotine and mint. The social worker in charge of my case. I shudder inside and push the memory away. My mind is back. Back in Mouse's comfortable flat.

'Come on, Erica, I'll teach you how to play chess,' he says, flicking his grey-brown locks.

4

Faye

Home from the gym. In my bedroom, trying to rescue my hair.
I have managed to wash it. But Georgia has woken from her
morning nap, so drying it will be a problem.

'I'm not Georgia any more,' she tells me. 'I'm a kangaroo.'

She bends down, face plastered in a mischievous grin. 'I need
to do my hopping practice.' She begins to hop around our
bedroom. Even though she is only three years old, she is heavy
enough to make the floorboards vibrate. I shouldn't have let her
sleep for so long. Now she is full of energy. She picks up my
Chanel perfume.

'Kangaroos like perfume,' she announces, spraying it into the
air around her.

I snatch it away and put it in a drawer. 'They don't like
perfume. They like grass.'

'Come on then, Mummy, let's go outside and get some.'

'I can't go outside, I need to dry my hair.'

'Well I'll go then,' she says, jumping towards the door.

I lean across and lock it. 'No. No. You can't go alone. I'll come
outside with you later.'

'OK, Mummy, I'll wait.'

She jumps up and down on the spot. She bounces towards
the dressing table, and picks up my new eyeshadow.

'Kangaroos like wearing make-up too.'

'No they don't. Kangaroos like sitting on their mummy's bed watching films.'

I sweep her into my arms and lift her onto the bed. I snap the TV on and find *The Jungle Book*, her favourite film, on Amazon Prime. I sit at my dressing table, brush my hair and switch the hairdryer on. She slips off the bed and moves towards me. She shakes my leg to get my attention.

'Where do shadows come from?' she asks.

I snap the hairdryer off. 'Go back and watch the video. Ask Daddy tonight,' I suggest. 'He knows that sort of thing.'

Phillip knows so many weird random facts. As soon as I met him I admired his intelligence.

She tosses her head disapprovingly. 'You just want to dry your hair, not talk to me, Mummy.'

'I *need* to dry my hair, Georgia — it's wet.'

She stoops into her kangaroo position again, hands like paws, bent in front of her chest. I scoop her in my arms and place her on the bed again in front of *The Jungle Book*. I sit next to her with my arms around her, to try and calm her. Then when she is engrossed in the movie, I creep away and continue to blow-dry my hair. When I have finally finished smoothing my hair, I turn the TV off.

'Come on, we're off to the shops,' I announce.

She wriggles off the sofa and slips her hand in mine.

'Can I walk, Mummy? Leave the buggy here?'

Her walking is more of a totter than a walk. But she smiles at me, and as soon as I see her smile, I melt. So after wrapping up against the rain, brandishing a brolly this time, we leave our modern town house, holding hands. Georgia is now tired of being a kangaroo. Just when I would like to go quickly, we move like snails. Turning the corner past the line of fine Victorian houses, towards the high street. Right onto the main road. Past the green, beneath the bridge. Dust from passing traffic spitting into our faces as we slowly progress towards the centre of town.

At last we arrive at a narrow doorway between the bank and the chip shop. The entrance for Serendipity Model Agency. The scent of the chip shop assaults my nostrils as I press the buzzer. The speaker attached to the buzzer vibrates. I lean my weight on the door and we tumble inside.

Slowly, slowly, still holding hands, we pad upstairs to Serendipity Model Agency, run solely by my agent, Mimi Featherington. She has ten clients, and a room above the chip shop that always smells of burnt fat.

I knock on the glass door at the top of the stairs.

'Come in,' Mimi invites, opening the door to welcome us. 'How lovely to see you.'

Georgia stares at Mimi's purple Mohican hair. Mimi, a forty-year-old punk rocker, with a neat face spoilt by a plethora of pins sticking into it. We follow Mimi into her office.

'So good to see you,' she simpers.

My heart sinks. Mimi always simpers when she hasn't any news. And I so wanted her to be telling me I had a new modelling contract.

'I just thought I'd pop in and see how things were going,' I say with a shrug of my shoulders.

'Do sit down,' she says gesticulating to the chair in front of her desk. I do as she requests and Georgia scrambles onto my lap.

'What did you want to know?' Mimi asks.

My insides tighten. It's obvious, isn't it? When will she send me some decent work? I've done reasonable work before, haven't I? I need the Serendipity Model Agency to really, really pull their finger out. To get me the work I deserve.

'Just wondered whether you'd heard from the estate agent yet?' I ask, putting my head on one side in an attempt to look as nonchalant as possible.

Mimi's eyes flicker. 'I'm afraid it's a no. They liked you a lot but . . .' She crosses her legs and folds her arms.

I wrap my arms around Georgia and pull her towards me. 'But what?' I ask, smiling bravely.

'They wanted someone a little younger.'

The words I have dreaded for so long, finally spoken. I inhale the scent of Georgia's young skin and for a second, instead of loving her, I envy her.

'But I'm only thirty-four for heaven's sake,' I splutter.

Mimi shakes her head. 'Mid-thirties – a difficult age group to market.'

Anger incubates inside me. If I do not leave quickly it will erupt.

My smile stretches tightly. 'Well let's just hope something else crops up soon. I'd best be off. Time to pick Tamsin up from school.'

'Mummy, Mummy, please can we buy sweeties first?' Georgia asks.

Too weak to argue, I reply, 'Yes. Yes. Of course.'

5

Erica

I look out of the window. It is still raining. I am still in Mouse's flat. Still playing chess. Or at least Mouse is playing. I'm pretending to, but not really concentrating. I am thinking about you, Faye. About wanting to be like you. A better version of myself.

For you look like the woman I might have been, if I'd had a solid start in life. The day I first saw you, walking past my flat, after you had turned in to the school playground I sat on the sofa in my musty home, and yet again studied my mother's photograph, now creased and faded with time. I found myself staring at the once fine lines of her face, knowing that many years ago she must have looked like you. I glanced at my chubby face in the mirror, and knew that I could look like you too, one day, if I wasn't so overweight.

Inspired by your glamour, my first step to improve my looks was a visit to the local Oxfam shop. As soon as I walked in the scent of stale clothing assaulted me. The shop assistant was paler than pale. Frizzy brown hair. Pinprick eyes. Looking bored and sorry for herself, as if she would rather be doling out food in Africa, or building pot-bellied children a new schoolhouse.

I began to flick through the racks of clothes. What had happened to the people who used to wear them? Where were they now? Alive only in other people's memories? I stroked a jaded green party frock and tried to imagine the party it went to. A tea dance in an upmarket hotel. A young girl waltzing with her partner, looking into his eyes wistfully.

I looked across at the row of tweed sports jackets, imagining the elderly men who used to wear them, oppressed by the reminder that the father I never knew has probably died too.

I rummaged through the mixed racks. There was nothing I liked. I sighed inside. Even though I hardly had any money, I wanted to treat myself to something special.

Giving up on the racks, I began to walk around the edge of the shop, looking at the wall displays. Second-hand books. Antique wine glasses too small for modern life. Greetings cards, I didn't have anyone to send to.

Then I turned the corner and came across handbags and shoes; rummaging to try and find something right. Too big. Too small. Too frumpy. I finally found a pair of suede boots: trendy and grungy. I pulled my trainers off and thrust my feet into them. One glance and I knew I'd buy them. But my feet would be so much more attractive than the rest of me, and I knew I needed to start work on everywhere else.

'Are you all right, Erica?' Mouse asks, grey-brown eyes darkening. 'Are you playing chess, or are you sitting looking out of the window and daydreaming?'

I squirm in my seat. 'I'm thinking about chess of course,' I lie.

Mouse grins. My stomach twists. Mouse has a lovable grin.

'I can tell you're not concentrating because you are giving away pieces too easily. If you were concentrating properly I think you would win.' There is a pause. 'It's your turn now; show me what you've got.'

I grin back at him. 'OK then.' I deliberate for a while and then move my knight to take one of his pawns.

'Not too bad, I suppose.'

He starts to plan his next move. I begin to daydream again. I'm going to be slim, and beautiful. Like you, Faye. I have started a diet. And a few weeks ago I went jogging for the first time. Fifty paces walking slowly. Fifty paces walking fast. Fifty paces jogging. Twice around Marble Hill Park.

Because I've not been able to follow you today, Faye, I'm imagining your movements in my head. Monday. Legs, Bums, and Tums. Stomach crunches galore at the Anytime Leisure Club. If I had enough money I would join a club like that.

'Checkmate,' Mouse announces. 'I've beaten you for the third time today.'

Mouse is grinning at me, dimple playing to the left of his broad mouth. Mouse with his pondering personality that slows the movement of his face.

The alarm on my watch beeps. Twenty-five past three. In five minutes I'll watch you walk past again.

6

Faye

Sitting at the dining table in our living room, the girls settled in bed.

'How was your day?' I ask my husband Phillip, as I watch him spooning pasta into his mouth.

'Fine,' he replies, without looking up.

'Oh come on, I'm at home with the kids. Give me a break, let me hear something about your work environment,' I say.

He looks up and frowns. 'Are you trying to tell me you're bored at home?'

'Did I say that?'

'Not exactly.'

'Not at all.' I pause. 'I just asked about your day.'

He leans back in his chair. He shrugs his shoulders. 'I drove to work. Parked the car. Walked across the car park.' He pauses and smiles. 'And then, the really exciting bit, I fastened the top button on my coat.'

'Did you get a good parking space?' I ask, trying to keep my voice light.

'Did the buggy wheels rotate smoothly today?' he replies.

I take a deep breath. Did I ever find quips like this interesting?

'Is this really how you want to communicate with me this evening?' I ask. 'When I've had a problem arise that I would like to talk about?' His eyes soften in concern. 'For the first time, a client said I was too old for the job,' I continue.

Repeated, the barbs of these words penetrate my mind more deeply. He leans across the table and takes my hands in his. 'You're still beautiful, Faye.' There is a pause. 'But that day was bound to arrive.'

'So you agree?'

'I didn't say that.'

'Oh yes you did.'

7

Erica

Saturday morning. On my own for the weekend as Mouse has gone to see his dad. His dad's name is Angus. Angus is tall, much taller than Mouse. Handsome, like a grey-haired Robbie Williams, with a ready smile and a rectangular face. Mouse looks a bit like him but not quite. Everything about Mouse is not quite. His problems really messed him up when he was younger, but now he is thirty, after special schooling and help from his father, he has learnt to cope with living in society. He recognises signs of emotions now. He understands how he needs to respond to comply. He has a raw honesty in his reactions that I find refreshing.

Saturday morning. Up super-early. Yoghurt and fruit for break-fast. Out for my run.

I count to ten, take a deep breath and start. Fifty paces walking slowly, watching my legs wobble as I move. Fifty paces walking quickly, heart beginning to pound. Running next, breathing quickly. The running hasn't killed me yet. Walking again, the fat on my legs vibrating. Quickly, quickly, heart pulsating. Running again, stabbing pains lacerating my sternum. A stitch-like pain like an iron staple to the right of my groin making me bend over as I walk. How am I going to make it twice around the park?

Visualise. Visualise. I try to picture my rolls of fat. Visualise. That is what it says in my self-help book. I visualise the rolls of fat that circle my back. The lumps of cellulite nestling on my buttocks. The loose skin folds on my inner thighs. Visualising.

Forty-nine. Fifty. Walk fast. One, two, three . . . Jogging, jogging around the park.

I end up doubled up at the park gate. About to vomit. Heart pumping. Chest aching. Feeling light-headed, as if I am about to faint. When I have recovered a little I amble home.

The musty smell of my flat crawls into my bones and cradles my nostrils as I limp towards the shower. I turn the water on and wrap myself in a towel whilst I wait for it to warm up. The plumbing grunts and creaks, like an old man climbing stairs. The water runs brown before it turns clear.

I test the water with my fingers. It still feels like ice. I am tempted not to bother, to just get dressed without a shower, but that is the start of a sort of slovenliness that I don't want to be guilty of.

I wait another five minutes and then I step into the shower. The water is hot and satisfying now. It pummels my body and the more it presses against me, the more I relax. I soap myself with the lavender shower gel that Mouse bought me last Christmas. I start by lathering my generous thighs. Not taut and firm like yours yet, Faye, still dimpled with cellulite; down, down, towards my tree-trunk calves and broad ankles.

I massage and rub. It feels so soothing. So liberating. Upwards, upwards. Fingers circulating around my gelatinous breasts, my rolls of stomach fat. Fingers soaping into skin crevices. One day, Faye, if I keep working hard, my fat will dissolve, and I will be toned and slim like you. Showered and dressed. Jeans and a jumper. Grey duffel coat that I have had for twenty years, and a black beanie hat. I step out into a cold sunny morning and wait at the bus stop across the road from your house. Every time a bus comes I ignore it.

Your front door opens and your Zac Efron of a husband steps out carrying a suitcase. A weekend bag. He waves his car keys. Lights flash. The boot opens. He flings the suitcase inside and drives off.

I continue watching your house. Buses that I do not get on continue to lumber past. I look at my watch. Nine a.m. Your curtains still haven't opened, but the girls must have been awake for hours by now. Are you ignoring them? Rolling over in bed and trying to catch a little more sleep?

Nine-thirty a.m. The living room curtains are opening and you are standing looking out at the day wearing your short velvet dressing gown, displaying perfectly tanned golden legs. How have your legs become so golden? I didn't see you going to the tanning shop. I must add it to my places to watch.

I wait and wait. Sitting in the bus cubicle, blowing onto my hands to try and keep them warm. The 33 arrives. An elderly man stumbles off. The 270 thunders past. The 490 stops. Three teenagers who have been smoking and chatting stub their cigarettes out on the pavement and alight. Mid-morning now. The bus stop is becoming busier.

At last I see you, Faye, emerging from your house with Tamsin and Georgia. I got close enough the other day to hear you say their names. You are wearing skin-tight black jeans, black stiletto heels and a black suede jacket. Very nice, Faye. And I like the pink cashmere scarf and pink lipstick to brighten things up. On this cold Saturday morning, the world needs brightening up.

Holding Tamsin's hand, pushing Georgia along in the buggy, striding purposefully out of your front gate and turning right. I cross the road and walk behind you at a distance.

8

Faye

'You can choose a big bag of sweets later, as long as you go into the Bentall Centre crèche now and behave yourself,' I beg Tamsin as we walk hand in hand towards the railway station to catch the train to Kingston upon Thames. With my other hand I am pushing her baby sister along in the buggy. Georgia is fast asleep.

'But, Mummy, why? Where are you going?' Tamsin asks, clinging on to my hand more tightly.

'I've got to go to the hairdresser's, and a few shops, to get ready for tonight.'

'What's tonight?'

'A party.'

Tamsin's eyes widen. 'Will Harry Styles be there?'

I wish, I say to myself as I shake my head. 'Not exactly!' I pause. 'But I've got to look my best.'

Tamsin jumps up and down. 'You always look good, Mummy.'

Good, but not good enough.

Cheered by the promise of sweets, Tamsin climbs cheerfully onto a seat on the train, staring out of the window eagerly. She clings tightly to my hand as we arrive in Kingston, and progress slowly through the hordes of Saturday morning shoppers, towards the Bentall Centre. She trips cheerfully into the crèche, blowing me kisses, as I deposit Georgia who is fast asleep in the buggy. Relieved to have dropped them off with so little fuss, I set off into the main body of the shopping centre, towards my appointments. Eyebrows. Nails. Blow-dry. Boring but necessary. Tedium is the first part of this job; perseverance the second. One scout to spot me. Making contact with the right agent. That is all it would take. And Jamie Westcote will be there tonight.

9

Erica

I follow you into the shopping centre. I hover behind you as you drop the children into the crèche at the entrance, pretending I am queuing to pick someone up. Georgia is fast asleep in her buggy. Tamsin clings on to your hand so tightly. Oh, Faye, is that because you are leaving her again? So many Saturdays spent in the crèche. Half their lives playing with children they don't know, and will never see again.

You drop your girls off and leave the reception area with a shrug of your shoulders, looking relieved. You wait for the lift. When it arrives, I follow you in.

I like your perfume, Faye, a musky combination of vanilla and ginger. I look across at you in the lift. I do not allow myself to stare at you when I am close. A rule I break today. Today I treat myself. Your violet eyes catch mine. I lose myself and smile. You smile back. Two friendly women, about to go shopping on a Saturday morning, smiling at one another. How natural is that?

The lift stops on the second floor and you get out. You disappear into the nail and brow bar. I watch and wait in the coffee shop opposite.

10

Faye

Sophia and Ron's party in their Victorian house in Strawberry Hill. I arrive and kiss my hosts, handing Sophia a hand-tied bouquet from the local florist's.

'Thank you for the flowers, darling,' Sophia says, placing them on the marble table in her generous hallway. 'Come and say hello to everyone,' she instructs, putting her arm around me and guiding me into the living room.

I am only half an hour late, and already the room is teeming with people. People shoulder to shoulder, glasses in hand, chatting and laughing. She pushes me towards the first group we come to, closest to the door.

'This is Faye,' she announces, 'a famous model.'

Conversation interrupted, they turn to look at me.

'Hardly famous,' I mutter.

'But a model though?' a woman with a high forehead and protruding teeth asks.

'Yes.'

I feel hot with embarrassment. What qualifies me to say I'm a model? An agent? Having been paid for three photoshoots? When will my attempts at this profession seem real?

The woman smiles at me, and takes my arm. 'Let me introduce you to a friend of mine then.'

She leads me across the room and taps a man on the shoulder. He turns round and smiles at her. He has short black curly hair, and dark eyes like pinpricks in his pale face. He is wearing russet corduroy trousers, and a shirt decorated in brown and red concentric circles.

'Jamie, let me introduce . . .' She stalls as she realises she doesn't know my name.

'Faye Baker,' I say, offering my hand to introduce myself.

'Jamie Westcote.'

It's him. Jamie Westcote of Top Models. The man I came here to meet. This is it. My big opportunity. The woman who introduced me disappears.

'I'm a model,' I say, 'with the Serendipity Agency. Let me give you my card.'

Hands trembling, I fumble in my handbag, pull it out and hand it to him. But he does not accept it. Instead, he leads me to the side of the room, away from the group.

'I need to explain why I can't accept your card.' There is a pause. 'I don't put people on my books unsolicited,' he announces. His eyes meander slowly up and down my body. 'And I think it is only fair to tell you that your looks are too regular. Even if you approached me through the correct channels I wouldn't be interested.' He pauses. 'We're looking for something – a bit different.' I feel hot, and know I am blushing. 'You could try for catalogues, I suppose. But you need to be a standard size for that.' Another glance. 'And I guess your chest is too big.' There is another pause. 'In actual fact breasts are out of fashion, as are over-contrived looks.' He smiles a half-smile, head on one side. 'Sorry. I'm only being honest. At least you've had a free appraisal.'

Before I have time to pretend to thank him, he shrugs his shoulders, turns and walks away. Back to his group who lean towards him, sharing a joke, laughing. He puts his head back and joins in, leaving me standing at the edge of a room of noisy people with no one to talk to and no glass in my hand.

Feeling empty and low, I move past shoulders, across the drawing room into the hallway. I step into the cloakroom for privacy, and sit on the toilet seat, head in hands, trying to compose myself. Over-contrived looks. How stupid I have been. How naive. The thought of meeting this man has been keeping me buoyed up for weeks. I press speed dial on my mobile phone to try to get through to Phillip. He doesn't pick up. Pity. Just hearing his voice would make me feel better, or would have made me feel better in the past. The words we spoke to each other a few nights ago reverberate in my head.

'A client said I was too old for the job.'

'You're still beautiful, Faye, but that day was bound to arrive.'

I pull myself up from the toilet seat and splash cold water on my face. I freshen my make-up and step out of the cloakroom into the hallway. Time to get myself a stiff drink.

A man is walking towards me. Jonah. Phillip's oldest friend from school and university. Not only Phillip's close friend, but our architect as well. The man I suggested should supervise our loft conversion.

'Faye, how lovely to see you.' He pulls me towards him, irradiating me with an overdose of aftershave and kissing me on both cheeks. 'A vision of beauty to liven up a boring party.' He holds my eyes in his. 'Is Phillip here? I haven't seen him for ages. I'd love to have a chat with him.'

'He's away at a conference; you'll have to chat to me instead.'

11

Jonah

'Away at a conference,' I say. 'I see. I'll have to catch him another time.'

You are looking more beautiful than ever, with your colt-like legs. Your tiny waist. Your ample breasts. I stand looking at you, imagining, as I have so many times before, their shape unfettered by the confines of a bra. Tip-tilted. Large alveoli. Bell-like. Your hair and your eyes shine. Like Elizabeth Taylor, you are exotic and colourful. The excitement that simmers whenever I see you rises inside me.

'This Prosecco diluted with orange juice is a bit insipid,' I say raising my almost empty glass. 'Would you care to accompany me to the kitchen to find something proper to drink?' I manage to ask, holding your violet blue eyes in mine. 'What about it?'

You pause. You swallow. I watch your Adam's apple move up and down your pretty throat. 'Good idea,' you reply.

Together we move away from the main party, out of the hallway and through the children's sitting room – plain sofas, large TV and an Xbox with surround sound – into the kitchen.

The kitchen is a hive of activity. The catering company are buzzing around like flies, putting the finishing touches on trays of canapés, loading the dishwasher with used glasses. A tiny woman, wearing a blue uniform, with a face so delicate she looks like a flower ambles towards us. 'Any chance of some whisky?' I ask.

25

'Of course, Sir, I'll find you some. Ron has quite a collection. Any particular brand?'

'Glenmorangie is my favourite.

'What about you, Faye?'

'Red wine please.'

The catering assistant reaches into a box stacked in the corner, pulls out a bottle of red wine, and opens it expertly with a flick of her wrist, pouring you a glass and leaving the bottle on the counter. Then she pads over to a cupboard in the corner and pulls out a black and orange bottle containing my favourite tipple. She pours a generous amount into a crystal glass.

'Ice? Ginger?'

'No thanks.'

I sweep the wine bottle from the counter, put a hand on your back to guide you, and carrying our drinks we step back into the children's sitting room.

'Let's just stay here, away from the riff-raff,' I suggest, sinking into a sofa to the right of the door.

You laugh, kick off your killer heels and sink gratefully next to me onto the sofa. It sags in the middle and my body has slipped to lean against yours. I want to bury myself in your scent.

'You are so beautiful, Faye. But you know that, don't you? People must always be telling you that.'

You lean more closely against me. My right hand hovers near the small of your back.

12

Faye

Sitting on a sofa with Jonah, feeling light-headed and floaty because I've had too much to drink. Jonah's hand is massaging the base of my spine and I know I should be pushing him away, but he is making me feel relaxed. So relaxed. The image of Jamie Westcote's eyes running over my body keeps rolling across my mind, alongside Phillip's words. I am playing a game in my head, imagining Jamie Westcote is leaning towards me and speaking, his words contorting to say what I wanted to hear, Phillip standing beside him nodding his head.

'I love regular looks,' Jamie whispers. 'Your breasts are magnificent.' His whisper rises to a shout. Everyone at the party is listening. I see faces turning towards him. 'Regular looks are where it's all at now.'

But it isn't Jamie Westcote who is speaking, it's Jonah. Jonah is speaking, and massaging the base of my spine. He pulls me towards him and kisses me. When he has tried to do this on previous occasions I have pushed him away. But tonight, I find myself kissing him back. It is so long since anyone except Phillip has kissed me that the novelty of someone else's touch burns my skin like fire. Jonah is looking at me admiringly, making me feel special. Admiration is incendiary tonight.

13

Erica

The moon is high. An owl hoots from the trees in the park across the road. I yawn and tighten the top button of my duffel coat. People have been leaving in dribs and drabs, the host and hostess seeing them off.

The door opens. It is you at last, wrapped in a blond man's arms.

'Don't worry, I'll walk her home,' the man is saying, smiling at the hostess.

The front door closes. You walk down the drive, stones crunching beneath your feet, holding on to the man for support. Loose-limbed. Face flushed. When you reach the end of the drive you turn left not right. Where are you going, Faye?

14

Phillip

At the Digital Marketing Conference in Harrogate. The hotel is large and Victorian and has seen better days. The dinner is held in a function room in the basement, with no windows. Dark red patterned carpet. Violent red walls. White linen tablecloths and solid silver cutlery add a touch of sophistication. The man sitting to my left has a pale face and stale breath. The woman to my right is punchy and interesting, so punchy and interesting she makes me feel tired. The food is as it always is at conferences. Acceptable. Unremarkable. But I am not a foodie, so it doesn't matter to me. I wash it down with plenty of wine. The speeches aren't too bad. One of them is quite amusing and makes me laugh.

And now dinner is over and we are free to proceed to the bar. The man on my left at dinner sticks to me like a leech. He buys me a large glass of wine and himself a double whisky, and slurs his words as he eulogises about Professor Torrington's lecture on algorithms earlier.

I excuse myself by pretending I need to go to the toilet, and return to my room, where I drink two cups of peppermint tea in an attempt to sober up, and watch the Sky evening news. I text you twice. You don't reply. I hope you're having a good time. You were worried about going to the party alone. I want to touch base and speak to you. I never feel right when I can't reach you. Tired but restless, I try to settle to sleep but my mind is too alert. I miss your warm body lying next to me. I think back to the day we met.

I was twenty-five. You were twenty-three. I was a digital marketing executive for a small company that had offices on Upper Ground, between Waterloo Station and the river, round the corner from The London Studios. You had just joined the company as PA to my boss. I got chatting to you as I waited to go into a meeting with him. Asking you to come for a drink tripped naturally off my tongue; the pretext for me to tell you about the company. You agreed readily, and a few evenings later we met on the pavement outside the office and hailed a taxi to *Tattershall Castle*, an old paddle steamer converted into a pub restaurant, moored on Victoria Embankment.

It was a soft summer evening, warm breeze from the river caressing our faces and arms. The grey Thames sparkling to silver and diamonds. You sat opposite me and leant forward. I was mesmerised by your violet eyes.

'Tell me everything about Digital Services Limited. All the gossip. The full rundown,' you demanded.

Before I could begin to hold forth, we were interrupted by a waiter asking us what we wanted to drink. I ordered pale ale. You ordered a white wine spritzer. Do you remember, Faye? And then I told you everything I knew. The services we provided. The names of our major clients. The personalities and foibles of our managers. Somewhere in the middle of my diatribe our drinks arrived, and a small dish of cashew nuts. I wolfed the nuts down; you didn't touch one.

We ordered another drink each. The alcohol was beginning to relax me; soften my edges. You put your hand on my arm.

'Phillip, you know so much.'

Desire rose inside me like an electric current. 'What about you, Faye? Tell me about yourself. I've rabbited on for long enough.'

'I want to be a full-time model. So far I've just had a few jobs.'

First and foremost, you've always wanted to be a model. You still want to be a model. However hard I work to give you a comfortable lifestyle with the girls, our life together isn't enough to sustain you. You want others to admire your body. The more time goes on the more I question how comfortable I am with that. Sometimes I wish you were less good-looking and we didn't have all this angst.

15

Jonah

You are sitting on a sofa, in the middle of my drawing room. I've admired you for so long I can't believe you are here in my home, visiting me alone. The first time I saw you was ten years ago, when I visited Phillip in London. You were, and still are, the most beautiful woman I have ever seen, with your long dark hair, your chiselled cheekbones and violet eyes. It was your eyes that unnerved me most; the way they slipped into mine, like velvet.

I hadn't met up with Phillip for a few years at that point and was surprised my computer geek friend had managed to attract such a glamorous girlfriend. He'd never been much of a ladies' man. The three of us met up in a Pizza Express near Charing Cross – Phillip's suggestion, not mine – I don't usually frequent pizzerias or chain restaurants. I survived the ordeal by looking into your eyes as I choked on an overdose of basil and tomato.

Tonight, so many years on, still besotted, 'Would you like a nightcap?' I ask.

'Just a small one thanks, nothing too strong.'

'Gin and tonic OK?'

'Lovely thanks.'

My hand slips as I pour the gin, so I give you quite a slug. We sit next to one another on the sofa sipping our drinks. Softly, gently, I put my arm around you. You lean in to my body. I hold you more tightly and take your hand in mine.

16

Faye

I am standing in front of Jonah. I feel confused; sad and happy at the same time. I know I ran into him at the party and that I have gone back to his house. His sitting room is spinning around me. Slowly. Quickly. Slowly. Now I am holding on to him to keep standing.

'Let me look at you, really look at you,' he says.

His arms are behind my back and he is unzipping my dress. I work so hard toning my body, working on almost every muscle, or at least every muscle I know about, so I want to show him, really show him. I am not embarrassed. I am proud of my shape.

I feel my dress slip over my skin and fall to the floor. I am standing in front of him in my new red silk bra and panties, decorated with Chantilly lace. The room is slipping from side to side, making me feel as if I am on a boat. He is admiring my body. He is smiling. His eyes are caressing me, just like they have always done. I know he thinks I am beautiful. I need to be beautiful tonight.

17

Jonah

You are moaning beneath me, neck stretched in ecstasy. So tight around me I can hardly breathe. I've never known a woman who wants me so much. And I cannot believe, after waiting so long, that woman is you. I try to close my mind to all sensation so that I don't climax too quickly. I pretend I am back at school, standing behind my desk, reciting the alphabet backwards. Before I reach V, you are finished, spent. And I can relax again.

My crescendo starts gently, slowly, a sweet sensation that feels electric. I pump into you more deeply and it intensifies into a burning heat. Pain and pleasure merge. You are holding me so tight. Your legs and feet push into my back as if you want to force me more deeply inside. It is delicious. Too much. I am not sure how much longer I can bear it. It's rising, it's increasing. I am soaring. One last thrust so sweet I feel ready to die in your arms right now. And it's over. Tangled in your arms I gasp for breath, and wait for my heart to calm.

18

Faye

I wake up, Beethoven pounding in my ears. Mouth parched. Head throbbing. My hair is damp and I am naked, clamped in a stranger's arms.

Heavy inside, I untangle myself from him and sit up. No. Not a stranger. Jonah, my husband's old friend, our architect, who I ran into at the party last night. What have I done? I squint at my watch in the dark: 3:30 a.m. I pull myself up to standing, panic rising inside me.

My marriage. My children. The babysitter.

I snap the light on. I look down at Jonah, sleeping like a baby, penis withered into a small crinkled knot. He doesn't stir. What happened? Jonah has never been my type. The first time I met him he said he thought footballers were overpaid wide boys. I asked him what he thought architects were then, and he gave me a supercilious grin that tightened the knots in my stomach. His long-vowelled voice smacks of superiority, even though he went to a local comprehensive, like me and Phillip. I had a drunken aberration last night, one I will regret for the rest of my life.

Heavy with remorse, I reach for my clothes. I find them scattered across the sitting room, and pull them on. My coat and handbag are in the hallway. I remember leaving them there. I wrap my coat around my shoulders; its familiarity comforts me a little, as I step outside into a bright moonlit night.

35

I pull my iPhone out of my bag. Fifteen missed calls. Thirteen from the babysitter. Two from Phillip. What am I going to say? I need to get used to making up lies. First I text our babysitter. *On the way home. Sorry. Party went on really late. Got carried away.*

Then I check on Phillip. Only two missed calls, and not too late. Just didn't hear those because of the noise of the party. Nothing to explain. I exhale with relief.

We live so close to Jonah it isn't worth calling a taxi. My footsteps resound across the pavement, as I stride through the solidity of darkness towards home. At least it is so late no one I know will see me. Five minutes later I am walking up the steps to our front door, turning the key. I step straight into our living room and turn on the light. The familiarity of my living room surrounds me like a sanctuary. My behaviour is out of step. But nothing here has changed. My normal world is waiting for me.

Lucy, our babysitter, stretches her arms in the air from the sofa, and sits up. Her long brown hair is tangled and crumpled. Her eyes blink as she becomes accustomed to the light.

'I was so worried. Are you OK?' she asks.

I walk towards her and sit on the sofa next to her. I shake my head slowly, and raise my hands a little.

'Sorry. So sorry. Had too much to drink. Stayed too late. Got carried away.'

'Are you sure you're OK? Has something happened?' she asks, looking shocked at my dishevelled appearance.

'Course not,' I reply. 'I fell asleep on the sofa at the end of the party, that's all. A bit embarrassing but all OK.'

'As long as you're all right,' Lucy says, slipping off the sofa and reaching for her bag and coat, which she's placed on the floor beside her: obviously keen to get away as soon as possible.

I rummage hurriedly into my handbag and pull out £100 to give to her. I hand it across.

'That's far too much,' she complains, trying to hand it back.

'No. Let me give it to you. I want to. I've inconvenienced you.'

'Not really,' she says.

'But I worried you,' I splutter.

'A bit. But you're a grown woman. I know you can look after yourself,' she says, leaving the notes on the coffee table. She smiles at me as she pulls her coat on. 'Please don't worry. I'm cool. Everything's fine.'

I scoop the notes from the table and press them into her hand.

'I'm not accepting no for an answer. I want you to have this money. You must take it. Otherwise I'll only send it to you in the post.'

This time her hand closes reluctantly around the notes. As soon as she has gone, I text Jonah:

We need to talk.

19

Phillip

Sunday evening. I pull the car into our drive. Lights smoulder down from the top of the house. I have flowers for you, Faye, and a soft toy each for the girls.

I let myself in and switch on the light. The hallway is filled with its usual clutter. The buggy. A row of shoes. A pile of old clothes to take to the charity shop. This evening the house is eerily quiet. Silence presses against me and the vision I had of you rushing to greet me, smothering me with kisses, echoes towards me making me feel sad.

Perhaps you are having difficulty settling our offspring. I leave my gifts on the dining table and slowly, quietly, move through our living area, and tiptoe up the stairs. Past Tamsin's bedroom, past Georgia's nursery. The lights are dim. I hear the repetitive sound of their gentle breathing. Into our master bedroom with its state-of-the-art bathroom, only recently installed, which I am so pleased to have been able to afford. More dim light. This time I hear electronic music. Pounding and trance-like. You are sitting, back arched, cross-legged on your exercise mat, arms stretched out like a ballet dancer. Not that I am an expert at this, but it's Pilates I guess.

As soon as you see me, you snap the music off and slowly unwrap your body.

'The wanderer returns,' you say as you stand up.

'Not a very exciting wander, I can assure you.'

'It must have been much more exciting than staying at home,' you say with a grimace.

'Haven't you had fun then?'

'Depends what you call fun.'

'Well I don't call sleeping through lectures about computer algorithms fun.'

'And I don't rate being cold-shouldered by a sanctimonious prick who owns his own modelling agency.'

Your eyes are wide and glistening with tears. I take you in my arms and pull you against me. You clamp against my chest as if the world is about to end.

'I ran into Jonah at the party,' you murmur between sobs.

20

Erica

Did you really think no one would see you, Faye? I followed you, hiding in moonlight shadows. How could you disappear behind his shiny front door when you have a husband like yours? Handsome, in a solid way. Supporting you. Helping you with the children. I watch him through my binoculars whenever you leave the curtains open, hugging them and putting them into bed, reading them bedtime stories. I've seen him so many times walking up your drive with takeaways and flowers. Most women would give their right arm for a man like that.

How do you think your behaviour will affect your children? Do you know what it is like for children to have a mother go off the rails? Can you imagine what it was like for me?

And I am back. Remembering. My social worker visiting me in my second foster home. My foster mother flinging plates into the dishwasher, tidying up piles of washing. The social worker had only given us an hour's notice. I helped her tidy up and by the time he arrived I was already drained and exhausted.

We sat opposite one another in the dining room. He sat hands together on his knee, mouth in a line. I knew something bad was coming.

'Erica, your mother is dead.'

'What happened to her?' I spluttered, heart racing in my chest.

'She died of a drugs overdose.'

There was a pause. 'She was peaceful, Erica. She is living with God. Happy in Heaven now.'

Living with God, not with me? I felt empty. Bereft. I had always thought she would come back and care for me. Now I knew I was alone. I was too choked to cry. Bitterness pushed the tears away. Tears would have given me respite. Tears would have helped. But back then, nothing helped.

21

Jonah

I am parked outside your daughter's school in my lilac Jag, waiting to see you. It smells of leather and money. That is why I like it so much. A present to myself for my thirtieth birthday, with some of the money I had just received from my great-grandmother's trust fund. Years ago I tried to let you know you would be better off financially if you chose me. Now so many years on, you are beginning to see sense.

You won't be long. School starts in ten minutes. I watch other mothers sidling past, looking so grey, so colourless. In comparison to you they all look dumpy and plain. I watch their body language as they talk to their children with a pious air.

My body sings as you come into sight. Walking past, coated in skin-tight Lycra. I am ready for you, ready and waiting, blood pulsating through my body. Waiting for you to drop Tamsin off. Waiting for you to get in my car and talk.

22

Faye

I slip into the passenger seat of his car, Georgia fast asleep in my arms.

'Jonah, I'm ashamed about what happened on Saturday night. We both made a terrible mistake. I expect you feel the same about our one-night stand. That it was a total one-off.'

He leans towards me, eyes gleaming. 'I was rather hoping we could go on seeing each other. When you've had a taste of perfection it's good to make it last as long as possible.'

I sit looking at his fine-boned face. His slightly effeminate good looks. How much had I had to drink? I have never previously found him attractive, but somehow suddenly he seemed so empathetic on Saturday night. Being with him felt so right.

'Please, Phillip's your friend too; neither of us want to hurt him. I love him very much. Let's just forget what happened.'

His mouth twists. 'Funny way of showing your feelings, shagging his best friend.'

'I know. I'm appalled by my behaviour.' Tears fill my eyes. 'And I don't want him to know what happened.'

Brown eyes darken. 'It's really not going to be that simple. I can't just let this drop. I'm in love with you, Faye.'

23

Erica

Where are you going? Why are you turning in the opposite direction to my flat? I need to watch you even more carefully now I know how irresponsible you are. Where are you taking Georgia? She needs stability. She's used to the crèche at your leisure club.

I reach for my coat, slam the door, and race down the stairs to follow you. The pedestrian crossing slows me down. The lights take so long. I wait at the crossing and see you walking in the opposite direction, further and further away from me. A car is trailing you. A shiny lilac Jag with a personalised number plate. You stop. The car stops. A blond head of hair leans out of the window. Your boyfriend, the blond guy from the party. Why is he meeting you at school? Is your relationship serious? Are you going to put your children through the trauma of coming from a broken home?

24

Faye

Back in the changing room, after my spinning class, reaching into my locker, I hear my iPhone buzzing. A new message. An electric current burns through me. Not him. Please not him. I told him I didn't love him. I warned him if he told Phillip I'd deny it, and Phillip would trust me over him. But as I stepped out of the car eyes shining into mine, he said, 'I like it when you play hard to get.'

My whole body stiffens when I remember the wolf-like look on his face, his usual veneer of sophistication dissolved away. I take a deep breath. If he causes trouble I'll just have to deny it. Deny. Deny. Deny. No one can prove that he is right. The phone continues to buzz. I sigh with relief as I reach across and pull it towards me, and press green. The agency.

Mimi wants to see me.

As soon as I arrive, she ushers me in. Mimi is dressed down today. Her hair, although still purple, is not gelled into a Mohican. She has forgotten to put the safety pin in her nose. I sit opposite her wondering why she's taken it out. Does it get in the way when she makes love, when she kisses? She smiles at me, and the skin around her eyes crinkles.

'I've got a job for you,' she says.

I open my mouth and close it again.

'Don't look so surprised, I do place people sometimes,' she says.

'What is it?' I ask.

She leans back in her chair and folds her arms as her smile widens. 'An assignment for the local ice-cream company.'

It's not a national campaign, but it's a start. Just the start I needed. A reputable local company. My heart soars.

'What do they have in mind?' I ask.

'A photoshoot. Two days at most. You walking in the local woods wearing a floaty dress licking one of their ice creams, soft-focus lens. "*Dreamy and creamy*", will be the tag line, "*Making you feel as if it's summer all year.*" They're intending to run an ad on the back page of the *Richmond Magazine*, and make a film advert for local cinema.'

'Dreamy and creamy sounds fine to me. I accept.'

'Don't you want to know about the money?'

'Of course I do, just didn't like to ask.'

'Four hundred pounds.'

Four hundred pounds. Not a lot but a job. Something beginning to happen at last. This is a big step up. Maybe my career will take off at last. Maybe one day, in the scale of things, my problem with Jonah will seem irrelevant.

25

Erica

'What's the matter?' Mouse asks, as I sit at his breakfast bar sipping a cappuccino. 'Your lips are curling downwards. Are you in a mood again?'

'Sorry.'

'Don't apologise, just tell me what's wrong. That's what's supposed to happen, isn't it? You worry. Then you tell me about it because I am your friend.'

'It's just that life's so unfair,' I say with a shrug of my shoulders.

He laughs, his strange laugh, like a braying donkey. 'There's nothing new about that.'

'Is that supposed to make it any easier?' I ask.

He puts his arm cautiously around my shoulders, as if he wants to be friendly but is not quite sure how to be.

'Please try and explain.'

'It's the children. Faye's children. How come she's been able to have them when she can't even look after them properly?'

He looks at me intently and his eyes widen. 'Is that what's happening?' he asks.

Yes, I think, but don't reply. It is too painful to speak about. A tear begins to trickle down my face. Yes. These children, who've had such a good start in life, will not get the backing they need because Faye has become distracted.

Look at what happened to me. Did my life start to go wrong,

the minute I was born to a mother who couldn't look after me? Or was it always a disaster from the start?

No. My mother loved me. She looked after me as well as she could, for as long as she could. As a young child I remember her sweet scent as she held me. Sitting, snuggled up on the sofa together, watching Disney films.

'Erica,' she would say, 'always remember, there is nothing as strong as a mother's love.' Then she would pause, and hold me against her more tightly. 'I want to wrap you in cotton wool and protect you for ever.'

If only she had.

Once upon a time, my mother cooked a mean spaghetti bolognaise and knew how to dip strawberries in melted chocolate. I never had a dad. Mum just had lots of boyfriends who came and went. Mike, Steve, Francis, Robert, Sam, Jake and Rod. Rod was my favourite – funnier and kinder than the rest. He built a Morgan car with a kit, and sometimes took me for a 'spin' around the block in it.

I was happy back then. But happiness is a funny word. What does it mean? Is it an idea? A feeling? Is it real? Was it the warm contentment that began in my stomach and radiated through my body, because I had my mother and I knew she loved me? She was the pivot of my life. Maybe she still is, even though she is only a memory now.

The first day my life began to fragment I was walking home from school with my friend Geoffrey. He lived near me and every afternoon when school had finished we ambled along the road together on our way home until we parted at the third corner. Memory plays tricks. I remember sunny afternoons; frost, wind, and rain, all dissolve into oblivion.

On one such sun-dappled afternoon, we heard shouting behind us and turned around to see two boys from the year above marching quickly towards us, shouting, 'Slag. Slag. Slag.'

Tommy Hall and John Allan. Tommy was large for his age with

a broad slack face, always redder than it should have been. Always looking as if he had been running and was out of breath. John was wiry. Petite and mean. Boys to keep away from if you could.

'Slag. Slag. Slag.'

Getting nearer. Grinning and pointing. Pointing at me. We turned away from them and continued to walk. But they stepped in front of us and blocked our path. Eyeball to eyeball. Eyes scalding ours.

'Erica Sullivan, your mother's a slag,' Tommy said.

'Like mother, like daughter – slag, slag, slag,' John continued.

Geoffrey puffed out his pigeon chest and stepped towards them, chin up defiantly. 'Shut up, you two. I hear you're not the sharpest knives in the drawer. Leave Erica alone. She's worth ten of you.'

Tommy clenched his fist, pulled his arm back and rammed his hand, like a hammer, into Geoffrey's stomach. Geoffrey bent double. They ran away laughing, and shouting, 'Slag, slag, pussy, pussy.'

I put my arm around Geoffrey's bent shoulders. 'Are you all right?' I asked.

'Just about, I think.' There was a pause. 'What a pair of knobs.'

'Thank you so much for defending me.'

We began to walk slowly along the road, but Geoffrey was struggling, holding on to my arm. 'Why do you think they said that?' I asked.

He turned his head and pressed his eyes into mine.

'Don't take any notice of them – there's always a few knobs about in life.'

We staggered to our parting corner.

'Thank you again,' I said. 'I hope you feel better by tomorrow.'

He laughed. 'I hope I feel better long before that.'

I watched him walk away, still holding his stomach. Then I turned and ran home to my mother.

My mother and I lived in a block of flats on the council

estate, on the edge of the leafy part of town where Geoffrey lived. The same estate as Tommy Hall and John Allan. I ran through the under passage that crossed the A road, trying to ignore the rancid smell of stale human urine. Into our homeland of 1960s concrete. Solid and grey and ugly. Up the concrete staircase (the lift never worked), along the balcony to number 64, Bluebell Rise, our small, square, characterless flat. At least we had a bedroom each. Mum said we were very lucky to have been allocated that.

She was in the kitchen in her fishnet nightie dancing with Rod, the radio on full blast – a half-empty bottle of gin on the kitchen table.

So you see, Faye, life isn't always easy when your mum is a slag.

26

Jonah

Sitting in my office, tapping my carefully manicured fingernails together, thinking about you, Faye. On Saturday night you seemed so interested, so attainable. I think back to the moment we stepped out of Sophia and Ron's house, anticipation crackling in the air between us.

I have been infatuated with you since we first met. During that time you have always been with Phillip, but I know deep down you are in denial and would rather be with me. Your eyes bubble when you look at me. A surreptitious smile plays across your lips when your head turns towards me.

Do you remember when Phillip went away on a business trip, before you were married? I took you out on a boat ride one hot summer evening, along the river from Twickenham, and we ate at a gastro-pub next to the Skiff Club, opposite Hampton Court. Watching the river meander past; ducks and swans ambling, and bobbing their heads into the water for food. An eight gliding proudly along, coach instructing the rowers with a megaphone from the safety boat. We were so relaxed and comfortable together. Time seemed to stop.

I ordered a full-bodied white burgundy. We downed one bottle and then another. As the sun began to set across the water, a million shades of ochre and orange melting into the horizon, you said, 'Thanks for a wonderful evening, Jonah.'

'How's it going with Phillip?' I asked, trying to sound nonchalant.

'I think it's fine, but he has been rather distracted with his work recently.'

I leant across the table and took your hand in mine. You didn't pull away.

'You'd be better off with me,' I said.

You frowned a little and smiled a slow smile. 'I'm not after money. I'm after Phillip.'

But now, so many years on, you are tired of Phillip; otherwise you wouldn't have betrayed him with me. It is my turn now. To date I haven't had a meaningful long-term relationship, only short-term ones that have lasted a bit too long. I have only tolerated most of the women I have been with because I enjoy sex.

But, Faye, you are different. I love everything about you. The way you speak. The way you think. The way you move. And the sex I had with you was the best sex I've ever had. You wanted me so much. You made me feel I mattered when we were making love. Our destiny is sealed. From what you said to me in the car I know you are still in denial. But I know you have always wanted me, and at last this weekend you succumbed to your desires. Now you have tasted me, soon there will be no holding back.

I type your address into my computer. Drawings of your house begin to spread across my screen. Your bedroom. The place you lie with Phillip. Can he make you climax like I can? Has he ever heard you really, really gasp? Any man can impregnate you, give you children, like Phillip has, but it takes a man like me to make your mind and clitoris pulsate. Come to me. Get real, Faye.

27

Phillip

I watch you as you unload the dishwasher. Your news today, the modelling job, has made you look different. It affects every muscle in your body; you even stand differently. You turn towards me, back arched, hand on hip.

'And another thing that's good is that Jamie Westcote's model didn't get the job.'

You step forward and cling on to me. I hold you; your lithe body hard against mine. I think back to all the male attention that has been lavished upon you during the time I have known you. I was hardly the only man after you. I know I am punching above my weight. Eyeballs slide as you walk across a room. Whether you are a successful model or not, you are beautiful in the eyes of the opposite sex. You don't need to do this any more. We are older. You need to look after our children now.

'Faye, you're beautiful,' I whisper in your ear. 'You're beautiful to me whatever happens. Try not to care so much.'

28

Faye

'Try not to care so much.'

What are you talking about? Modelling is my life. My vocation. Of course I care so much. You are looking at me with condescension. As if my job is not real to you. What is the matter, Phillip? You never used to be like this.

29

Faye

I am on the way to the photoshoot; butterflies in my stomach. It is over a year since I've had an opportunity like this. At least, Phillip, despite beginning to bristle with disapproval these days when I talk about my job, you are being as helpful as usual; I suspect out of a sense of duty. You have taken Tamsin to school today and organised a place for Georgia in your workplace crèche. A new crèche experience for her. You have always been helpful but I used to think it was because you were as passionate about my work as I am. That is not true now. What will happen if you find out about Jonah? But you will never find out about Jonah. I will never admit the truth.

I push my worry about both you and Jonah away as I park my car. The trick is to develop a male brain, compartmentalise, I tell myself as I step outside to admire the vista of Bushy Park. Such a cold October day, almost no one else here. Grey sky, and grass so damp it looks as if it's decomposing. I gaze across the park towards the make-up tent, by the woods, where we will do the filming, and see mist floating through the bare trees. The conditions will have an eerie effect on the photoshoot.

I walk along a muddy path towards the tent, wrapping my faux-fur jacket around my shoulders, and balancing on the tips of my new designer boots in an attempt not to damage them. Two men are standing outside it, drinking takeaway coffee, pointing at the trees beyond, nodding. They turn around as I approach.

'Natasha?' the one without a camera around his neck asks.

'Faye.'

He consults the piece of paper he is holding.

'Sorry,' he says as he stretches his hand towards me. We shake. 'Tim Turnbull, at your service.'

'And I'm Pop – the man with the camera,' his colleague says as he touches me lightly on the shoulder and pecks me on both cheeks.

'Pop?' I ask.

'Yes, my friends call me that sarcastically because I look so young.'

I laugh, but my laughter sounds frail. I flash him my best smile. The one I practise a lot.

'Well,' says Tim-the-Director, gesticulating towards the tent, 'do step inside to start make-up.'

I follow his instructions to find a young girl sitting at a plastic table sorting through a bag of lipsticks. She stands up as soon as I enter.

'I'm Daisy. Super excited to meet you.'

Super excited. Dressed in black. Not wearing any make-up herself.

'Do sit down and we'll get cracking. I'll need to remove all your own make-up first. I like to start with a blank canvas.' There is a pause. 'Try to relax.'

She wraps me in a black plastic gown and stretches a hairband across my forehead to pull all the hair from my face. I try to relax. But I cannot. Thinking about my body positions. My pout. Daisy rubs cream all over my face, with rough fingers. Then she rummages through a large leather holdall and pulls out a pot of foundation.

'Bamboo beige,' she announces, slapping her hands on her apron. 'Perfect.'

Slapping on layer after layer of bamboo beige. This seems to be taking for ever, but my head has been pushed so far back I can't reach to look at my watch.

'Where did you train?' I ask to pass the time.

'The London School of Make-Up.'

'Was it fun?'

'Yes but please don't talk – you need to relax your muscles so that I can deal with the crevices in your face.'

Crevices? My insides tighten. I didn't know I had any. Age again. She doesn't need to be smug about it. It will happen to her one day. She continues to massage and pummel. Foundation applied, now she attacks my face with brushes. A peculiar sensation runs across my eyebrows. My eyelids are being scraped by a knife. 'Eyeshadow,' she informs me. Just as I am not sure how much longer I can cope with this, she chirrups, 'Nearly finished!'

Finally, finally after administering eyeliner and mascara, she brandishes a mirror in front of me.

'There,' she announces. 'What do you think?'

'Good,' I reply. 'But a bit heavy.'

My words hang in the air between us.

'At your age it needs to be thick.'

Age. Age. Age.

'I'm thirty-four years old,' I snap.

Ignoring this information, she hands me a bag containing my outfit for the day.

'I'll step outside, give you space to get changed. Wait till we get to the woods to put the shoes on.'

She leaves. I unzip the bag and pull out a dress like gossamer. Soft grey silk, almost see-through, with matching underwear, and shoes with razor-blade heels that look as if they are made of candyfloss. I brace myself. Now I know why the make-up is so heavy. It's necessary to disguise hypothermia.

I put on the underwear, pull the dress over my head, and fuss over its arrangement in front of the full-length mirror in the corner of the tent. At least I'll be able to keep my jacket and boots on until we reach the woods. I fling my jacket across my shoulders, stuffing my candyfloss shoes deep into its pockets. Time for my grand exit from the tent. I step outside and shout across to Daisy, Pop and Mike, who are huddled together sharing a roll-up with the heady scent of cannabis. They do not hear me.

'Ready when you are,' I announce more loudly this time.

Pop turns around. He sees me and waves. He throws the joint to the ground and stamps on it to stub it out.

'Let's go,' he instructs. 'Daisy, get the ice cream.'

Ice cream. I shiver inside. I'd forgotten about that. She disappears back into the tent and steps out with an icebox I hadn't noticed earlier. We walk along the path to the woods. I have to tread carefully along the muddy path because of my boots and the length of my dress, so I am soon trailing behind the other three, who are striding out in their sensible clothes, well ahead of me.

Eventually, I catch up with them. They are smoking again. Cigarettes this time. I hold on to Daisy for balance whilst I pull off my boots, and slip the ridiculous candyfloss shoes onto my feet. They are not really shoes, just decoration. I pull off my jacket and hand it to Daisy. The cold air slices into me like a knife. The photoshoot starts. The wind picks up.

'That's nice,' Pop says. 'It makes your hair look fantastic.'

I try to smile as he instructs, through chattering teeth. I run through the trees — as much as you can wearing candyfloss. Slowly, slowly I walk, licking ice cream. Sitting on a tree stump. Climbing a tree. Leaning forward. Leaning back. Perky. Pretty. Pouting. Devilish. Body and mind numb with the cold, eating vanilla ice cream.

30

Erica

When my run is over, even though I actually enjoyed it for the first time, I feel light-headed, as if I am about to faint. I hobble back to my flat and collapse on my bed. I fall into a deep sleep and dream.

My dream is so sharp. So clear. I'm in my muddy blue track-suit, my pain has disappeared and I am running effortlessly, wearing gold Lycra and shiny purple trainers, which cushion my feet. People turn their heads as I pass, wanting to admire my fitness. My surreal body is perfect for a sportswear advert. I dream that Nike have asked me to model for them next week. I am running to pick Tamsin up from school. She steps from the classroom door and her face lights up as soon as she sees me; blue eyes with a sapphire shine. She runs into my arms. I hold her against me, wanting to protect her for ever. Tamsin, my heart sings, Tamsin my love.

Then I wake up in my cold damp flat. I look down at my body, my heavy arms and thighs, my baggy clothing that needs washing. Tamsin is not my girl. The dream was so beautiful that when I realise it was only a dream I almost cry.

My iPhone beeps. Twelve o'clock. Mouse has invited me for lunch. Time to go for beans on toast. Am I allowed beans on toast? I suppose so. Just one slice. I drag my exhausted body out of bed, swallow to push back my tears, and pull my hoodie on to go upstairs.

As I climb the stairs feeling as if I am walking through mercury, I know I am going to crack this. I am going to get fit and look like you, Faye. Then I am going to take both of your children away, one at a time, and be a surrogate mum. A far better mother than you.

31

Jonah

I am going to watch you from a distance whilst I finalise my plan to tempt you away from Phillip. You didn't see me this morning, did you? I didn't park outside the school. I hovered outside the Anytime Leisure Club. I know you go there every day. There are so many cars stuck in traffic along the road by the station, you didn't notice mine. But I saw you, your creamy body striding along the pavement, pushing Georgia along in her buggy. Lycra clothing tracing the cleft between your buttocks.

32

Erica

I arrive at the small side room to the church hall where the slimming group hold their meetings and step inside. It feels as if the temperature barely changes, and like my flat, this room is musty and damp. A small three-barred electric heater is plugged in and burning brightly, but I take one look at it and sigh. It will be completely inadequate in this challenging environment. The room smells of stale air and wet sawdust.

An elfin woman steps forward to greet me. Bony. Pointy. Smiley.

'Welcome,' she says with a broad-stretched smile. 'I'm Julia, the group leader.'

'Erica Sullivan,' I reply.

She ticks my name off a list she is holding.

'Do sit down,' she invites. 'The others will be here soon.'

I sit on one of the small wooden chairs pushed close to the electric fire. The chairs look as if they have been removed from a 1950s primary school. While Julia hovers at the back of the room flicking through a thick red manual, I sit looking at the electric fire waiting for the others to arrive. They arrive one at a time and every time someone comes Julia abandons her manual and ticks the person's name off the list.

They smile at me. Friendly smiles irradiate from pretty faces, figures distorted by body fat. Their eyes do not follow their smiles. I see in their eyes that, like me, they are desperate about their size.

'Is this your first session?' a short blonde woman asks.

'Yes,' I reply.

Julia's footsteps echo across the parquet flooring, as she walks towards us carrying a set of digital scales.

'This is a new class. It's everyone's first time.' She puts the scales on the floor in front of us. 'Who wants to be weighed first?' she asks.

I put my hand up.

'Come on then, Erica, step forwards.'

I stand up and feel eyes watching me. It makes me squirm with embarrassment. But I know I must improve the way I look. I know I must do this. I step towards the elfin woman. I hold my head high and stand on the scales. I know I cannot win a battle if I can't even face it.

Julia announces my weight, eyes holding mine.

My insides feel as if they are collapsing, I am so embarrassed. I am far heavier than I thought. Three stone to lose. A long way to go. Julia's eyes are shining into mine. Telling me that I can do it. Telling me to believe in myself. She smiles, a slow hesitant smile, and nods. I turn around and face the class. A woman at the front who looks to be a similar size to me begins to clap. Everyone joins in. I walk back to my chair surrounded by applause.

You can do this, Erica, I tell myself. *You really can do this.*

33

Jonah

Lunchtime. I walk out of my office past the bank, turn right past the doctor's surgery, then right again. The road curves into a cul-de-sac of 1930s semis. I slip down a cut-through passageway full of tree roots and cigarette butts, along a wider street lined with red brick Victoriana; to number 133 — the house at the end of the road. Beautifully kept. Garden manicured. I walk, the soles of my shoes resonating on slate, up the tiled pathway and ring the doorbell.

Anna must have been waiting for me because the door opens immediately. As I step into the red-carpeted hallway, she gives me a tired smile.

'Sally is ready. You can go straight upstairs.'

Sally invites me into her bedroom with an artificial smile, and a thick Brummie drawl. She is wearing a silk dressing gown that is too busy; duck egg blue with birds flying across it. Too many beaks and feathers.

'Welcome,' she says taking my coat and hanging it up behind the door.

'Did Anna tell you I want you to wear a wig?' I ask, looking into her pale green eyes.

'Yes.'

I rummage in my briefcase and pull it out, black tresses freshly washed and styled.

'If you sit at the dressing table I'll help you put it on.'

She walks towards the dressing table, continuing to smile. I step behind her. She sits down and shakes her shoulders a little to relax them. I lift the wig carefully in my fingers, holding its crown wide open and gently, gently, starting at her forehead, coax it onto her head.

'What do you think?' she asks, standing up and shaking her head so that the bottom of the wig vibrates lifelessly against her shoulders.

'Not bad. But your eyes are the wrong colour. They need to be violet.'

'Next time I'll wear coloured contacts,' she says as she walks towards me, and starts to undress me. When I am naked she pushes me onto her bed, onto her floral counterpane that has seen better days, and removes her dressing gown, revealing sagging white breasts. So unlike your perfect curves that I have to turn her around and enter her from behind, burying my face in the wig. My crescendo takes a while as the girl is so unresponsive. In the end I manage, by playing with the curls of the wig and imagining I am rubbing up against your sweetness, Faye.

34

Erica

On my way back from my morning run in the park, it feels as if someone is pushing a steam roller across my stomach. I can't keep moving. I have to stop for a break. I rest awhile and find myself staring at the noticeboard pinned to the school gate.

<u>Lunchtime assistant required.</u>

My stomach lurches in hope. They need help to serve the school lunches and help to wash up afterwards, for two hours a day. Fair pay, minimum wage. I re-sat my maths GCSE last year and managed to gain a B. My maths teacher even wrote me a glowing reference to help me get a job. Serving food. Washing up. Nice and simple. I know I've not managed to get a job for ages but I could apply for this. Oh yes, I could apply for this job watching over Tamsin. Getting to know her first.

35

Faye

Georgia and I are holding hands, tripping slowly through town, on the way to the agency. Georgia is clutching her weekly treat, her oversized bag of sweets. She chose one of almost everything in the shop, and six white chocolate mice.

My stomach tightens as I think I see Jonah's car. I haven't seen him for a while. Much to my relief, ever since I explained my feelings honestly, he hasn't been waiting for me at the school. He must have accepted my decision. But I have been feeling guilty. A leaden heavy feeling pulling me down.

All the times he has approached me and I have brushed him off successfully – why did I succumb to his advances in the end?

Because of Jamie Westcote. Because of Phillip.

Phillip suggesting my modelling career is drawing to an end, before it's taken off. Jamie Westcote putting the boot in. The tightening in my stomach becomes painful as I remember what happened between Jonah and me.

For whatever Phillip's current views about my career, he is the centre of my family, my rock. And I do not want my family life to disintegrate. I feel as if I am suppressing a constant volcano of panic, as if my life as I know it is about to end at any moment. But however awful this feeling is, my behaviour caused it. I am going to ride through it. Live with it until it fades. I will move through it in the end.

What is Jonah doing here now, hovering in the traffic near

the agency? Is he on the way to make an architectural visit? I do not want him to wind the window down and talk to me, so I sweep Georgia into my arms and walk around the block to approach the agency from the other direction.

Mimi's hair is more flamboyant than ever today. Purple and pink and green. A triple-tipped Mohican. More of her head is shaved. Her piercings are multiplying. Georgia sits on my knee, looking at her, transfixed by her chains.

'The ice-cream photoshoot was a success,' Mimi says, smiling at me and folding her arms. 'They're using the film for an ad in the local cinema, a large still will be up on a bill board by the library.' There is a pause. 'Plus the local magazine ad, as was originally discussed.'

'When will I get my fee?'

'Soon. Soon. They won't let you down. I'll chase it,' Mimi promises, leaning back in her chair and stretching her legs out in front of her.

'Now – you've been offered another job.'

I lean forwards, keen to listen.

'It's to advertise some riding stables in the next county. But you need to be able to ride a horse.'

'No problem,' I lie, wondering whether Jonah is still in the vicinity, 'I learnt when I was a child.'

36

Erica

'So, Mouse,' I say as I sink into his sofa, 'my first job interview in years is over.' I pause. 'And I have to tell you I felt sick with nerves.'

'What happened?' Mouse asks, standing in front of me, looking down. 'Your face is flushed; you're pleased. You're excited aren't you?'

The grin I cannot contain widens. 'Yes. Very. They asked me if I could start as soon as they had done a background check.'

'Fantastic, Erica.' He grabs my hands and pulls me to my feet. 'May I have the pleasure of this dance to celebrate?'

His face is so serious, and his suggestion so flippant, I can't help but giggle. Frowning, he turns his speakers on and a waltz begins to play. He takes my arms and leads the way. One two three, one two three, one two three. I get in a bit of a muddle and stand on his feet.

'No. No. No, Erica.' He shakes his head. 'Let's start again.'

He starts the music from the beginning, puts his right arm around my waist and guides me around the room again, leading with his left foot and arm. We manage three times around the room perfectly before I stand on his feet again and we collapse in giggles.

'No. No. No. Erica, stop laughing. We need to get this right. I am going to make you do it again.'

37

Jonah

Because I can't have you yet, I am only managing to contain myself with help. She opens her bedroom door slowly with a wary smile. Her blue contacts do not compare to the Liz Taylor violet of your eyes. The sultry wig too limp to match your hair. Her face is not yours. But I need this. I step into her room and close the door.

'Take your dressing gown off,' I command.

It slips to the floor. She is naked. She moves towards me, and kneels in front of me. She unzips my trousers, pulls my pants down and tries to take my coil of softness in her mouth. I push her head away.

'No,' I bark.

She looks up at me, strange blue eyes sad and pleading.

'What do you want?' she asks.

'You know what I want to do to you.'

Her eyes cloud with fear and that turns me on. I feel myself becoming erect. I grab her breasts and twist her nipples so hard she cries in pain. My erection is throbbing now. I grab her by the shoulders and throw her onto the bed. I kick her legs apart and thrust into her dryness. I thrust and thrust. She cries because I am hurting her. I am hurting myself too, but there is a fine line between pleasure and pain, and I am really enjoying this.

38

Erica

Slimming club again, sitting shivering by the electric fire, waiting for the other weight watchers to arrive. Julia, the elfin woman, pointy and ethereal, is standing at the back of the church hall, texting on her iPhone. The others start arriving in dribs and drabs, laughing and chatting, making small talk. Their laughter surrounds me and makes me feel lonely. Faye, you and I are two of a kind, aren't we? Never quite part of the group.

I think of you, and your irresponsibility, and how much Tamsin and Georgia need to be taken away from you.

'Time to start,' Julia announces, putting her iPhone in her pocket and walking across the hall, to stand in the middle of the space in front of us, beyond the chairs.

She stands next to her major weapon, the scales. Her body is small and neat, but her grin is wide and fixed. 'Let's weigh ourselves first.'

We come every week. We know what to do. We queue in front of Julia, holding our record books. Chattering still envelops me, without including me. I watch the woman in front of me stand on the scales, her ample thighs pushing against the material in her skirt and stretching it.

'Same as last week,' Julia announces. 'You're stabilising. Don't lose heart. That often happens after the initial weight drop-off.'

71

But despite Julia's encouragement, the woman turns to go back to her seat, eyes facing down.

'Remember keeping slim is a constant battle. We are not on a diet, we need to live a healthy lifestyle – all the time,' Julia continues. 'Next please.'

I step forward, wriggling out of my jumper and kicking off my trainers. I step onto the scales.

Breathe out. Pray. Pray I am losing weight.

The numbers on the digital scale reach a desirable weight, and do not rise any further.

'Congratulations, Erica, you've lost a stone in a month.'

39

Faye

I enter the office, which looks like a stable itself, a wooden barn of a place with copious beams and a high ceiling; difficult to keep warm. A young girl is standing behind a wooden counter looking cold and bored. The counter is decorated with leaflets, trinkets for sale, baskets containing packets of crisps and biscuits. There is a coffee machine behind her and a shelf laden with fizzy drinks.

'Kate's running late.'

'OK – how late?'

'About twenty minutes.'

'That's fine. I'll just sit and wait.'

'Can I get you anything to drink?'

Having taken note of her additive-laden selection I immediately snap, 'No thanks.' My skin can't tolerate drinks with additives.

I sit on a bench that runs around the edge of the 'office' and, feeling bored already, pick up a leaflet about the riding school. I flick through shiny photographs of young girls sitting on horses decorated with a plethora of rosettes. Of horses running freely through open fields. My stomach contracts. Why have I agreed to this? I've always been frightened of horses. I don't even like walking past them if we meet them in a field on a country walk. And it's not as if I'm even a country walk sort of person in the first place. I push my fear away and fiddle with my iPhone, engrossing myself in Facebook gossip and BBC News.

When Kate finally arrives she is short and stocky, with a grin so straight it could be mistaken for a grimace. But deep-voiced and square-fingered, there is something resonant and reassuring about her.

'Sorry to have kept you waiting. Let's get started.'

I stand up and walk towards her.

'You'll have to leave that in a locker,' she says, pointing to my iPhone. 'Sure-fire way of making a horse bolt.'

'Thanks for telling me.'

'Don't worry. I'll soon get you licked into shape for the photoshoot. They only need a few photographs, don't they? I've got the most gentle horse in the world ready for you. She's a beauty. Her name is Whisper.'

When I am deemed to be correctly dressed and briefed, I am allowed into the arena to meet her. Dappled white and stream-lined, saddled up and ready to go. She is eyeballing me, head high, neck arched. My insides quiver as Kate holds her reins and barks instructions.

'One foot in the stirrup, swing your other leg over.'

I do as I am instructed and somehow find myself sitting in the saddle on Whisper's back, feeling unprotected and vulnerable. Despite the hard hat that is pressing into my skull and giving me a headache. Despite Kate's eagle eye watching me.

Nothing is holding me.

I should be wearing a seat belt or a safety strap. Whisper is stamping her right front hoof, moving her head and neck from side to side, making me feel dizzy.

'Horses and ponies are very sensitive,' Kate says. 'They sense fear and lack of confidence. You must sit tall and calm, and let her know who's in charge.'

I straighten my back and tighten my thighs against her body.

'Is that better?' I ask.

'Taller, calmer,' Kate replies. 'Squeeze your thighs and she'll walk forwards, pull the reins and she'll stop. Off you go. I'll watch.'

I look down at the ground and my dizziness increases. I look up again at Kate, who nods at me. Taking a deep breath, I squeeze my thighs against the horse's flanks. She sets off slowly. So slowly. But my stomach churns at her every move. Even though she's only just started to go, I want her to stop. I pull the reins. She keeps moving. I pull them again. She moves faster. What am I doing wrong?

'Let her know who's in charge,' Kate barks from the edge of the arena.

I feel my heart thumping in my ears. I pull the reins so hard I think I could be cautioned for animal cruelty, and she finally condescends to halt.

'Praise her for doing the right thing,' Kate instructs.

I lean forward, stroke her neck and mumble 'Good girl,' into her ear.

'Now you need to learn to trot,' Kate continues. My hands and legs are trembling. 'Squeeze your thighs twice and she'll trot.' There is a pause. 'Lift up and down with her movement like I showed you.'

Whisper begins to go. My stomach tumbles as I bounce. I grit my teeth and do as I am told. Up and down, up and down, butterflies in my stomach, the movement making me nauseous. In the end I can't stand it a second longer, so I tug on the reins and Whisper stops. I need a break.

'I need the loo,' I lie.

Kate saunters across the arena towards me, and takes Whisper by the bridle. She talks me through my dismount. Much to my amazement I manage to reach the ground without cricking my neck or damaging my back.

I walk across the arena feeling bruised and shaken. Stepping into the cloakroom I catch sight of my face in the mirror. Puffed and swollen. Pink piggy eyes. Not only am I terrified of horses, I am allergic to them too. I'll have to dose myself up with antihistamine for the photoshoot.

40

Phillip

This evening you managed to get a babysitter, and we have broken free from home. Arm in arm, we step into the new wine bar in town. Quirky and stylish. Empty wine casks instead of tables. Candles instead of electric light. In an old basement, which has been made to look like a wine cellar. Stepping inside is like stepping into another world. A world of romance and secrets.

But not quite.

A man is ignoring his wife and staring across at you, as you edge behind the wine cask we have chosen. I watch him, watching you, and instead of romance and secrets I realise this wine bar is just full of the same thing as usual. Men who want to look at you. His eyes rest on your legs, then your buttocks. Then inevitably your breasts. His wife notices me watching him and looks embarrassed.

It's always like this; everywhere we go, someone finds you attractive. The constant attention makes me feel tired.

The waiter saunters over, flashing a full-beam smile.

'What can I get you, Madam?' he asks, eyes brimming into yours.

Your eyes shine back into his. What is happening? Are you flirting with him, Faye? I clench my jaw and pinch myself. Of course not. I must stop doing this. We've always been disproportionately attractive. Thinking about it too much will drive me mad. But I don't need to worry about looks; you like me for my mind, don't you, Faye? You've always respected my opinion, haven't you?

The waiter returns with a bottle of claret, and pours us a glass each, flamboyantly, from a great height, a thimbleful of wine in an oversized glass. You ignore him this time. Perhaps you sense the way I am feeling. I sit admiring the contours of your face, flickering in the candlelight across the barrel.

'How's the horse riding going?' I ask as I take a sip of my wine.

You snort. 'I'll get away with it, as long as the pony they provide for the photoshoot is old and knackered.'

'It won't be. What's the point of photographing a good-looking woman on a clapped-out horse?'

Your eyes darken and your face stiffens. 'Well you think I'm old and knackered. So there is every point. Two battle-axes together.'

I sigh. 'Why are you saying that, Faye?'

'Can't you remember what you said to me, Phillip?' Your voice is sharp. Eyes spitting.

'Yes I can.' I lean back. 'And I didn't mean you were old and ugly and looked like a battle-axe. You are putting words in my mouth.'

You lean across the barrel towards me. 'What did you mean then?' you ask, lips thin and stretched.

'Just that we are entering a new phase. Early middle age. We need to put more emphasis on the children.'

Shoulders raised. Arms crossed. 'Are you saying that I don't look after them properly?'

I close my eyes for a second in exasperation. When I open them again your eyes stab into me. 'No. I didn't mean that. I just think they're more important than your modelling career. It doesn't matter to me whether you're modelling or not, Faye. To me you are beautiful anyway.'

You shrug your shoulders like an awkward teenager. 'You just think I'm getting too old, losing my looks. That's why you're commenting.'

I shake my head. 'No.'

'This is my career you're mauling. You're behaving like a chauvinist, not supporting me.'

The word chauvinist sears into me. 'I have always done everything to support you. Taken the children to the crèche. Dropped them off and picked them up from school.' My voice is raised and barbed.

I look across at you frowning towards me, the perfect lines of your face contorted, and I realise why I am more possessive about other men looking at you than I used to be. Because you always seem exasperated with me. I feel vulnerable because you don't respect my opinion any more. You used to adore me just the way I was. I never had to try too hard. Now I say or do something wrong every day.

41

Erica

The school dinner I am serving looks good today. The children's favourite. Pizza and chips, followed by jelly and ice cream. Nothing like school dinners in my day when everything seemed to be accompanied by boiled cabbage so fresh from the field it still had bugs in it. Pizza is not only the children's favourite, it is my favourite too. But I have to deny myself such things now, as I am the upcoming star of the slimming club. Slimmer of the week.

I am standing behind the counter brandishing my serving slicer, waiting for Tamsin to arrive. I used to think she wasn't as pretty as you, Faye, but the more I see of her the more I grow to love her looks. She is as beautiful as you, it is just her beauty is more subtle, more delicate. Her attractions discreet. I have been smiling at her every day and now she is beginning to look out for me when she comes to collect her lunch. Yesterday, for the first time, she smiled back. And that is a big thing for a child who seems to be inherently shy. The extra portions of pudding I have been giving her have helped.

Tamsin's class are filing into the dining room. I am so used to looking out for them I am beginning to recognise some of her classmates. There is a chubby girl who looks rather like I used to when I was young. Her hair is dull. Her clothes need washing. But she is always smiling, showing too much of her red gums. When she tries to talk to Tamsin, Tamsin moves away. Tamsin hangs around with a tall skinny boy with owl-like glasses, who always seems to wear navy and black, and a tiny girl they call Ashley – whose real name is Ashmolean – with shoulder-length blonde hair, and brown eyes. The class seem to dote on the girl with blonde hair so it seems to me that Tamsin is in with the in crowd.

She is entering the dining hall holding hands with the owl boy and laughing. They are both chatting to Ashley. As usual their teacher accompanies them. Mr Parkinson – nicknamed 'Parky' – a jaded middle-aged man with a red face, whom they all seem to adore.

Today as every day, he sits at one of their tables, pouring himself a glass of water, waiting for his food, while the children queue. One of the cooks scuttles over and places an extra-large portion of school lunch in front of him. He smiles as he thanks her, his dry face almost cracking as he moves it. I think he must have psoriasis. It really isn't normal to have a face as red as that.

Tamsin and the owl boy are standing together in the food queue, heads together, discussing something serious now. Are they talking about you, Faye, do you think? About the way you are too involved in your infidelity and never seem to do your duty?

The queue moves quickly. Tamsin is standing in front of me, raising her plate towards me. Fine black hair brushed and shiny. Wearing a pink dress patterned with rabbit shapes and matching cardigan. Pink tights. Pink patent leather shoes with large white bows. Party clothes. Not suitable for school. But that is your influence isn't it, Faye? Trying to turn your daughter into a model like you, repressing her individuality, her freedom. You are damaging her personality with your vanity.

My heart lurches as she looks at me with piercing eyes like yours. You are so lucky to have a daughter like this. So gentle, so fragile. Someone to love and protect. Slowly, slowly, looking into her eyes, I balance a piece of pizza onto my slicer and place it carefully onto her plate.

'Would you like another slice?' I ask.

Her eyes widen. 'Parky said we were only allowed one.'

'Well it's a secret that only I know. Special girls are allowed two.'

'Am I a special girl?' she asks with a giggle.

'Of course,' I tell her as I balance another slice onto my utensil and lean towards her.

I lean across so close I am almost touching her pale skin. The slice wavers as it tumbles onto her plate.

'Thank you,' she says and gives a smile that is a replica of yours.

'My pleasure.'

I watch her walk away, towards the woman serving chips. Watching her frail body, which needs my protection so very much.

42

Phillip

'Jonah rang me today. The planning permission for the loft came through – he wants to come and check the measurements again, before he brings the builder to meet you next week,' I say as we sit eating our supper, after the girls are in bed.

You stiffen.

'What's the matter?' I ask.

'I've been meaning to talk to you about that. I think the loft conversion is a waste of money.' Your voice is strained and waspish.

'But . . . But . . . You were so keen on this project. It was your idea in the first place.' You don't reply. You sit looking at your almost empty plate. 'What's made you change your mind?' I ask.

You sigh and lean back in your chair. I watch you bite your lip. 'I think it's too expensive.'

'It's a lot cheaper than moving.' I pause. 'Look, Faye, we discussed this, really carefully. I thought the decision was made. You wanted the extra room so that your parents could come and stay from time to time. Give you a break. Help you look after the children.'

You bite your lip again. 'We've been managing pretty well on our own.'

'Faye. You're confusing me. You wanted this so much.'

'If we do go ahead, I don't think we need Jonah to supervise the building work.'

'Why are you being awkward about Jonah? You've always got on well with him. I'm flabbergasted. It was you who suggested we use him in the first place.'

You raise your hands as if you are pleading with me. 'I've just had second thoughts. We hardly need a loft conversion and we can't afford to have Jonah to supervise. I'm getting too *old* to be a model and I didn't ever earn much money in the first place.'

I sigh inside. Not the age thing again. 'He's included his fee for that in the price we've already paid.' I shake my head. 'I thought you knew that.'

'If that's the case, get him to pay us some money back.'

'Faye, what on earth's the matter with you? You know things don't work like that.'

43

Jonah

I am walking up the steps to your front door, carrying my briefcase containing your plans. Your loft conversion. What a good excuse for keeping in touch with me without Phillip becoming too suspicious. Is that why you dreamt up the idea in the first place, because you were besotted with me? But actually he took a while before getting back to me with official permission to come today, so maybe he is beginning to guess about our relationship? It always used to be Phillip and I who had a relationship: at school, at university, drinking and chatting. He was always so quiet. I was always buoying him up until he got the upper hand. You.

In my dreams, my fantasies, I see you every day. Then, as we make love, you are so clear, so greedy for me, so passionate. I savour the expression on your face at my every touch, as we make love. I know what you like, Faye. The memory of your pleasure sears across my mind. The way you moved, the way you breathed. I only have to close my eyes to feel you close to me.

The door opens and you are standing in front of me, wearing your skin-tight jeans, and a pink cashmere jumper that caresses the curves of your breasts. I step into your compact hallway. I can see through into the living area; Phillip is not around right now.

'Hello,' you say, face crumpling in embarrassment.

'Hello,' I reply, trying to hold your eyes in mine.

But your eyes do not want to play games today. You close the front door behind me, and lead me into your living room. Your house is so small. Downstairs you really only have one room; no wonder you need an extension. We stand in the debris of your life. The living room floor cluttered with toys. A plastic tea set. A row of Barbies. Soft toys. Scattered jigsaw pieces. Books.

'I think we need to clear the air,' you say. 'I regret what happened and there is nothing between us. That's all. That's it.'

'Do you really think it's that simple when I've wanted you for so long?' I ask. 'I'm a patient man, Faye, I can wait until you change your mind again.'

Your eyes harden. 'I do think it's that simple, and if you don't you'd better leave.'

I shrug my shoulders. 'You've commissioned me to do a job – so I'll have to stay for a while, at least.'

There is a pause. You shrug your shoulders. 'OK. Go upstairs and look at the loft again. There is no need for me to come with you. I'll stay down here. I've got a few phone calls to make.'

I make my way upstairs alone. The landing walls are crowded out with photographs of your family. The arty-farty type. All four of you tumbling together in lines and laughing, hands on the person in front's shoulders. Looking so casual, so relaxed, so modern, and yet so quirky in faded brown and white.

Your pretence of a happy life.

I walk past Tamsin's bedroom with its frilly pink counterpane, and flouncy curtains. Fluffy cushions, soft toys, books about Jemima Puddle-Duck. Past Georgia's tiny snug. The door to the master bedroom is wide open. I step inside and close the door. I close my eyes and inhale your scent. Vanilla and musk. You must have just put your perfume on before you came downstairs.

I open my eyes and pretend you are here with me, reaching your hand out to pull me towards the bed. The bed looks dishevelled; you haven't made it properly. I throw myself onto it and put my head on your pillow. I can smell your hair, your breath. I rummage beneath your pillow and find your nightdress. I hold it to my face and smell you on it. My breath is coming quickly as I slide off your bed and stuff your nightdress in my briefcase. Now all I need is some underwear. I reach into your bedside drawer and help myself, before smoothing down your duvet and leaving your room.

Up one more floor to re-inspect the loft area. The loft is walk-in. Through a cupboard in the top bedroom. I step inside and switch on the light. Boxes everywhere. I'll check the contents of these boxes next time. I've been gone too long. I'm coming back downstairs to talk to you again, Faye.

44

Faye

As soon as I walk into my bedroom after he's gone I feel confused because I don't remember making the bed so carefully. I was in such a rush to get Tamsin to school and Georgia to her play date. I don't remember leaving my knickers drawer open. I never leave it open – I hide my private things in there. My contraceptive pills. My vibrator for when Phillip is away. I shudder inside as I snap the drawer closed. Surely Jonah would not have dared to come in here? But then again his behaviour has always been worrying. Maybe I have been too naive not dwelling on it; always reckoning he would find a woman of his own, not just spend for ever ogling at me.

I step back in time, remembering all the times he has come on to me over the years, whenever Phillip's back was turned.

A group of friends, on a cold winter night, walking into central Twickenham to a restaurant. He and I were chatting and ended up behind the others. To catch up we cut along the pathway at the side of the old bakery, out of sight of passers-by. As soon as we were alone, he put his arm around me. I stiffened. He clamped his arm more tightly across my shoulders.

'What's the matter, Faye? I'm only being friendly.'

Only being friendly. He was invading my personal space. Touching me like that made me feel uncomfortable. Looking back I realise he has always made me feel uncomfortable. So what happened the night after the party? Did he tap into my vulnerability? Or had he spiked my drink?

45

Erica

No need for all that fifty slow steps, fifty fast steps palaver, I am jogging, really jogging now. Really beginning to enjoy it. It refreshes me. Makes me feel calmer, happier. It must be true what they say: exercise releases hormones that give you a high.

I jog every afternoon for forty minutes, after I've finished serving school lunch. Making sure my route always goes past your house.

Taking it slowly past your house.

Today as I admire your neat modern home with its mock-Georgian front door and double-glazed windows, winter pansies spilling from a pot by the door, I see a man leaving, wearing a grin so wide it almost cracks his face in two. His blond hair shines in the watery winter sunlight.

Why are you still messing with him, Faye?

46

Phillip

As soon as I arrive home from work, you step towards me, eyes burning.

'Jonah's been in my knickers drawer,' you announce.

I frown, confused. 'Jonah?'

'Jonah. Your best friend. Our architect. Do you remember him? Did you forget he was coming?'

I wince at the way you are speaking to me. You sound like a fishwife, Faye.

'What happened?' I ask.

'He's been here, snooping on me.'

'Snooping?'

'You don't have to repeat everything,' you snap as you throw toys that are littering the floor into the basket in the corner.

I begin to help you. 'I wasn't aware I was. What happened? What did he do?' I ask.

'He's been in our bedroom. Some of my things have been moved.' Tears begin to fill your eyes. 'You know he's always pestered me. I've told you so many times. You don't believe me do you?'

I step towards you. You push your body against mine, clinging to me. Crying and crying. I wrap my arms around you. What is the matter, Faye? Why would Jonah be snooping on you, after all these years of friendship? All my friends fancy you a bit. Is that so surprising? But no one's infatuated with you enough to be snooping on you. I hold you against me and worry. I worry you are becoming paranoid. Over-focused on the power of your looks.

47

Erica

I've dyed my hair black like yours and I'm growing it. It's a bit edgy at the moment, sticking up on top, but when it gets a bit longer I think it'll settle down. One day I want it to be as long as yours. I'm already a stone and a half lighter. Halfway there. Same again to go. And as I want your children to take me seriously I need to buy some new clothes.

I am rummaging through the racks at the Oxfam shop again, looking for a bargain. The selection here hasn't improved at all since my last visit. A row of limp blouses mourning their owners. And then on the next rack I stumble across something that doesn't look too bad. A baggy corduroy dress in reasonable condition. I try it on. It hides my stompy figure and looks quite nice with the grungy boots I bought before. Looking at myself in the mirror of the changing room, in the poor lighting of the shop, I could be mistaken for a chubby yummy mummy.

I pay for my clothes and then leave the shop wearing them. All I need now is an expensive coat. I step into the Italian restaurant on Church Street, so popular even though it's the middle of the afternoon. A number of young retireds are already drinking wine and eating pasta. People always seem to be eating and drinking and whiling away time in here. Every time I walk past I wish I could afford to join them. A smiley young woman dressed in a black miniskirt and a white apron steps towards me.

'Can I help you?' she asks.

'I hope so. I just popped in because I think I left my coat here last week.'

She stands weighing me up, hand on hip.

'What's it like?' she asks.

'A dark bluish black,' I reply as non-specifically as possible.

'I'll go and have a look.' She shrugs.

She disappears through a doorway behind the bar, leaving it unmanned, and returns a few minutes later carrying two coats. One a black raincoat that looks like a man's, the other an expensive bundle of dark blue cashmere that I could never afford in a million years.

'That's mine,' I snap, pointing at it. 'Thank you so much.'

I must have sounded convincing because she gives it to me without hesitating, looking as if she is pleased to have been able to help. I slip it on. Fortunately it is a large size and fits perfectly. I walk out of the restaurant slowly, trying to look as nonchalant as possible, but my heart is beating like a trapped bird's wings.

I walk home, cradled in luxury, on my way to show Mouse.

48

Jonah

I step upstairs towards Sally who is waiting for me, lying on the bed wearing nothing but the wig and contacts.

'Put these on quickly,' I instruct, throwing a bag at her, containing the clothes I stole from you, Faye.

She gets up and bends to pick up the bag. I watch her walk to the bathroom. As I wait, I sit on the bed surrounded by imitation Sanderson prints; genetically modified roses and camellias. On the curtains, the duvet, the wallpaper. A fresh country look, so innocent and sweet. A masquerade in case the police come.

Anna is masquerading as a normal landlady. Sally is masquerading as a normal girl, who works in a supermarket. I've seen her there, at the till, handling people's groceries several hours after opening her legs for me.

There is an undercurrent of sex games in every small town. Only the blind cannot see this. Sex games masked by the pretence of routine. Behind lunchtime trips to buy sandwiches that take too long. Supposed visits to the pub with long-lost mates. Madonna was right all those years ago. It's sex that keeps the world turning, nothing more erudite or meaningful.

Sally is taking her time in the bathroom. I can hear rustling and wonder what she is doing. She was naked in the first place; all she needed to do was to slip a thong and a nightie on. Maybe she is pepping herself up with some pills, leaving me alone in her boudoir, which gives away nothing about her. The busy floral pattern takes attention away from the fact that otherwise it is bare, no remnants of an ordinary life. Does she have a personal life, a world away from here?

She is an empty vessel, except for what happens between us. I never think of her between encounters. As soon as I step out of her bedroom door, in my mind she no longer exists. It is another person who sits at the till at Tesco. A person I will never know.

Not like you, Faye. I want to know you inside out; everything about you. Your thoughts. Your fears. Your every sexual fantasy.

49

Erica

Sitting in my flat, studying myself in the make-up mirror I bought in Boots this morning. So highly magnified, it shows every burst blood vessel, every pore, every blemish. Despite my shortcomings, analysing my face at such close quarters is fascinating. I really need to concentrate on looking after myself.

And I've had a spending splurge on Rimmel. I lay my purchases on the dresser by my mirror. A khaki eyeshadow palette. Mascara. Eyeliner. Bronzer. Lipstick. Slowly, carefully, I begin to apply the eyeshadow, drawing and then colouring in almond shapes across my eyelids. Moving on to the bronzer, stiff brush strokes from cheekbones to ear. Carefully shaded lips. A final flourish with eyeliner and mascara.

Make-up done, I bound upstairs to see Mouse. I knock on his door, and without waiting for a reply, turn the handle and step inside. He is tidying his bookshelves. Mouse likes his possessions to be in order. He looks up.

'Wotcha. Good to see you.' He steps towards me, eyes softening. 'Oh, Erica,' he says. 'You look really, really, nice.'

50

Faye

Rushing to the school pickup, bumping Georgia along in the buggy. It was a battle to force her into it, as now she always wants to walk. But we were so very late, after picking her up from her play date, that I didn't have any choice. I ignored her screams of protest, the way she stiffened her back and arched her neck, as I lifted her in.

Now, as I enter the school playground, I am still paying for it. She remains wailing with temper. The other mothers have taken one look across at my screaming child, and as usual, are keeping well away from me. Will I ever become one of them? Part of the school-gate banter?

The other mothers seemed to know each other before their children started at this school. I am not sure how. From church? From nursery school? Whatever. They seem like quite a clique.

I stand a little away from them and strain my ears over my daughter's wailing to try and listen to what they're saying. I think they are talking about the headmistress.

'She always supports the teachers,' a woman with rabbit-like front teeth announces, with a snarl on her face.

Is this wrong? For a head teacher to support her staff? Their words merge together in my mind as Georgia finally stops crying. If they asked my opinion, what would I say? What do I think? Then the snarly woman – Ashmolean's mother – makes an announcement.

'Ashmolean is going to St Paul's Girls' when she leaves here. We think it's the best school for miles,' she announces. 'What do you all think?'

And now they are all nodding their heads and talking so fast I cannot make out any individual words. I sigh inside. How does she know which secondary school Ashmolean is going to? Ashmolean is only six. I am standing watching them all when I notice an Amazonian woman walking towards me. She has square features and perky hair sticking out at odd angles that rather suits her. She looks a bit quirky, wearing an expensive cashmere coat and shabby old boots.

'Hi,' she says, 'I'm Erica, Rosalie's mother.'

'Tamsin's mother,' I reply.

She raises her eyes to the sky. 'Is that all we are, somebody's mother these days?'

I laugh. 'Sorry, my name's Faye.' I pause. 'And this is Georgia. She has only just stopped screaming.'

Erica. Different from the other braying mothers. Smiling down at Georgia. Beaming at me intently, as if she finds me interesting. We are interrupted by Tamsin running out of class, running towards us. She stands stock still as soon as she sees Erica and gives her a high-wattage smile, then she tickles her sister, and runs to hide behind my legs. Erica bends down to Tamsin's level and peeks around my legs.

'Peek–a–boo,' she says.

51

Erica

Tamsin hides, giggling, behind your shapely legs. She looks so vulnerable today, so much in need of my love.

'Well,' you say, 'nice to meet you. Best be going home. Stuff to do. Tea to cook.'

And then you walk away holding Tamsin's hand. I think Georgia has fallen asleep in the buggy. You are leaning your head towards Tamsin, listening to what she is telling you.

But you don't deserve to have her to listen to, do you? Two-timing whore, with a high opinion of yourself. Adulterer. Liar. You deserve to lose your children, like my mother lost me.

I close my eyes and that ache engulfs me. The ache I get when I remember the children at school calling my mother a slag. The jeering and bullying, which began on the walk home from school when Tommy Hall hit Geoffrey, spread like wildfire, in the classroom, in the playground. I had to tolerate it for the rest of my primary school life. From that day forward I regularly heard, 'Her mother's a slag,' like a whisper on the wind, wherever I went. Geoffrey stopped walking home with me. He didn't want to get hurt again.

52

Phillip

'Jonah wants to come around again tomorrow,' I say, unbuttoning my shirt, as we get ready for bed. You are pulling off your underwear and slipping into your negligee. The black lacy one with the rosebuds around the collar that I bought you last Christmas. As soon as I mention the word 'Jonah' your gentle curves become hard-edged. Neck taut. Head raised.

'With the builder?' you ask.

'No. On his own again.'

Your violet eyes darken to purple.

'That's ridiculous. He only came last week. He shouldn't need to come again. You know I think he stole my nightie and some knickers.'

I sigh inside. I don't believe you. Why would he do that? Jonah and I go back a long way. He was always surrounded by women. One new woman after another, even though they never hung around very long. With so much sexual opportunity in his life, why would he need to do something weird like steal a pair of your knickers? But I really don't want this argument to start again, so I toss my shirt into the laundry basket, and ignore your statement.

'He just wants to check the measurements, one last time,' I reply.

You stand staring at me, hands on your hips, as if you are about to shout at me like a fishwife. Again.

I sigh inside. 'Faye, what's worrying you?'

'You know. I told you. He's a pervert and a thief.'

'That's quite an accusation.'

You sit on the bed and burst into tears. For years I have put up with men ogling you, friends fancying you. I have never had your glamour, your allure, so it is hard for me to understand just how careful you have to be, but I really do hope it's not pushing you over the edge.

53

Faye

He is upstairs again, pretending to check the loft measurements but I guess, like before, he is rifling through my things. I had to agree to his visit otherwise Phillip would have asked me even more questions about why I was reacting against him. I cannot bear for Phillip to know the truth about what happened between us. If he does he will never trust me again. Lack of trust is a killer, damaging even the best of relationships. I am living on a knife edge because I need to preserve my family life. I need to fight to keep us together.

I so want to forget what happened, but it's clear that Jonah does not intend to allow me to do that. He seems quite content with the idea of ruining my life, my relationship with Phillip. I am so surprised by his attitude. I know I made a terrible mistake but I would have thought it was quite clear that it was just a casual fling.

The truth is I don't remember very much about the evening. I remember him kissing me at the party. His kiss excited me. We walked back to his house from the party, arm in arm, laughing and chatting. I remember him unzipping my dress and it falling to the floor. Proud of my body, I wanted him to admire me. I needed admiration that night.

I think I was culpable, lying on the floor, naked, pulling him towards me, allowing him to enter me. I don't remember his climax. I don't remember mine. I woke up, mouth parched, head throbbing, disgusted with myself. Still disgusted with myself. I will be disgusted with myself for ever. What happened to me? Why did I do this? I am beginning to question whether I was in control, or whether I was pushed.

54

Jonah

Phillip, although academically bright, with a maths degree from Cambridge, is very gullible. Fancy believing I still need to check the measurements of the loft. Maybe the press are right: most university degrees are not what they're cracked up to be; not designed to sharpen the mind. My architecture course at the same university was much broader. Encouraged more lateral thinking.

I never quite understood why you were so attracted to him in the first place, Faye. He was always too amiable and pleasant; the sort of man women pushed around. Initially, that was why I enjoyed his company so much. He was bland and easy. He soothed my edges. Calmed me down. I used to envy him his lack of colour, the way he always blended in, like a chameleon. I was always a bit too obvious. A bit too standout. I am trying to forgive you, Faye, for becoming entangled with such an average guy, when someone like me would have been far more stimulating. But we all made mistakes when we were young, didn't we? And you were far too young when you met him. You should have waited until you had ripened, before you allowed yourself to be tied down.

I move past the sycophantic family photographs, smiling down on me from your landing wall. I don't like to look at them. I don't like to see a still of your husband touching you. I do not want other men to touch you, Faye. Soon you will be mine, and mine alone.

I stop outside your bedroom door and my heart quickens. This time I'm after some perfume. Smells are evocative. If I take some of your perfume, I'll be able to take a little whiff of your scent wherever I go. I turn the door handle but it won't move. I clench my fist and force it. But it still won't move. I lean my shoulder against the door and rattle it. The door is locked.

Oh, Faye, why are you trying to shut me out of your life? You can't lead me on and push me away. I am a full-blooded man, not spineless like Phillip.

I know the measurements off by heart. I do not even need to take my tape measure out. I stand by the window of your compact fourth bedroom and look down to the pocket hand-kerchief garden below. Hardly any room for your girls to play. When they come to live with me they can have whatever they want. A tree house. A tennis court.

I move across to the wardrobe, climb through to the loft space and flick the light on. At the moment it is cluttered with pile upon pile of plastic boxes. They'll have to go in the garage when the work starts. Real hoarders you and Phillip. A lot to sort out when you split up.

I climb over some of the boxes and push some aside so that I can sit cross-legged in the midst of them, on the floor of the loft. They are labelled in your handwriting, Faye, bold and curly. Phillip – school reports. Phillip – memorabilia. Phillip. Phillip. Phillip. No thanks. Not interested. Faye – photographs. Now you're talking. I stand over the box labelled to contain your photographs and pull the plastic lid off. A horizontal line of A3 manila envelopes, individually marked. Hands trembling, I pull a handful out. Holidays. I open that envelope and pull a few photographs out. The first one is of you as a teenager, sitting in a rock pool grinning at the camera. So curvy. So cheeky. So devilish. A brief bikini. Not a stitch of make-up.

Perfect.

I put all the other photographs and envelopes back into the

box and snap the lid back on. I have so many photographs on my phone of you and Phillip, but not one as special as this, of a younger you, totally alone. Holding my treasure carefully against my chest with one hand, I clamber out of the loft and snap the light off. I stand and look at the photograph. If I had met you then, before you met Phillip, you would not have been saddled with him. I slip the photograph into my briefcase, and pad downstairs to look in your violet eyes again.

55

Faye

At last. I hear his footsteps thumping down the stairs and I brace myself to escort him out of the house with as little interaction as possible. He steps into my living room and stands in front of me, half leering, half grinning.

'Thanks,' he says. 'Next time I come I'll bring the builder with me.'

'Fine. Good,' I reply, beginning to move towards the hallway to lead him straight out.

He puts his hand on my arm. I turn to face him.

'It's not fine, good, the way you are treating me, Faye.'

My insides tighten.

'You have lied to Phillip by not telling him about us.'

'There isn't an us.'

'You know there is and it's just a matter of time before I tell him.'

'How many times do I have to warn you I will just deny it, so it's hardly worth your effort?'

'How do you know I'm not recording this conversation?'

'You wouldn't dare.'

He steps towards me and tries to take me in his arms. I stiffen my body and push him away from me but he overpowers me and presses me against the wall. He tries to kiss me but I close my mouth. He continues to kiss my face. I cannot move. I cannot speak. My heart is beating in overdrive. He breaks off from kissing me, and laughs.

'So demure now, but no one knows as well as me, what happens when you let go.'

He is pressing me against the wall more tightly now. I feel his erection through his trousers, pulsating against my stomach.

I scream, as loud as I can for help. He holds his hand against my mouth so that I can hardly breathe. 'The next time you scream for me it will be in pleasure, again.'

56

Jonah

I hold my hand across your mouth and feel your body trembling. My erection pulsates and I want to open your legs and enter you right now. But that would be too sweet. Too easy. I want to prolong this. I pull my body away from yours, pad through the hallway and let myself out.

Next time you will give me what I want. You know that don't you, Faye?

57

Faye

Just when I think Jonah is about to rape me, he releases my body from his grasp. I slump to the floor. Is this what happened? Did he rape me in the first place and just leave me feeling guilty about it? Or am I in denial, wanting to blame him instead of myself for what happened? I hear his footsteps pad through the hallway. I hear him open and close the front door. I pull myself up to standing, feeling as if I am wading through lead. As if I am distant from the rest of the world, enclosed in a bubble. Forcing myself to walk to Georgia's play date to pick her up. Past houses where normal people live. People who haven't been unfaithful to their husbands.

I manage to breathe deeply in and out, and smile in front of Sophie's mother as I collect my daughter. She answers the door in a denim apron and invites me in to her large pine live-in kitchen. Sophie and Georgia are sitting in front of a Disney video, a plate of untouched sliced apples and bananas between them. Georgia looks up and smiles, head on one side.

'Please can I just watch the end of this, Mummy?'

I look at my watch. Half an hour to school pickup. I look uncertainly at Sophie's mother.

'It's only got ten minutes to run. Why don't you just stay for a quick cuppa, if you think you've got time? I don't need to dash today – Jodie Cooper is picking Hermione up – we have a drop and pickup share. Such a big help.'

Hermione is in Tamsin's class. That is how Sophie's mother and I got to know each other in the first place. Georgia and Sophie love each other. Hermione and Tamsin clash.

'Lovely thank you,' I reply.

'Thank you, Mummy,' Georgia says blowing me a kiss.

Georgia must like Sophie very much. On her best behaviour today. No screaming. No pouting.

Sophie's mother makes a pot of tea and we sit on opposite sides of the pine bench table that runs through the elaborate living kitchen of this fine Victorian house.

'I want to talk to you about the school lunches,' she says. 'A group of us don't think they are healthy enough. What do you think?'

I lift my teacup to my mouth, hand trembling, and take a sip. Still feeling Jonah's erection pressing against my stomach. Still feeling my heart beating like a trapped bird's wings.

'Well, Tamsin hasn't complained so far,' I manage.

Sophie's mother leans towards me across the table. 'Well she won't will she. Children like chips with everything and greasy burgers ladled with all sorts.'

'All sorts?' I ask limply.

'Processed cheese. Ketchup.'

'I see. I didn't realise.'

'Don't you look at the menu?'

'No. I erm . . . where would I find it to look at?'

'It's pinned to the noticeboard every Friday afternoon, for the next week.'

Sophie's mother is looking at me, eyes wide, as if she can't believe my negligence. 'A group of us go and check it every Friday and then we complain to the Head, immediately, in the hopes she will alter it. But she always ignores our comments.' She sipped her tea. 'I was just wondering what you think?'

I feel dizzy and sick. 'Now you've pointed out the problem I will take a look. Thanks,' I say and smile weakly, holding my hands together on my knees so she won't notice their tremor. I slide my eyes across to the clock. I know I need to leave in less than three minutes. She follows my eyes.

'The film will be over in two seconds,' she says. 'Life's such a rush, isn't it?'

I nod my head. Relieved to hear the theme tune of *Beauty and the Beast* resonating around the kitchen, I stand to leave. For a second, as I glance through the kitchen window, I think I see the back of Jonah's head as someone walks past outside. My already palpitating heart beats faster. It isn't him, I realise as I watch him turn to cross the road. In fact this man looks nothing like Jonah. I must be becoming paranoid. I breathe in and out, slowly, deeply. My heart begins to slow a little.

'Thank you, thank you,' Georgia exclaims as she leaves.

She has had such a good time with Sophie that she skips all the way to the school gate, helping me push the buggy. When we arrive I think for a second I see Jonah's car parked on the double-yellows. But when I look again the car has gone. It wasn't him. I tell myself. Please. Please. It wasn't him. But then not many people drive a lilac Jaguar. So my heart pulses again, like a forge hammer, loud and all encompassing, beating against my eardrums.

Standing in the playground now, I look down at Georgia, sitting peacefully in her buggy, eating a healthy snack that Sophie's mother gave her, waiting for my other daughter – feeling empty inside. As if I am walking on the edge of an abyss. If I fall the wrong way I won't survive.

The other mothers are standing heads together talking quietly, almost whispering. Oh no. Erica is here, walking towards me brandishing her high-wattage smile. I am not in the mood for Erica. But it's not her fault. I'm not in the mood for anybody right now.

'Wotcha,' she chirrups, standing too close to me.

'Wotcha,' I reply, feeling so sick I might vomit.

'Would Tamsin like to come and play with Rosalie one day next week?' she asks, eyes glittering with enthusiasm.

I swallow to push back vomit. 'That's very kind. I'll ask her,' I manage.

'No. Don't ask her. Keep it as a surprise. I want to take them on a special treat.'

I am feeling so shaky and confused. 'A special treat?' I ask.

'It's Rosalie's birthday you see.'

'Which day?'

'Well it's her birthday on Wednesday – but I'm not sure which day I'll be able to arrange the treat.' She puts her hand on my shoulder and leans towards me. 'I'll have to let you know at short notice.'

'Thanks,' I mutter, relieved to see Tamsin coming out of school and walking towards us.

As soon as she sees Erica, her face lights up, like before. I grab Tamsin's hand and rush away as quickly as possible. I need to get home away from the School Gate Mafia and try to relax. I walk home holding Tamsin's hand.

'Are you friendly with a girl called Rosalie?' I ask.

'No. I don't know anyone called Rosalie.'

'Are you sure? Erica's daughter?'

'Sure I'm sure. I can remember everyone's name in class.' She takes a deep breath. 'Jane, Juliet. Ann S. Ann T. Sophia. Cathy. Jeremy . . .'

'OK, OK, Tamsin, I believe you. You don't need to recite the whole register. Rosalie must just have a preferred middle name, or nickname, or something. That lady Erica definitely has a daughter called Rosalie. She wouldn't come to school to pick up an imaginary girl now, would she?'

Tamsin giggles. 'Course not, Mummy.'

Back home, still feeling sick and trembly, I cook fish fingers and beans for the girls' tea. Tamsin and Georgia relax in front of *The Lion King*. As soon as I have cleared up, I join them. I close my eyes to listen to the soundtrack. 'Can You Feel The Love Tonight' resonates in my head. The love I have for my family builds inside me. It sears across my mind and pushes my fear of Jonah away. I will not let Jonah destroy my family.

58

Phillip

Sitting in the Horse and Hounds, my favourite pub in town; oak beams nailed with horseshoes, sipping a pint of Adnams, watching Jonah walk towards me. Jonah. My oldest friend, who I have known since nursery school. The first words he said to me were: 'I'm three and a half. How old are you?'

Today he is overdressed as usual, in what looks to be a Brooks Brothers suit and double-cuffed shirt. The smartest man in the pub. Even though he went to the same state school as me, I developed superior tastes as we grew older. His accent changed overnight before we had finished celebrating getting into Cambridge, his Southern Counties accent suddenly posh enough to rival members of the aristocracy. But he was always such fun; the life and soul of the party. Sometimes when I was with him I would laugh so much I almost cried. The laughter has faded. He hasn't made me feel like that for a long time.

He rang me at work today wanting to come to our house again, because of some discrepancy with the plans. So he doesn't get your back up any further, Faye, I've arranged to meet him for a quick drink after work to sort things out.

He flings his coat across the chair opposite me, his aftershave almost giving me asthma. When did he start overdosing on aftershave?

'Can I get you a drink, mate?' he asks with a grin.

'Just got myself one.'

'Asked at the right time then,' he says and laughs.

He ambles to the bar, and returns with a whisky. He sits down on top of his coat and starts to sip it.

'What did you want to talk to Faye about?' I ask.

'The sequence of the job.'

I frown a little. 'But we've already agreed it, with the builder, by email and copied you in.'

'I just wanted to make certain we're all on the same page,' he replies spreading a copy of the plans across the pub table. 'Are you happy with the plans?' he asks.

'You know I am. I've confirmed by email.'

He leans towards me, holds my eyes in his and frowns. 'I just wanted someone to take a last look.'

'Is there something in particular that's worrying you?' I ask, casting a cursory glance over the drawings.

'No. No. I'm just very thorough.'

Thorough or pedantic? Has someone sued him? Has something gone wrong? He usually has such an air of confidence.

'I tell you what, I'll check them again at home one last time and then email you? Please don't worry. It's all cool.'

'Well, we do need to check the order of works, as well.' He smiles, a long slow smile. 'If you're too busy I can easily run through them with Faye, in the day?'

I stiffen. 'That won't be necessary. I'll run through them again, and get back to you. Is there some aspect you're particularly concerned about?'

'The whole running order needs to be precise. For example what about storage?'

'Storage?'

He sips his pint and then looks up at me. 'Where are you going to put all those boxes of photographs, while the work is going on?'

'In the garage.'

How does he know they are photographs? Is Faye right? Has he been snooping?

'What will you do with all that stuff if you split up?'

His words burn into me. 'What do you mean? Why would we split up?' I snap.

A leering smile. 'Women as good-looking as Faye don't tend to be reliable.'

What has got into him? 'Of course Faye is reliable – looks don't affect reliability,' I say, aghast. 'You've known her for years. Almost all the time we've been together.'

'Good-looking people have more sexual opportunities,' he continues. 'More self-confidence. More likely to experiment with different partners.'

Anger incubates inside me. 'Are you trying to tell me that's what Faye's been doing?'

'Why don't you ask her? Ask her yourself.'

59

Phillip

You step into the hallway to greet me.

'I owe you an apology,' I begin.

'What for?'

'You're right, Jonah is behaving strangely.'

Your violet eyes tighten. 'He's over-interested in me, Phillip. I know from the way he looks at me.' There is a pause. 'Why? What has he done now?'

'He asked to come here again and I thought you would be annoyed so I arranged to meet him at the pub.'

'Why did he say he needed to see us this time?'

'Some discrepancy with the plans. It turned out that there was no reason to meet up. He was just going over things we've all discussed ages ago.' I pause. 'He made some rather weird comments. He said women as good-looking as you don't tend to be reliable. Basically implied I should ask you whether you were playing around.'

Your lips begin to tremble but the rest of your face is still. Unreadable. 'I keep trying to tell you he's gone off the chain. His behaviour's become seriously weird.'

60

Jonah

Faye, it must be so boring living with Phillip. He is so sincere. So biddable and pleasant. Women prefer a man who is more assertive. More dominant. A man like me. He must bore you stiff. I am keeping myself hot for you while you decide how you are going to tell him you are leaving him. Lying on my bed cradling your photograph. The one of you in the rock pool. You don't have many clothes on. The photograph must have been taken almost twenty years ago, but you still have a hard body, don't you?

Lying naked on the bed thinking about you, reaching for my cordless telephone. I need to hear your voice, Faye. I need to hear you now.

61

Faye

Ashmolean is here for a play date with Tamsin, and I am hovering, trying to stop Georgia from spoiling their games. Georgia is a pickle. Every time I remove her from the older girls and try to distract her, she escapes from my attention, and when I turn around she is back. Misplacing pieces from the jigsaw puzzle they have almost finished. Climbing into the den they have built from sheets and pillows in the middle of the living room. Interfering with whatever they are doing.

'I don't mind,' Ashmolean says, hugging Georgia. 'I wish I had a sister.'

And now all three of them are pretending to be ballet dancers, skipping around the living room, pointing their toes and stretching their legs. I am watching them, feeling exhausted. The telephone rings. I pick up.

'Hello?'

No reply. But I hear someone breathing.

'Hello?' I repeat.

Still no reply. I put the phone down, and walk to the kitchen area to put the organic chicken nuggets with homemade breadcrumbs in the oven. Just as I close the oven door the phone rings again. I pick up.

'Hello?!'

I know I should put the phone down but I stand and listen,

transfixed by the sound of the breathing becoming heavier and heavier. Heavier and heavier until it sounds as if a man is climaxing. I slam the phone down, feeling sick.

62

Faye

I drove here this morning, countryside flying past in a blur, reliving the moment Phillip came home and told me that Jonah said he should ask me whether I'd been playing around. So my denials had to begin. Reliving the way Phillip took me in his arms. The way he held his body against mine. The way I want to step back in time, to before I slept with Jonah.

That sinking feeling I experienced when I first woke up in his house and realised what I had done now follows me wherever I go. It surrounds me as I sit here, dressed and ready, waiting in the stables' changing room, wearing my skin-tight beige pants, my black leather boots, and tailored black jacket. As I sit dosed up with antihistamine, and black coffee to keep me awake, make-up plastered onto my skin, blow-dried hair tickling my face. Pushing away the panic that is rising inside me. My panic ran into overdrive yesterday when he telephoned me. I know it was him, playing with himself. This man who I have known for so long, who is no longer my friend. Even the mention of his name makes me feel sick.

'Photographer's here, chop-chop,' I hear someone shout in the distance.

One last look in the full-length mirror. One last comb run through my hair. One last application of lipstick. I step outside. The sun is high in a cornflower blue sky. I inhale fresh air and for a second it calms me as the photographer walks towards me, and introduces himself as 'Sandy.'

Sandy. Shoulder-length hair the colour of honey, and soft brown eyes. White Wrangler jeans. Suede ankle boots.

'Are you nervous?' he asks.

'Not at all,' I lie.

He pushes his verdant hair back from his eyes. 'We need you to ride for about an hour.'

I thought it was five minutes. My heart races but I manage to smile.

'Come with me. It's time.'

I follow Sandy across the yard, to the arena, where my mount is waiting for me saddled up, stamping his right hoof. Phillip was right. He is young and lively, rippled with shiny muscles, gleaming from beneath his coat. Mrs Matterson, the owner of the stables, who has commissioned the adverts, is waiting for me too. She glowers at me, and nods. I widen my smile and nod back.

63

Erica

Faye, now I am exercising and eating properly, my weight is dropping off. I'm on a diet of fish, chicken, fruit and vegetables. Proper food, which keeps me feeling full, and despite feeling satiated, I'm losing a few pounds every week. I feel lighter in mind and body. More confident. More positive. Finding the confidence to plan the abductions. Tamsin first. Georgia in a few weeks.

Tamsin was in a chattery mood when I volunteered to help readers in Parky's class last week. Bright little thing, isn't she? She even knew the name of the farm you are going to for your photoshoot. But then you are so self-centred, I expect you have talked about it a lot at home.

So I know it's today, and I know where you're going. I've taken the day off work, having borrowed enough money from Mouse to hire a car, and I'm following you.

I follow you out of Twickenham, along the A road, onto the M3. Twenty miles down the motorway. You haven't noticed you have a tail. But you never really notice anybody else. Every day you stand away from the other mothers at the school pickup. Every day when I try to talk to you, you hold me at a distance. Why won't you communicate with me, Faye? It's not as if you're friendly with anyone else.

You turn off the motorway. You stop to queue at the exit roundabout. You are checking your hair in the rear-view mirror.

Hey, Faye, I want to tell you, don't worry – you're beautiful, you always look beautiful. Beauty isn't your problem, it's your lack of responsibility. We wind for another five miles along a B road dappled with gnarled trees and barn conversions. Until you slow down and turn right into Home Farm. I drive past. I need to give you a few minutes to park and get out of the car.

My body is clenched and tense. This part of my plan is pivotal. I can't afford to take too long now. What if I can't find a turning place for twenty miles? What if the photoshoot is over before I've arrived? Eventually I come to a picture postcard village, with a church, a duck pond, a pub and a shop. I turn around on the side road that lines the village green, and wend my way back.

I find the entrance to Home Farm again without any problems. The riding arena is well away from the car park. I know because I looked it up on Google Earth. As long as you are well occupied with the shoot you won't see me. I pull in and park my car right next to yours. Your car is a tribute to your vanity: glamour magazines, mirrors, nail polish, a bag of spare tights.

I take the screwdriver out of my pocket and stab it against the side of your front-passenger-side tyre. The rubber doesn't pierce. I bend down, hold the left side of the tyre to steady myself, push the screwdriver into the rubber as hard as I can, and twist it. I feel the release of air against my fingers as the screwdriver pierces the rubber. The sweet, sweet sound of hissing air.

But this damage is not enough. You might have a spare. And even though you don't look the type, you might know how to change a tyre. I change sides and raise the screwdriver again. But I am interrupted by the sound of an engine coming closer. A car is arriving, pulling into the car park. I run and hide behind the oak tree in the corner of the parking area, crouching behind the wide girth of its trunk.

I close my eyes and listen. I pray silently to a god I don't believe in. Whoever you are, be unobservant, go away quickly. Don't go in and tell her she has a flat tyre. Do not give her time to call the AA.

The car engine slows and stops. A car door opens and closes. Footsteps scratch across gravel. When the footsteps have faded I peek out from behind the tree trunk. Not a car but a van. A red post office van parked next to the car I've hired. I sigh inside with relief. A delivery. Soon the van will be gone.

I remain crouched behind the tree and time stops. I try to relax by stiffening my whole body and then relaxing parts of it slowly, individually, starting with my fingertips. But I try three times and it doesn't work. My body is as tight as a coiled spring. I count to one hundred and breathe slowly. But I still feel as if I am about to hyperventilate. Why doesn't the postal worker come back? Is he or she a friend of the family stopping for coffee? I fiddle with my iPhone but there is no 3G here, so I can only look at old messages. At last when I am just about to risk carrying on anyway, I hear footsteps on gravel and guess it is the postal worker coming back.

The sound of feet crunching into gravel becomes louder. I hear the van door open and close. The engine begins to purr, and tyres scrape across the gravel. I dare to peer from behind the tree trunk, and yes, the van has gone. I take a deep breath and step out from my hiding place, back to the driver's side front wheel of your car. I clutch on to the screwdriver in my pocket, pull it out, stab it into the rubber at the edge of the tyre, and twist again. It bursts immediately, air rushing out.

So far, so good, but still panic rises inside me. I run across to my car, open the door and turn the key, praying silently that the engine will start. It coughs and splutters. I turn the ignition again. The engine begins to throb. I push my foot down on the accelerator, and escape from the farm car-parking area as fast as I can.

64

Faye

My mount, Jack, is not a horse but a giant. He towers above me as I walk towards him trembling inside. I stroke his neck. He snorts and shakes his head as if he is trying to push me away.

'Steady, boy,' I say.

But he does not steady. He carries on snorting and shaking his head. I move back towards his belly and holding the front of the saddle with my left hand, just as I have been taught, put my left foot into the stirrup and lift myself over his back. I sit trying to be assertive, trying to remember everything Kate has told me. Firmly, calmly, pressing my bottom down. Sitting proud, shoulders flat, back straight. Holding his reins firmly. He lifts his neck back and whinnies, almost throwing me off.

'First we want you to walk him around the arena a few times,' Sandy instructs, standing legs wide, knees slightly bent, adjusting his camera. 'Then rise to a trot and finally a canter for as long as you can stand it, so that I can get as many shots as possible.' He pauses. 'If I've not got enough we'll need to start the whole process again.'

I manage a nod and a hesitant smile, and squeeze my thighs against the brute's sides to get him to walk. Walking forwards distracts him. He stops throwing his head back and whinnying. Maybe he is calming down. Maybe everything is going to be all right.

I stroke his neck. 'Nice and easy,' I purr softly.

'Trot now,' Sandy says.

I squeeze his flank tightly but he carries on walking.

'Use your whip, woman. Tell him who's boss,' Sandy barks.

Slowly, slowly I lift my whip. Slowly, slowly, I lash it down. He bolts from walk to trot to canter, in what seems like a matter of seconds. I lean forwards, holding on to his neck. A few more strides and he is galloping.

'Pull the reins,' Sandy shouts.

'Pull the reins,' Mrs Matterson calls through a megaphone.

He is moving so fast, vibrating my whole body, the reins have slipped from my grasp. Too frightened to move towards them in the saddle, all I can do is hang on to his neck. And scream.

'Stop screaming,' Mrs Matterson shouts. 'You're making it worse.'

I hang on more tightly, and my screaming increases. The gate to the arena is open and Jack thunders through it. The rhythm of his hooves is pulsating through my brain and stopping me from thinking. I don't know what to do. He races through another gate and into the field beyond.

The pounding of his body is settling, becoming more consistent. I am getting used to the beat of his gallop. I manage to lean forward and grab the reins. To sit more proudly in the saddle and tug them. His head jerks back and he begins to slow. Round and round the field he canters. But at least it is only a canter now. I pull and pull, leaning back, and the canter diminishes to a trot. Up down, up down like Kate taught me. I am guiding him by the reins now.

I guide him past Sandy and Mrs Matterson, who are standing at the edge of the field. Sandy has the camera on me. I ride him back into the arena. I dismount and stand holding his bridle, trying to disguise the tremor in my hand.

'That was awesome,' Sandy says. 'I got some amazing action shots.'

My body aches as I leave the arena and make my way back

to the changing room to collect my things. But I am pleased; proud of myself for coping with this. When I am almost there, Sandy catches up with me. He puts his hands on my shoulders. I turn around and find myself looking into his soft brown eyes. He pushes his hair back from his face.

'I thought that was awesome,' he says.

'Thanks.'

He stands, staring at me. 'But Mrs Matterson didn't, and she's the client,' he continues. He pauses. He swallows. 'I am afraid she said we need to reshoot with a model who can ride.'

I smell the faint aroma of cigarettes on his breath, and wish for a second that I hadn't given up when I was pregnant with Tamsin, and that I could have a smoke right now.

'Thanks. You win some and you lose some,' I say, hoping he can't hear the wobble in my voice.

I turn away from him, towards the changing room, burning with anger, pushing back tears. I worked so hard for this. I need to pull off my riding clothes and get back in time to pick Tamsin up from school. My fashionable riding clothes are tight, so tight, they cling to my skin. They take some peeling off as my anger is making my fingers tremble.

Half an hour later as I walk back to the car park, it's drizzling. A steady bone-chilling drizzle to match my mood. I should never have accepted this job in the first place. From now on I will not accept projects that mean I am punching above my weight.

As I approach my car, I know something isn't right. The car looks to be at a funny angle. As I walk closer my heart sinks as I realise I have two flat tyres.

65

Jonah

Sitting in my car outside school, waiting. Scrolling through the photographs of you on my phone; all marred by Phillip. Then I find the photograph I took the night we made love and my heart lurches. I took it as a selfie, just before you climaxed. What amazing sexual prowess, to be making you come and taking a photograph. As soon as Phillip sees it your marriage will break up. It is my 'pièce de résistance'. My trump card.

I look out of the window. Where are you, Faye? Why are you so late today? I need to have you near me now. To inhale your breath as it brushes across my face. To feel the heat of your skin, as you caress me. I take the photograph I stole from your house out of my wallet and sit looking at it. If I'd known you then, we wouldn't have had to wait this long.

I close my eyes and see you standing in front of me. The way you are now, with a slightly softer body that has filled out. Liz Taylor eyes. Strawberry lips, slightly parted. You lick your lips. You open your legs. I put my hand down my pants and begin to play with myself.

66

Faye

Two flat tyres. No spare. I don't know how to change a tyre anyway. Hands trembling, I pull my phone out of my bag to telephone the AA.

'Please send help as quickly as possible,' I beg. 'I'm a woman alone, in the middle of nowhere.'

It's not true, but I can't face going back to spend time with the harridan Mrs Matterson, and to face Sandy, who had such high hopes of doing a good photoshoot with me. He will never want to work with me again.

I look at my watch. An hour before school pickup. If the AA come quickly I should just about be all right. Sitting inside the car to keep out of the drizzle, exhausted after the disastrous photoshoot, listening to iTunes shuffle on my iPhone. Before too long I fall asleep and dream.

Jonah and Phillip are wrestling one another in a ring, but Jonah's body has become super-sized. The muscles in his arms are the same shape as a rugby ball. He throws Phillip across the ring, so that he lands on his back, then sits on top of him and begins to pummel his face. Phillip is screaming. I try to move towards him to help him, but my limbs won't move.

The sound of the AA van's engine wakes me up, and I sit watching it come into focus, worrying about Phillip. It parks next to me. I watch the mechanic step out and walk towards me, beginning to realise that Phillip must be OK, because it was just a dream. The mechanic knocks on the car window and I step outside into air still thick with drizzle.

'Thanks so much for coming,' I manage to say.

'That's what we're here for.'

I smile. 'Third emergency service, and all that.'

He smiles back. 'Exactly.'

A middle-aged man, with a substantial stomach and a reassuring smile. He busies himself inspecting my tyres. He stands a while staring, head on one side. He turns towards me, face stern.

'You'd better call the police, this has been done deliberately,' he announces. 'The holes are in the wrong place for nails or glass on the road.'

I go cold inside. My chest tightens. Is Jonah here watching me? Waiting to attack me? Waiting to attack my husband, like in my dream? But I cannot call the police. I need to try and placate Jonah myself.

'Thank you,' I say, not able to explain how much I need to keep my problems to myself.

He meanders to his van and returns with two temporary spare tyres. I stand and watch as he removes my damaged tyres and replaces them. Thinking about Jonah. About what he could do to me. To Phillip.

'All done now,' the AA man says. 'These tyres won't last long but they'll get you home. You need to get new tyres as soon as possible.'

'Thanks.'

'Are you all right? You look so pale.'

'It's been a busy day, that's all.' I shake his hand gratefully. 'Thank you so much,' I gush.

I look at my watch. I'll have to ring the school and ask them to keep Tamsin in the After-School Club.

67

Jonah

Still sitting outside your daughter's school waiting for you. You are usually here by now. Why are you late today? The other mothers are all arriving, warmly wrapped in their frumpy coats. I need you to arrive I need your colour, Faye.

68

Erica

The mothers, interspersed with the occasional father, are congregating like gannets. Chatting and laughing, but only the in crowd understands the joke.

Parky, red-faced and eagle-eyed, as responsible and protective as ever, is letting children out of class. One at a time, as soon as he sees their parents hovering at the classroom door. I beam my best smile at him, step forward and introduce myself.

'Hi, I'm Erica. A member of staff.'

'School dinners?' Parky asks with a smile.

I nod. 'And I'm a close friend of Faye Baker's. She's been delayed and just telephoned me to ask me to pick up Tamsin. She's coming out with me later anyway for my daughter Rosalie's birthday treat.'

Parky beams back.

'How lovely,' he says. I sigh inside with relief.

He steps to the side and Tamsin walks towards me. She smiles. I think she is pleased to see me.

'Where's Mummy?' she asks.

'She's been delayed at the photoshoot. She asked me to pick you up.'

Her face crumples a little. I take her by the hand, and start to walk her through the playground.

'Mummy always picks me up,' she says, trying to pull her hand away from mine.

Why is she being so whingy?

'She'll be here soon,' I say, gripping her hand more firmly.

I tug her arm a little, in an attempt to make her move more quickly. Through the playground, past the climbing frame and swings. Past mothers walking the other way, towards pickup. Past the annexe. Past the school office. We step out of the school gate and I see your boyfriend, Faye. Car slung across the yellow zigzags. Wearing a black cashmere coat with a velvet collar. Very City. Very polished. He'll have a long wait today to see you.

Still holding Tamsin's hand, I rummage in my pocket for my car keys.

'Parky says we should never get in cars with strangers,' Tamsin says.

'I'm not a stranger. Your mummy and I are good friends. We can wait here if you like,' I say, smiling, 'but I've got chocolate shortbread and juice for you in the car. And it's much warmer in there.'

She is looking at me wide-eyed, unsure what to do. My heart is pounding. Why is she scared of me?

'I normally walk home,' she says.

'We're not going far.'

Holding my breath, I scoop her in my arms, her cheek pressed against my face. Her skin smells fresh, of cherry blossom. So young. So smooth. So perfect. I open the car door. I lift her into the child seat I bought in the Oxfam shop and strap her in. I hand her a bottle of juice and the chocolate shortbread.

'Thank you,' she says.

I turn the key in the ignition and drive off – locking the childproof door locks. Left onto the main road, right at the lights by the garden centre, weaving our way towards the A316 and the motorway. Watching Tamsin, demolishing her shortbread, through the rear-view mirror, crumbs all around her mouth. As I settle in the middle lane she starts to swig juice from the bottle.

After a while she announces, 'I need a wee.'

'You'll have to hold it in.'

'I can't. I need to get out.'

'We can't stop here.'

'I can't hold it in.'

She begins to cry. To shriek. I turn the radio up loud to drown out her noise. After a while, much to my relief, she falls asleep.

At last we arrive at the Premier Inn I've pre-booked in Camberley. It is costing me all my savings to stay here for a few nights. Then I will have to lie low with her. Quite where I haven't decided. Somewhere no one knows us. She will have to be home-schooled. A tremor of panic runs through me, as I realise I have not thought this through. All I did was plan to abduct her. I didn't consider the practicalities of caring for her afterwards.

As I lift her from the car seat, she wakes up. 'I need a wee. Where's Mummy?' she shrieks.

'We're going inside now, so you'll soon be able to go to the toilet.'

'I can't wait. It's coming out.'

I put her feet down on the car park tarmac, as she stands and wets herself. She is sobbing, shoulders heaving, gasping for breath between sobs.

'Don't worry. I'll wash your knickers. It doesn't matter,' I say, lifting her back into my arms and stroking her hair.

Her sobs begin to soften and quieten. They stop.

'You've got a giant house,' she says pointing towards the Premier Inn, and wiping her nose with the back of her hand.

'It's not my house, it's a hotel,' I tell her.

'A hotel? Why aren't we going to your house?'

'It's on the way back from the photoshoot, so it's easier for your mummy to come here.'

Large eyes become larger still. 'Will she be here soon?'

'Very, very soon,' I try not to snap.

She begins to struggle to pull from my arms and get her feet on the ground. I hold her tightly, so tightly.

She continues to struggle while I check in. And even though I am fit, still doing plenty of exercise, her energy is already making me tired. The receptionist is wearing virulent purple to match the Premier Inn logo, clashing with her scarlet lipstick, which cracks as she smiles. She hands me a plastic key card.

'Thank you,' I say, exhausted.

Back aching, struggling with Tamsin in my arms, luggage slung across my shoulders, I move slowly in the direction of our bedroom. When we arrive it opens out before me: a giant double bed with a purple counterpane, ultra-modern TV. I place Tamsin on the bed, throw my bag on the floor and pop to the bathroom. I splash my face with cold water to try and relax. When I step back into the room Tamsin is sitting in the middle of the bed, watching a silly cartoon. A man with a sponge for a face. When we get back home she will have to watch something more erudite. My child will be educated properly. To make up for the education I never had.

'Will Mummy be here soon?' she asks.

'Very, very soon. But please stop asking that.' I pause. 'And I think you'd better take your knickers off so that I can wash them.'

I haven't got any spare clothes. I haven't got any toys for her to play with. I haven't got hold of the food she likes. I can't drive home; the police will soon spot me. What was I thinking? How I am going to look after her without getting caught?

69

Jonah

I cannot see you, Faye, but I can see Tamsin. Stepping out of the gates, holding another woman's hand.

A big woman who looks familiar, wearing a cashmere coat, with quirky pointy hair. Where do I know her from? I turn my mind in on itself to concentrate. The more I concentrate, the more I figure that I just keep seeing her around. Is she your friend, Faye? But I've never seen you talking to her. Where does she live? Where is she going? Where is she taking Tamsin?

She lifts Tamsin into her car, looking as if she is inhaling her, and bends inside to strap her in. Then she stands outside the car and looks around as if she wants to know who's watching her. She has strong cheekbones, a roman nose and small eyes. After she has scanned the surrounding area, she opens the front door of her car and slips inside. She seems to spend quite a while looking through the rear-view mirror before she starts the engine, as if she is checking up on Tamsin.

She pulls away from the school. I start my engine and follow her.

70

Faye

'You don't need to worry about Tamsin,' the school secretary informs me over the hands-free car phone. 'Our staff member Erica told us about the special treat she had planned for her. Erica told us you had contacted her to ask her to collect Tamsin for you.'

My mouth is dry. My heart stops beating.

'I didn't contact Erica,' I shout at the speaker, trying to keep my eyes on the road ahead.

'But . . . but . . .' the school secretary splutters.

'I don't even have her phone number,' I interrupt.

A lorry overtakes me on the motorway. It catches my car in its slipstream and pulls it to one side. When I have held the wheel steady and escaped from the pull of the lorry, I bark into the phone, 'Find out where my daughter is!'

'Yes. Yes. Of course.'

Nausea overcomes me. I retch as I hang on to the steering wheel. Was it Erica, or Jonah, who let down my tyres? I press the phone to contact Phillip on speed dial.

71

Phillip

By the time I collect Georgia from my workplace crèche and arrive at the school, the place is no longer a school but a crime scene. Police cars slewed across the gate. Police officers milling and hovering. I walk towards one of the officers in slow motion, as if I am walking through a dream scene.

'I'm Tamsin's father – Phillip Baker. What's happening?' I ask.

The officer's face is silent, immobile.

'We can't contact Erica; she's not picking up. We've been to her house and no one is there.'

I swallow. 'So you're treating this as an abduction?'

'Yes. But please keep calm. We are doing everything we can to find her.'

Keep calm. How can I keep calm? My heart and my mind are on fire.

72

Faye

Phillip, Georgia and I are in the head teacher's study, sitting together on a low-slung fawn sofa. The head teacher is sitting opposite us wearing tweed and kindness, eyes jaded and sad.

'Why did you let my child go home with someone without my permission?' I ask.

She shakes her head. 'I'm so sorry.' There is a pause. 'We believed her. She's a member of staff. We had carried out careful background checks.'

'When is Tamsin coming home?' Georgia asks, wriggling as she sits on my knee.

'Soon, soon,' Phillip says snuggling her closer to him. 'We're just trying to sort it out.'

Georgia relaxes her body against his. So trusting. And my heart explodes as I worry about where my other daughter is, and what is happening to her right now.

'Perhaps there has just been a misunderstanding and they're on the promised treat right now,' the head teacher says. But I know from her empty eyes that that isn't what she thinks.

73

Phillip

Back home with only one child, living through every parent's nightmare. The house feels empty and cold. Everything looks and feels wrong. We have put Georgia in front of a film, and are sitting at the dining table holding hands across it, eyes locked, bodies gripped by fear.

'Who is this woman?' I ask for the fiftieth time.

For the fiftieth time you reply, 'I don't know. I hardly knew her. I only spoke to her a few times. I didn't even know she was a dinner lady. She mentioned she wanted to take Tamsin for a special treat. She told me she had a daughter called Rosalie. I had no idea Rosalie didn't exist.'

Do you think you should have paid less attention to your modelling career, and more attention to what was happening at the school gate? I think this but don't say it. I look at you, bereft. We are both drowning, Faye.

74

Jonah

The square-faced woman is speeding down the motorway in her VW Polo. A bad driver. She must be making Tamsin car sick, driving too close to other drivers in the fast lane, forcing them to pull into the middle. Moving in and out without indicating. It is very hard to keep following her. But I am hanging in there and managing.

She turns off at junction three, without indicating. Good job I have excellent eyesight and a powerful car. She only brakes just in time to avoid ploughing into the car in front at the first roundabout. She follows the road and eventually turns right into the car park of an older, more characterful than usual Premier Inn, which looks as if it once was a large pub. I park in a space in the row opposite.

She opens the car door and steps out, face and shoulders strong and determined. There is something powerful about her, like a handsome lioness about to go hunting. She opens the back door and bends to lift Tamsin out. Tamsin is struggling and crying. She is wetting herself. Leonine woman lowers her to the ground and hovers above her, face like thunder, hand stretched as if she is about to slap her. But she manages to compose herself, and take her in her arms once again. Tamsin is crying. Tamsin is struggling. The woman is holding her so tight she can hardly breathe and is taking her into the hotel.

75

Phillip

We put Georgia to bed on automatic pilot. We are not living life, just moving through it. I can hardly bear to look at you. Seeing your pain intensifies mine. Silence presses against us, louder than sound, as the phone remains quiet, no one ringing to tell us Tamsin is on the way home. Silently, unthinkingly, I am blaming you, Faye.

76

Faye

I look at my watch. It is past Tamsin's bedtime now. If Tamsin is dead, I can only cope by killing myself. Then I think of Georgia and know I will have to be strong for her sake, and her sake alone. I will have to pretend to continue – to give her a chance, but the person that I used to be would no longer exist. I look across at the photograph on the mantelpiece of my two girls together, and my heart lurches. The one we took when Tamsin came to visit Georgia in hospital when she had just been born. Heat and nausea rise inside me. This is a punishment for what I have done. A debt for my behaviour, which I am being forced to pay. It is my fault you have gone.

77

Erica

I wash Tamsin's knickers in the bathroom sink and dry them with the hairdryer.

'I want Mummy,' Tamsin says, as I get her to step into them and pull them up.

'She'll be here soon.'

'When?' Tamsin demands, twisting and curling strands of hair between her fingers.

'Very soon,' I reply.

'I want to ring Daddy. He always comes when Mummy isn't there.'

'You'll have to put up with me for a while. Shall we do something fun until she arrives?' I ask with a soft smile.

'There's nothing fun here,' she says edging away from me and climbing back onto the bed.

Nothing fun here. The most expensive hotel I've ever stayed in. No. The only hotel I have ever stayed in.

'We could go and get something to eat in the restaurant. They have chicken nuggets and chips.' I pause and give her my gentlest smile again. 'I'll let you have ketchup.'

She wriggles and frowns. 'Mummy always lets me have ketchup.'

No self-restraint, Faye. Ketchup has sugar in. Haven't you read about the diabetes risks young people are exposed to today?

'Come on – shall we go downstairs to the restaurant then?' I suggest.

Tamsin sits, knees huddled to her chest, in the middle of the bed. I hold my hand out towards her. She shakes her head.

'I'm not hungry.'

'Well then, let's sit and watch the TV together,' I say, trying to snuggle next to her, resigning myself to take an interest in the cartoon character with a sponge for a head.

'No.' She shakes her head and bursts into tears. 'I just want Mummy.'

Her body is shaking and heaving in distress.

I sit on the bed and slide towards her. I try to put my arm around her shoulders but she pushes me away. 'Go away,' she shouts.

'I can't go away. I'm here to look after you.'

'I hate you. Go away.'

She kicks and screams. I do not know what to do to calm her. A knock at the door. My heart races. Police? Room service? Another knock, louder this time.

'Please open the door, Erica Sullivan,' someone shouts.

I slip off the bed, limbs like lead, mind frozen, move to the door and open it.

Three police officers. Two men. One woman. Barging straight in. The woman sweeps Tamsin into her arms.

'I want my mummy. I want my mummy,' she is yelling. Yowling and crying.

I stand watching her ungrateful behaviour, feeling like slapping her. Isn't she going to tell them how kind I was? How I was looking after her?

The woman rushes Tamsin out. Holding her tightly against her body as if she is protecting her from gunfire.

I am cuffed. Hands behind my back. Wrists burning.

'You are under arrest on suspicion of abducting Tamsin Baker. You do not have to say anything. But, it may harm your defence if you do not mention when questioned something which you later rely on in court. Anything you do say may be given in evidence.'

'I was taking her on a treat. Her mother knew about it,' I shout.

They bundle me out, down the long carpeted corridor of the Premier Inn, its psychedelic colours making me feel sick. Past the purple-clad receptionist who is checking some people in. People who turn to stare at me. Their eyes burn into my skin. I look the other way.

'What have you done with Tamsin?' I shriek at the officers holding me. 'Where is she?'

'Being taken back to her family.'

'I've not harmed her.'

'Good. That's something.'

Out of the hotel, cool evening air scraping across my skin. Into the back of the police car, which is slewed across the entrance to the hotel. Why do the police never park like normal people? One officer is sitting in the back of the car with me. The other in the driver's seat. He turns the key and starts the engine. The car sets off, siren blaring, advertising my distress to the world.

78

Phillip

The telephone rings. My stomach simmers with dread. I pick up, hands trembling.

'Mr Baker?'

'Yes.'

'Police Constable Vickers here. Good news. We've found her. She's safe.'

79

Faye

Tamsin is back in my arms. Wearing some spare clothes that had been provided at the police station. Hers had been taken in evidence apparently. And instead of smiling I am crying. With relief. With happiness. With an overdose of emotion. Holding her fragile body against mine. I want to hold and protect her for ever. Georgia, who has woken up with all the commotion, is clinging on to her too. And Phillip. Tears stream down Phillip's face. I have never seen him cry before. Not even when his father died. Not even when we got married.

We are moulded together in a tight, caressing ball. Conjoined, we move and sit together on the sofa.

'Can I sleep with you tonight?' Tamsin whispers.

'Of course,' I reply.

'Did that woman hurt you, Tammy?' Phillip asks.

I tighten inside.

'Did she?' Phillip pushes.

'No, Daddy. But I was frightened. I didn't know where you were.'

Tamsin clings to me more tightly, and despite my joy and relief I am angry inside.

80

Jonah

I know Tamsin is home. I saw the police arrive with her. Watched you come to the door and take her in your arms, wearing your black jeans, and a black T-shirt with a diamante spider on the front. She clung to you so tightly. Phillip holding Georgia, hovering uncertainly behind you.

Why did you let that woman take your daughter? You need me to protect you, Faye. Phillip isn't doing a good enough job. Never did really, did he? Even the speech he made on your wedding day was disappointing.

Now I have rescued Tamsin, you will be even more impressed by me, won't you, Faye? I will be your hero. Your knight in shining armour. You have always been attracted to me, but now you will finally realise my advantages are overwhelming.

81

Faye

A moonlit night. An electric moon poking its fingers between the gap in the curtain, irradiating my daughter's face as she lies between us, sleeping in the middle of our double bed.

You are fast asleep lying on your side, facing the wall, inhaling and exhaling deeply; almost snoring. I am amazed by your ability to sleep after such emotional turmoil. You used to be so empathetic and sensitive, but since Tamsin was taken, you have seemed so cold and distant, so far away.

Tamsin. Lying so still. Like a sleeping angel. I lie next to her, feeling every pulse of her breath. Every pulse of her life, her energy.

I close my eyes. My daughter's features fade. All I can see now is the spectre of Erica's face, moving closer and closer to mine, in the school playground.

'I'm taking Tamsin on a special treat,' she taunts.

I see her hand clasping my child's hand, pulling her through the school playground. Her arms holding my child against her body, so tight she is squashing her, as she pushes her roughly into a waiting car. She steps into the driver's seat and the car engine starts.

I am running after the car as it drives off. I have no car, no quick way to follow. I run and I run after the car, but the car pulls away, and however fast I run, I fall further and further into the distance. The car becomes a dot on the horizon. The car disappears over a crest at the edge of the earth.

I see Tamsin in the Premier Inn, calling for me and trembling. I see Erica moving towards her, about to suffocate her with a pillow. I wake up in a cold sweat and pull her body against my chest to comfort me. As my breathing calms, part of me dies inside. It is my fault. I should have checked out Rosalie. I should have realised Erica was a sham. I shouldn't have slept with Jonah. My life is a nightmare that I have to keep wading through.

82

Erica

The middle of the night. Hours since I heard the police siren slow and stop, and felt silence pierce into my head; silence sharper than sound. Hours since the burly officer who was sitting next to me in the back of the car bundled me in here, into this small holding room at the police station. Hours since he locked the door.

I am sitting on a bench in a small cell. No bed. No toilet. No wash facilities. Thinking about Tamsin. How sorry I am I couldn't help her. Why are they taking her back into danger? She would have soon got used to me.

I see her face as she enters the dining room at school with owl boy and Ashmolean. As she skips out of school and hides behind your legs. As she steps past Parky to hold my hand. I should have taken her further away. Somewhere they would never find us.

The cell door is being unlocked. The burly officer – the large swarthy man who put me in here – is standing in front of me, eyes burning into mine.

'Time to come with me,' he barks.

Trembling, I slip off the bench and stand up. He takes my arm and frog-marches me from my cell, along a long low-ceilinged corridor, into a check-in area.

'Erica Sullivan – the child abduction one,' he announces in a deep crackly voice to a young female officer sitting behind a counter.

'Can I ring my friend Mouse?' I ask as I stand in front of the counter trembling.

'Yes. You are allowed to ring your next of kin to tell them where you are. Otherwise they'll be worried,' the female officer says, handing me a cordless phone. 'Dial 9 for an outside line.'

'You're not allowed to ring anyone who may have acted as an accomplice,' the burly officer adds darkly, looking at the wall beyond my head, as if I am invisible. Irrelevant.

I have to concentrate to remember Mouse's mobile number. Despite the tremor in my fingers I manage to dial it. It rings. He picks up.

'Hi, Erica. Where are you? I was expecting you for supper. Did you forget?'

The sound of his voice, sounding so near down the phone line, yet so far away, makes my stomach rotate. Tears begin to stream down my face.

'I'm at Camberley Police Station.'

'What on earth are you doing there?'

'Please, please help me, Mouse,' I beg, between tears.

83

Phillip

I sit up in bed. I reach for the cricket bat that I keep at the side of the bed and sit holding it tight, ready to whack an intruder in the face. I lift the bat and bang it across my body with my right hand, catching the blow from it in the palm of my left. I continue to do this repeatedly. You have no need to worry, I tell you silently, no one is going to frighten my family again.

84

Erica

I have been allocated a proper cell with a bed and a toilet. I was only there a short while before the burly officer arrived to accompany me to the interview room. Fortunately, as soon as we arrived he disappeared.

So now I am sitting with the female police officer from last night, and a sergeant. A grey plastic table stretches between us like a battle line. The duty solicitor, whom I met briefly last night, arrives looking red-faced and flustered. She sits next to me. A middle-aged woman. Thin as a pipe. Nails bitten to the quick. Wiry hair scratching her face. I wish she looked more confident.

The sergeant turns the recording machine on.

'Third March 2018, 11:30 p.m. Sergeant Tiller present,' he announces.

'Constable Thackery,' the female officer chirrups.

'Sarah Tideswell,' the duty solicitor enunciates.

I announce my name, but as I do my voice cracks. For the benefit of the tape recording, the sergeant arrests me all over again. My stomach begins to churn.

'Why did you take Tamsin, Erica?' Sergeant Tiller asks, pushing his marble grey eyes into mine.

The churning in my stomach increases. 'Please give me my girl back,' I spit. 'She's mine.'

He leans back and folds his arms, taunting me with dancing eyes.

'But she's not your girl is she, Erica?' There is a pause. 'Her parents are Phillip and Faye Baker.'

I begin to cry. 'Give her back to me. I just wanted to help her.' My fingers are tightening. So tight I can't stop them. I bang my fist on the table. He does not flinch.

The duty solicitor, Ms Tideswell, shakes her head.

'I want to be a better mother to her.'

My sobs are becoming thicker, heavier. I begin to scream at the top of my voice. I scream and scream, so loud I can hardly breathe. I am screaming and suffocating, doubled up in pain, gasping for breath, pins and needles burning up my left arm, right across my chest.

Ms Tideswell leans across the table towards the sergeant. 'We need to terminate this interview.'

'I'm requesting a full psychological report before we continue,' Sergeant Tiller says into the microphone. He switches off the recording machine. 'Get a psychiatrist here as soon as possible,' he barks at Constable Thackery. 'And an appropriate adult.'

Ms Tideswell puts her hand on my arm. I push it away. 'Try to keep calm. We're only here to help.'

85

Jonah

I am sorting through a pile of post when the doorbell buzzes. I reduce Beethoven's Ninth to background music, and pad through the hallway to answer it.

I open the door to find a policewoman standing in front of me. Brown wavy hair cascades to her shoulders. She is young and pretty. Too young to be at work. She should be travelling the world weighed down only by a rucksack.

'Do come in,' I say.

She steps into the hallway. Medium height. Medium weight. Medium breasts.

'Hi there. I'm PC Linda Smith. I've come to talk to you about the child abduction you witnessed, if that's OK?'

'Of course.' I smile at her. 'Please follow me into the drawing room.'

Through my small hallway. Through my Georgian dining room, down into my sitting room, which opens onto my landscaped garden.

'Do sit down.'

She sinks into my Regency sofa and crosses an elegant pair of legs. I sit in a chair opposite her.

'I just want to ask you a few questions,' Linda Smith says.

I smile at her. 'Please fire away.'

'Could you run through what you saw again? If you don't

mind?' she asks, vowels precise and clipped. Not just shapely. Well educated too.

'I was driving past the school when I saw a woman leaving with a struggling child. The child looked really unhappy. I recognised the child: Tamsin Baker, the daughter of my close friends Faye and Phillip.'

Linda leans forwards, breasts pressed together like a comfortable shelf. 'And you decided to follow her?' she asks.

'There was no time to do anything else. If I had stopped to call the police no one would have known where they had gone.'

'It's such a good job you acted as you did, and telephoned us so quickly, after you had followed them. The parents were so grateful when we told them what you did.'

'I hope so,' I reply with a grin.

'We're all so very happy she's all right.' A pause. 'I just want to take your formal statement for the record. Is it OK if we do that now?'

'Fine.'

She smiles. Not as special as your smile, Faye. Don't worry, you put everyone in the shade. But a nice enough smile. Warm. Inviting. Men like to be invited. You know that don't you, Faye? I expect my next invitation is already in your mind.

86

Phillip

Georgia is in bed. I have just settled her and left her totally relaxed, lying flat on her back, arms splayed above her head. So pleased to have her sister home. She whispered that to me before she fell asleep. You and I are sitting in the living room, Tamsin dozing on your lap.

'I know Jonah has been a pain lately, but maybe we should invite him over for dinner to thank him. Cook a special meal? What do you think? He is my oldest friend and we really owe him now.'

Your face stiffens. But, 'Yes. Yes. You're right,' you say. 'He's been making me feel very uncomfortable lately but I suppose that's insignificant now he has helped get Tamsin back.' There is a pause. 'Invite him if you must.'

'Mrs Enthusiastic.'

You laugh an artificial laugh, letting me know my joke isn't funny. 'Just don't leave me in a room on my own with him, and if the evening docsn't turn out as you hope, don't blame me.'

You stand up, cradling Tamsin in your arms, ready to carry her upstairs and settle her. Your violet eyes catch mine. Violet eyes tangled with worry. Is inviting Jonah over a mistake? But I can't stop myself. He saved our daughter's life. He has been behaving strangely lately but I think we need to give him a break. Jonah and I go back a long way.

87

Erica

Lying on a plank-like bed, in a cell at the police station, waiting for a psychiatric assessment. Waiting to be formally interviewed. The bastards are blaming me for this, but it is your fault, Faye. How many men have you been to bed with? How unsuitable are your values?

I close my eyes. I am back, lying in bed with my mother. I smell lily of the valley. I feel the soft skin of her cheek as she lies next to me. When she took me in her arms I wanted to stay there for ever. But I could never stay lying in her arms for very long.

My mother had numerous boyfriends. I do not remember any of them clearly. I do not know which one was my father. They came and went, visiting her bedroom. The bedroom was a fresh lemon colour. When she had a boyfriend visiting in her bedroom I had to stay downstairs. I tried so hard to do as I was told, sitting downstairs watching TV.

But one evening I thought one of Mother's boyfriends was hurting her. She cried out in pain like an injured animal. I ran upstairs and burst into her bedroom to try to help her. She was lying on the bed naked. Her boyfriend was also naked, lying on top of her. Holding her wrists in his hands and forcing her arms apart above her head. He was pumping on top of her and she was screaming in pain. Another man who was fully dressed was standing above the bed watching.

'Get off my mother,' I shouted.

I picked up one of his shoes, which was lying on the floor in front of me, and threw it at him. It hit the back of his head. He pulled away from my mother, turned around, threw it back at me and missed. He moved towards me, face hissing with anger. His face was red and purple. I had never seen such an angry face. I tried not to look at the rest of his naked body. It scared me. I had never seen an erect penis before. The end of his penis was purple like his face.

'I'm not coming here again,' he shouted.

He picked his clothes off the floor, got dressed and left. The other man sat on the bedroom chair, waiting. I looked across to my mother. She had slipped her dressing gown on and was walking towards me.

She slapped me on the cheek, so hard, I could barely breathe. I began to cry. I wanted to run away, but my feet wouldn't move.

'Don't come in here when I'm busy with a man, ever again.'

I know what it is like to have a promiscuous mother. I didn't want you to damage your children, Faye.

88

Faye

'I'm not going to school today, Mummy.'

I groan inside. Tamsin is sitting at the dining table eating muesli, tucking in enthusiastically.

'I'm staying at home with you,' she continues.

Georgia is eating chopped banana with her fingers.

'You have to go to school,' I tell Tamsin, as I wipe Georgia's hands.

'Why?' she asks stretching her neat crocodile line of shiny milk teeth into a cheeky smile.

'It's the law,' I reply, taking a sip of coffee.

'What does law mean?'

'Rules. The rules we have to stick to.'

She shrugs her shoulders. 'Why do we have to stick to rules?'

'To keep safe. To make sure we do what is best for everyone.'

'But Erica wasn't sticking to rules when she took me.'

'And look what happened to her – she's in prison now.'

'Will I go to prison if I don't go to school?' she asks as she continues to eat her muesli.

I am so tempted to say yes, to frighten her into doing as I say. But if I frighten her she might freak out.

'No you won't go to prison, but the head teacher will be cross. And Parky will miss you.'

I look at my watch and my stomach tightens. Ten minutes

before we need to leave for school. Since the abduction, getting Tamsin to school has become harder every day.

'Come on, Tamsin,' I say in a bright, buttery voice. 'You've finished your breakfast. I'll clean Georgia up. You get your hat and coat.'

Tamsin folds her arms. 'No.'

I step into our kitchen area, soak Georgia's flannel in warm water, and gently wipe her face. Then I smile sweetly at Tamsin, pretending I haven't heard her.

'Come on, darling. I'll help you find your shoes and coat.'

Arms folded more tightly. 'No.'

'I have some chocolate buttons for you – when you've got your coat on.'

Her arms loosen. She slips off her chair and moves to stand in front of the coat rack by the door. I whisk her coat from its hook and help her into it. I hand her a few chocolate buttons from my secret stock.

'If I put my shoes on, can I have some more?'

'OK then.'

She puts her shoes on as quickly as possible. I hand her a few more.

We set off down the road, Georgia's face clean now, dropping off to sleep in the buggy. Tamsin is eating chocolate buttons. Not ideal. But at least she is going to school. I started off wanting to be the perfect mother, but these days everything is a bribe or a compromise, and I just manage. All the relationships in my life seem corrupt these days.

The walk is taking for ever. Tamsin is walking so, so slowly. After a hundred yards, she stops. Feet locked to the ground.

'I don't want to go to school. I want to stay home with you.'

I kneel down and hug her. 'The bad lady won't come again. It's OK, Tamsin.'

'I know the bad lady isn't coming. I still don't want to go to school.'

'Come on. Let's pretend you are a bird flying to school. I'll carry you.'

She giggles. I lift her up, beneath my left arm and try to carry her in a horizontal position, like a bird or an aeroplane, while pushing the buggy with my other hand. But she is too heavy. It doesn't work. I have to give up for a rest.

She sits on the pavement. 'I'm a bird having a rest,' she says. 'In a moment I am going to look for worms.'

Before she can do that, I find the energy to lift her up again. She flies for a while. We rest. She flies again. Finally we arrive at the school gates. She is still pretending to be a bird as I lift her past the School Gate Mafia, who look across at us and frown as we pass. We are late. They have already dropped their children off. The playground is empty. The children have gone inside.

She finds her feet.

'Bye bye, Mummy,' she says, stepping into her classroom at last.

89

Erica

The psychiatrist is sitting behind the plastic table in the interview room, waiting for me. She has black hair and looks tall above the table. Her face is long, and her hair falls shapeless and dark, like bland curtains on either side of her face. She smiles at me.

'Hi, Erica,' she says. 'Please sit down. I am pleased to meet you. My name is Jane Harrington.'

As I sit I realise that tears are streaming down my face. I attempt to wipe them away with the back of my hand. She passes me a tissue.

'Thank you.'

I sit wiping my face, looking at her. She has soft brown eyes, like Ashmolean's at school. I try to remember the colour of my mother's eyes, but I cannot. Were they violet like Faye's and Tamsin's? Is that why I have become so obsessed with them? No. I don't know. I push that thought away. A young officer arrives placing a tray of tea and biscuits in front of us. Custard creams. Mouse's favourites. What have I done? How long will it be before I see Mouse again? How is he managing without my support? I should have thought about that in the first place.

The police officer disappears. I take a sip of my tea. So sweet it bites into my tongue. But it is soothing somehow. I take a custard cream.

'Let's start with your crying,' Jane asks. 'Do you often cry like this?'

'No. It's just been sparked by this arrest when I was trying to help Tamsin.' There is a pause. 'I feel so guilty.'

Jane is making notes on a pad in front of her. She takes a sip of tea. She puts her head up to speak. 'Guilty about what you did?' she asks.

I shake my head, confused. 'No. Guilty I couldn't help.'

'We can talk about that later. First there are some questions I need to ask.' She consults a printed sheet she picks up from her desk. 'Have you ever been suicidal?'

'No.'

She ticks the sheet.

'Have you ever had suicidal thoughts?' she continues, looking up, eyes riddled with concern.

'No,' I repeat.

Her mouth flattens. 'But you have had a difficult past, haven't you?' she asks.

'If everyone who has had a difficult past killed themselves the human race would have died out centuries ago. What are you trying to say?'

Her mouth moves downwards. 'I am not trying to say anything. I am just trying to ask a few standard questions in order to assess you.'

What am I? A person or a protocol? 'OK then, fire away.' I grit my teeth and manage.

'How do you feel you get on with others?' she asks.

I sigh inside. 'Like who?' I ask.

'Well, let's start with your parents?'

'I can't remember my father at all. I'm not sure I ever met him.' A silent tear slides down my face. 'And I can only just remember my mother, but I think she was a bit like Faye.'

'In what way?'

'I'd prefer not to say.'

She swallows. She pauses. 'Why did you take Tamsin?' she asks.

'She needed to get away.'

'Like you did, Erica?'

'Yes.'

In the distance of my mind I am back in my council house. My mother has been taken away in an ambulance and my social worker is helping me pack. My clothes. My small golden teddy bear that I have had since I was three. A photograph of my mother. The one I still have, and treasure. Mother is standing by the sea wearing shorts and a T-shirt, wind funnelling her long black hair. Her grin is so wide, so cheeky. She loved the sea. She once told me watching the waves roll in made her feel free. I now understand the tragedy of her life. This picture encapsulates her before tragedy took over. If only she could have stayed like this.

Jane is talking to me, over the thin thread of my memory.

'We are going to help you. Antidepressants. Dialectic Behavioural Therapy. A form of CBT, which is very successful. The results we now have with talking therapies are phenomenal.'

Her words spin in my mind on automatic repeat. There but not there; swimming in the ocean with a young version of my mother.

90

Faye

School pickup. Parky's dark eyes burning with concern. I know he is devastated about letting Tamsin go off with Erica. He looks older, smaller, diminished in every way.

'We need to have a meeting with the Head.' He pauses. 'The classroom assistant is letting the children out and looking after Tamsin. Would you like her to look after Georgia too?'

After what happened, I don't want either of my girls looked after by a classroom assistant. But I have no choice. I can't have them listening to us discussing the abduction.

'Yes please,' I say.

Parky takes Georgia's buggy and wheels it into the classroom, then he comes back to fetch me and lead me across the playground. The School Gate Mafia's eyes light up, searing into my back, as I follow Parky, into the main entrance of the school, through the waiting room, resplendent with class photographs, and bold finger paintings. Past the school secretaries. He knocks on the Head's door.

'Come in,' she shouts.

Parky opens the door and we step inside. Mrs Worthington, the Head of School, is about forty years old, slim with sculptured hair, riddled with expensive two-toned highlights. Dressed like the lady captain of a golf club. Chinos. Tailored jacket. She is sitting legs crossed, to the left of her desk, in the sofa area of her spacious office. Her shoes are golden, soft leather pumps. Comfortable and expensive.

'Thank you for coming.' A pause. A smile. 'Do sit down,' she says, gesticulating to the sofa opposite.

I sit down; Parky sits next to me. The sofa looks comfy but the cushions are hard, pressing into my back.

'No one regrets what happened to Tamsin more than I do,' Mrs Worthington says.

Anger knots in my stomach. I am sure Tamsin, Phillip and I regret it more. Her attitude is too calm and complacent. 'School procedures are being investigated by the local authority, and I, as head teacher, face suspension if we are found to be at fault in any way,' she continues. 'I just thought you ought to know what was happening. Also, we are worried about Tamsin. We are having a few problems with her.'

Problems. The knots in my stomach rotate like pounding fists. What do they expect after their negligence? Problems they need to deal with.

I glare across at Parky.

'Would you like to explain, Mr Parkinson?' Mrs Worthington says.

'She isn't eating at school,' he starts.

I sigh inside. That isn't much of a problem – she eats so much at home. 'Maybe she isn't hungry in the day because she has been having a large breakfast,' I snap.

'Not eating is the tip of the iceberg,' Parky continues. 'She is ignoring her friends Tom and Ashmolean, staring through them all the time as if she is in a trance.' A pause. 'She isn't concentrating in class. She won't even sit still at story time and that used to be her favourite.'

My stomach feels as if it is about to implode. Parky's voice is soft and flat. Maybe story time is monotonous. Maybe he needs to make a bit more effort.

'She pinched Ashmolean's bottom three times and made her scream,' he continues. Another pause. Raised eyebrows. 'Then she sat screaming in the Wendy house, throwing plastic fruit.'

171

I cannot put up with any more of this. I stand up.

'She has just had a bad experience,' I shout, 'due to your negligence. Now she needs love and understanding. She gets it at home and I expect her to get it here.'

Parky stands up, face redder than ever. 'She does indeed. I completely agree. We all need to lavish her with as much love and understanding as possible. Children at this age are love sponges. They soak it all up.'

'That's right, Mrs Baker,' Mrs Worthington adds, rising to her feet, and crossing her arms. 'We just wanted to let you know that we think it is very important that we all work together to lavish her with attention right now.'

91

Erica

Mouse is here. Taking me in his arms for the first time. I am clinging on to him and crying. He is stroking my back to comfort me. What have I done? Why am I here? Why can't I just go home with Mouse?

92

Jonah

So pleased you have invited me for supper – like you used to in the old days. So busy with your own lives since you had the children, you haven't invited me for a while. I have been really looking forward to it. I walk up the steps towards the front door of your modern town house, almost tripping over the pot of winter pansies you always place on the top step. I knock on your roaring lion brass doorknob. Very faux-Georgian. As you know, Faye, you get the real thing at my place.

Phillip opens the door, wearing jeans and a Gant T-shirt. He hasn't shaved. His face is murky and messy, no designer stubble.

'Come in,' he says with a grin.

Phillip. I look into his eyes. Nothing hard-edged or controversial about him. And I am back remembering a summer night drinking vodka on the banks of the Cam, the river so hot it felt oily, daring him to swim and race me from Magdalene Bridge to Queens. He wouldn't rise to the challenge. He needs to rise to my challenge now, if he wants to keep you, Faye.

I step into your compact hallway. Do you remember the way you screamed, Faye? Soon you will be screaming for me in a different way.

And now you are here, pursing your lips and brushing them across my cheeks, gently in welcome, for Phillip is watching us. I step back to admire the lavender silk dress that clings to your body. Long black hair tumbling down your back.

'Thank you, Jonah. Thank you so much.'

'The least I could do,' I reply. 'What a trauma you have been through.'

Your eyes gleam with suppressed tears.

I follow you and Phillip through the tiny hallway that opens out into your tiny open-plan living room. Down the steps that run across the width of the room, into the sitting area, opening onto the pocket handkerchief of a garden.

I sit on a sofa, opposite you both. Phillip opens the champagne. The cork explodes from the bottle and hits the ceiling. You laugh. I wouldn't laugh if my house were being damaged. Even after three years at Cambridge the idiot doesn't know how to open champagne. One day soon, Faye, we will drink champagne together, in my beautiful home, incomparable to Phillip's, and celebrate the start of our new life. But tonight Phillip pours us a glass each and we stand in the middle of this cluttered room, raising our glasses.

'Cheers,' he says, 'We will never be able to thank you enough.'

'It was a no-brainer. Just lucky I was going past at the same time.'

We clink glasses and sit down.

I watch you lift your glass to your creamy lips. Your eyes are shining. Your cheeks are flushed.

Phillip offers me an olive. It squashes between my fingers as I raise it to my mouth. I play with it between my teeth before I bite into it. It tastes bitter, salty.

'I must just check the food,' you say with a smile.

Clutching your champagne, you make your way to the kitchen. As your hourglass figure sways across the room, I undress you with my mind. Your silky dress slips to the floor. Your lacy bra and panties. I want to walk up and take you from behind. You like that position don't you, Faye? You climaxed twice. And then I climaxed. The best climax of my life.

175

93

Phillip

I am grateful to Jonah, but you were right, Faye: I do not like the way he is staring at you. I've always thought he fancied you, and that his eyes lit up when you were around, but this is different. This is predatory. I try to distract him but he is so entranced by you, he doesn't move or speak until you leave the room. Then he places his champagne on the coffee table.

'Is Tamsin all right now?' he asks.

'Yes. Seems to be. But she's a bit clingy. Frightened if she doesn't know where we are.'

I sit sipping my drink. Saturday night. Why is he wearing a suit? He is always overdressed. I remember a time at Cambridge, when we took an old friend from school punting. Jonah turned up looking like a real plonker in a blazer and straw boater. Who owned a straw boater in 2004? You would have thought it was 1904. And tonight, wearing a suit on Saturday evening. Completely over the top. Look at his tie. A Cambridge club, and far too garish. He smiles and crosses his legs. His trouser leg rides up, well past his ankles. Bright orange socks. Always showy and flamboyant. I used to like him for that. It compensated for my dowdiness. He said and wore things that I would never dare. I could sit in the background and enjoy watching and listening, soaking it up. But I no longer need his colour. I have your colour, Faye.

'I suppose being a bit clingy after what's happened is par for the course,' Jonah says, with an inappropriate grin, so wide and glaring that these days it just sets my teeth on edge.

'I suppose so. But fortunately I haven't had to cope with my five-year-old child being abducted before.'

Silence settles between us.

'I recognised the woman who took Tamsin,' he announces after a while.

'You did? Do you know anything about her?'

'No. It's just I've seen her around quite a lot.'

'The police have informed me she's called Erica Sullivan. Does that ring any bells?' I ask.

He shakes his head. 'The name isn't familiar, just the face.'

'Maybe she's got one of those generic faces.'

He smiles. 'Maybe.' He presses his hands together, tapping fingernails against fingernails. 'Or maybe she's been stalking Faye.'

Stalking Faye. How would he know whether anyone is stalking you, Faye?

94

Faye

'Supper's ready,' I announce, placing the starter on the table. Asparagus wrapped in pecorino and prosciutto.

Phillip and Jonah walk towards the table. Jonah is smiling at me with his eyes. Phillip's face is leaden. Has Jonah said something?

Phillip pours the drinks. I take a large slug of red wine and cut into my asparagus.

'Jonah suggested Erica might have been stalking you. Do you think that's possible?' he asks.

'How would you know that, Jonah?' I ask, voice on the edge. High-pitched.

Jonah smiles a high-wattage smile and raises his eyebrows. 'Just a guess of course.'

My heart is racing. I cannot eat. I sit pushing my food around my plate.

'Did you say anything to the police?' I ask.

'No.'

I sigh inside, with relief.

'If it's what you think, why didn't you tell them?' Phillip asks.

'Because it's such a random guess.'

Just a guess. A random guess. When will Phillip guess? I look across at him eating his asparagus, looking so dear, so familiar. What have I done? Will I ever be able to move past this?

95

Jonah

The evening is dragging. Every time I ask Phillip a question his answers are monosyllabic, as if he is withdrawing from me like he used to at the end of a heavy night; too much alcohol making him silent and flat. Faye, you look so worried. So beautiful. Worried suits you – makes you look vulnerable.

You place a pot of coffee on the dining table, and a box of mint chocolates.

'I'm whacked out, after everything that's happened,' you say, rubbing the side of your head, as if you have a headache. 'I'm so sorry but I'm going to have to excuse myself and go to bed.'

'Are you all right, darling?' Phillip asks, standing up and moving towards you, body stiff with concern.

You smile, a half-smile. 'I'm fine. Just tired. It's all been so stressful. You know stress makes me tired. I can hardly keep my eyes open.'

Phillip kisses you. You kiss him back and run your fingers through his hair. Your gesture of affection stabs into me. You should not touch him like that in front of me. We need to talk. We need to sort this out. Then you step away from Phillip and move towards me.

'Thank you again, Jonah, you've been such a brick.'

I stand up and pull you towards me. I inhale your scent. I try and hug you closely but you stiffen, so I just breathe you in. One at a time your lips brush across my cheeks like feathers, almost too light to feel. This is not good enough, Faye.

179

'Goodnight,' I say as you walk away.

You disappear upstairs.

Phillip pours the coffee and offers me a chocolate.

'No thanks.'

'A liqueur perhaps? Drambuie, Cointreau? Or what about Glenmorangie, your old favourite?'

'Oh yes. Glenmorangie please.'

'Still a whisky boffin are you then?' he asks as he walks to the drinks cabinet in the corner of the living room and pours us a large tipple each, into chunky crystal glasses.

'Yes. Have a nightcap to help me sleep every night. You should try it. It's fantastic with my sleeping pill, zopiclone. Puts me in a trance. Makes me feel so relaxed.'

Ignoring my medical ramblings, he asks, 'Shall we sit in the comfy chairs?'

We settle ourselves on opposing sofas, with coffee, mints and whisky. The gritty silence that has fallen between us so many times this evening descends again. Phillip sips his coffee and stares into the air in front of him.

I look at the photograph of you, Faye, in the middle of the coffee table. Long hair pulled up into an elaborate bun. Smile pronounced. Wearing a purple silk evening dress that accentuates the colour of your hair. I stare at you for a second too long.

'That's Faye,' Phillip says. 'When I took her back to my college ball.' There is a pause as he takes a sip of his drink. 'You've always found her attractive, haven't you?'

I lean forwards and cross my legs.

'I hate to tell you, Phillip, but she finds me attractive too.'

96

Phillip

'. . . she finds me attractive too.'

His words jolt me. As if I have been attacked with a cattle prod. He sits on my sofa looking smug and self-satisfied, like he always used to when he boasted about making a conquest. Even though he may well have saved my daughter's life my fist clenches. I want to punch him in the face.

'What makes you think Faye finds you attractive?' I ask.

He grins a wolfish grin. 'Can't you see the pull between us? It has always been there but it has intensified recently.'

'No. I'm her husband, so obviously I assume she's in love with me.'

His sips his Glenmorangie and raises his eyebrows. 'In that case why has she spent so many years flirting with me, and finally managed to seduce me?'

I shake my head in disbelief. 'Seduce you? What are you talking about?'

'She came back to my house and we made love, the night of Sophia and Ronald's party. When you were away at a conference.'

I want to hit him so hard that I pulverise him into the carpet, but I clench my teeth, breathe deeply and hold back. Ultimately I trust my wife, not my friend.

'I don't believe you.' I stand up and walk towards him. 'Even though I'm grateful you rescued our daughter, I think you'd better leave our home right now.'

97

Faye

Tired. So tired. So glad to be away from Phillip and Jonah. There is an atmosphere between them that is draining, and after being so worried about Tamsin, my mind can't deal with any more stress. I am so scared that Jonah will tell Phillip but I can't police their every conversation. I will just have to deny it. It will cause a rift between them, but I have to trust Phillip will believe me, not Jonah. I will just have to be strong and stick to my guns. Dogmatic. Emphatic. Trusting that Phillip will want to believe me. Trusting that I can play on that despite the truth.

I drag my heavy limbs away from the living room, temples pulsating, leaving the men to put the world to rights, over coffee and chocs. I take some ibuprofen, clean my teeth, put my silk teddy on, and slip into bed.

But I can't sleep. I need Phillip's warmth in bed beside me. The reassuring rhythm of his sleeping breath. I lie, too tired to be downstairs socialising, mind buzzing too much to sleep. I will deny it. A denial so deep even I will start to believe it never happened.

Jonah won't dare tell Phillip.

If he does, Phillip won't believe him.

Even if he does believe him, I will deny it.

If I deny it, Phillip will believe *me*.

These four thoughts spin round and round in my head for what feels like hours. At last I hear footsteps padding up the stairs. At last Phillip is coming to bed. He opens the bedroom door and steps through it. I snap the light on and sit up.

'Has Jonah gone?' I ask.

'Yes.'

Phillip but not Phillip. A face with a look on it that I have not seen before. My heart begins to race. My stomach constricts.

'Did you sleep with him?' he asks.

'What are you talking about? Of course I didn't,' I reply.

His eyes shine in the electric light as if they are about to fill with tears. He raises his shoulders a little. 'Then why did he say you did?' Phillip sits on the edge of the bed, eyes burning into mine. 'He said you went back to his house and seduced him the night of Sophia and Ron's party.'

'In his dreams.' I pause. 'Your best friend is a weirdo, who's always had a crush on me. He is just jealous of you. Of our relationship. So he is deliberately trying to come between us. I will be insulted if you even think about believing him.'

98

Phillip

'I will be insulted if you even think about believing him.'

A defensive line. Not a good sign. My veins are pulsating with alcohol. I need to calm down. I need to lie down and think. Do I really doubt that Jonah is jealous of what I have, and wants Faye for himself?

'Please, Phillip,' you say. 'Jonah's a real bad apple. He's just trying to wind you up.' Then your voice weakens and becomes plaintive. 'Phillip, I'm so tired. Please let me go to sleep.'

I lean across and kiss you. Your lips feel thin. I switch the light off, and pad through darkness, to the bathroom to clean my teeth. You have been through so much; I know I must try not to put you through any more. By the time I get into bed, you are sleeping or pretending to. No guilty conscience to keep you awake? Is this what my life has been reduced to, looking for signs to try and determine whether or not I have been cuckolded?

I sink into bed, anger and alcohol pounding through me, and fall into a restless sleep.

99

Erica

Lying on my bed in my cell at the police station, so bored I feel like screaming. The electronic lock whirrs and a police officer appears. So many different officers.

'Erica, please come with me. I want to introduce you to your appropriate adult,' he says with a slight lisp.

An appropriate adult. They must be so worried about me. Don't they know I have spent my whole life looking after myself? That never once have I had an appropriate adult in my life? I slip off the bed and follow him, along the contorted corridor to the interview room where I slump into a chair and wait. He stands and hovers.

After about five minutes a young woman with honey blonde hair divided into two doll-like plaits enters the room. She is wearing denim shorts, a plain T-shirt and wedges. Her finger and toenails are painted bright green and doused with silver glitter.

'Hello,' she says, 'I'm Perdita.'

Voice high-pitched and thin. Appropriate adult. She looks like a child. With a child's appreciation of life. She sits next to me, pushing watery green eyes into mine.

'I've come to explain to you that you will be transferred to the remand wing of the local prison in the next few days. Do you know what remand is?'

'Yes,' I snap.

'Shortly after you have settled in, you will start a course of DBT.' She pauses. 'Do you know what that is?'

'Yes. Yes. The psychologist explained. Dialectic Behavioural Therapy.'

'Yes. But do you understand what it is?'

'It's a talking therapy that changes the way you think and behave,' I parrot from the leaflet I was given.

'But do you really know what to expect?' Perdita pushes.

'Not really but I know I need help.'

Perdita leans forwards and puts her head on one side. 'That's a good start, accepting you need help. But let me explain – it will help you replace negative thought patterns with positive ones.'

'They'll have a job on with my life.'

She leans across and takes my hand in hers. 'It worked for me and they had quite a job on with mine. I'm here to help you. Is there anything at all you'd like to ask?'

'Yes. When can I see my friend Mouse again? I need to see Mouse.'

100

Phillip

Days move on and still anger pulsates inside me. Do I trust you, Faye? Do I trust Jonah? One of you is lying. But how do I decide between my wife and my friend?

101

Faye

I move towards him. He smiles half a smile. His eyes shine into mine. Surely that's a good sign? He steps from the classroom door, and the classroom assistant takes his place, to slowly, carefully, let the children out. Parky stands in front of me, so close I can taste his breath. A smoker. I never realised that before. My face burns with embarrassment. The other mothers must be watching.

'How has she been today?' I almost whisper.

He shakes his head slowly. In despair? In exasperation?

'Variable. She's getting worse. I need you to come and see the Head with me again.'

My stomach rotates, as we repeat the same movements as before. Georgia is wheeled into the classroom to be watched by Parky's assistant. I am guided across the playground, watched by the School Gate Mafia. Into the Head's study; this time sitting on a sofa opposite the Head and Parky. Mrs Worthington begins.

'First, I want to let you know about the situation with the tribunal. We're still waiting to hear. Still waiting to present evidence.'

They deserve to be hauled over the coals for not dealing very well with the aftermath either. But I manage to suppress the anger that is building inside me.

'Thank you for keeping me informed. What else did you want to talk about?' I ask.

She looks across at Parky. She meets his eyes. They are deep blue, and shining with concern. He is not enjoying this any more than I am. He turns to me and blinks.

'We think you need to send Tamsin to see a child psychologist.'

'But . . . but . . .' I splutter, 'don't you think if we all work together, my husband and I, and the school, we can get her through this difficult patch?'

He shakes his head. 'No.' There is a pause. 'She needs professional help.'

Anger cascades. 'I don't want her labelled,' I insist. 'Pigeon-holed.'

The Head intervenes. 'She has had a bad experience. We think instructing a child psychologist would be the best we could do to help her through this as quickly as possible.' She smiles a curt smile; so smug, so used to being in control. 'Go home. Talk to your husband. If you agree, the school secretary can give you a list of recommended practitioners tomorrow.'

I feel like slapping her across the face and shouting *it's your fault, you sort it.* But I manage to clench my fingers together and suppress my feral instinct. It will not help me get a happy daughter back.

Parky leans across and puts his hand on my arm. 'Don't worry, Mrs Baker. Tamsin is a lovely girl. We'll soon sort this out. I just don't like to see things build. Best to nip it in the bud.'

I wince at the invasion of his touch and want to push him away. But then I look into his face and see a dear old boy, sixty at least, approaching retirement, much loved by Tamsin before this happened, and by many school children over many, many years. This school's version of Mr Chips. And I hold back.

'OK, OK, I'll go home and think about it.'

But as I sidle out of the Head's office, my anger turns to shame. I never thought a child of mine would need counselling. Counselling my own child, surely that is my responsibility? Five years old. Already needing counselling. Why has our life gone so wrong?

102

Erica

In the van, on my way to prison, trying to look out of the high window of my compartment to see a bit of sky, to try and stop myself from feeling sick. Locked up and cuffed in this small space, buffeted along a windy road, I feel extremely nauseous. The van is rattling. Rattling my stomach. Rattling my head.

103

Phillip

The children are in bed. I open a bottle of Merlot and pour us a large glass each. We sit together on the sofa. I put my arm around you and pull your body towards mine, but you pull away. I know what is happening. You want to talk. And when you want to talk you like to see my face. My face is the same as ever, but my heart has changed.

'What do you think we should do about Parky's suggestion?' you ask.

You hold my eyes in yours and sip your wine. 'I told you. We should go along with it.'

'Why?' you ask, eyes darkening.

'Why not?' I reply.

'Is that as far as you are going to go, to analyse this?' you snap.

I shrug my shoulders. 'He has spent forty years dealing with young people. The child psychologist will be a professional. These people really know what they are doing, Faye.' I pause. 'I'm in favour of any help we can get.'

Slowly, slowly you shake your head. You sit on the sofa, gripping your wine glass too tightly, and frowning. 'Don't you think professional counselling might cause more damage, be counterproductive?' you say raising your voice, chest heaving. You put your wine glass on the table. 'They can be condescending. Fitting people into boxes. Into pre-described patterns.'

Your frown deepens. You stand up, shaking your head.

'I'm fed up of this conversation. I'm going to bed.' You turn back when you reach the doorway to the stairs. A tear runs down your cheeks and your face crumples. 'I'm just frightened, Phillip. Frightened of making any more mistakes.'

Mistakes? With Tamsin? With Jonah? Or am I your mistake?

104

Erica

'Hi, I'm Jessica Bell,' my DBT specialist says as she sits down opposite me, next to Perdita, extending her arm in a friendly manner first to me, then to my appropriate adult. Jessica Bell is slim and elegant. She looks about sixty years old. Fine skin. Thin like tracing paper. Wearing a tasteful cream blouse and a tight suit. Flat black shoes with a large gold buckle.

'Good to meet you, Erica,' she says. 'I think we should start with the problem and work backwards. Do you agree?'

As if I know where to start. But I know I must try and cooperate.

'Yes,' I reply. 'That makes sense to me.'

She leans forwards in her chair and crosses her legs. 'First, and this will be painful, I want you to try and tell me why you took Tamsin.'

Her question stabs into me. 'It is painful.'

'Why, Erica?'

'Because I don't want to be punished for trying to help.'

'Stealing a child is a criminal offence, Erica. But I believe you that you wanted to help.'

My eyes are prickling, filling with tears. 'You believe me?' I mutter.

'Yes. And now we need to channel that helpfulness and work out how you could have behaved differently.' Jessica leans forwards, smiling at me enthusiastically. Her smile is genuine. It travels around her whole face and shines from her eyes. 'What were you trying to protect Tamsin from?' she asks.

'Her mother's promiscuity.'

'What made you think her mother was promiscuous? How did you know about it?'

My stomach tightens. My body feels bloated, as if it is about to burst. I shift awkwardly in my chair. 'I'll tell you why I know about Faye's promiscuity. I was following her.'

'Why were you doing that?'

The tightness in my body thickens. Pushing up through my throat, making me feel as if I am about to choke. 'It's so embarrassing,' I splutter.

'Please don't be embarrassed. I'm here to help you, not judge you.'

Jessica's voice is warm and soothing. Her words float towards me and envelop me. My words move towards Jessica from somewhere deep inside me.

'I'm infatuated with her. I wish I had her life.'

My words stand in the air between us, and I am proud of them. Pleased I have spoken.

'And then you saw some misbehaviour which poisoned your mind?'

'Yes. She shattered my illusions by sleeping with a man who wasn't her husband. And she has such a lovely husband. Such a perfect life. It triggered memories for me of my own mother's promiscuity and my difficult life. It made me want to take Tamsin away and protect her from the danger I have suffered.' I am crying now, tears streaming down my face. 'I only ever wanted to protect Tamsin. I would never have hurt her. Not in a million years. If I hurt Tamsin I would be hurting myself as well as her.'

Jessica leans forwards again, puts her hand on my arm and smiles. Her smile wraps around me and makes me feel a little lighter. The crying is helping. It is cathartic. Perdita passes me a tissue to dry my face.

'Thank you for being so honest,' Jessica says. 'There are so many positive ways to move forwards from this. We will have plenty of time to discuss them over the next few months, as we are going to see each other several times a week.'

105

Faye

I am sitting in the waiting area in the vestibule of the local hospital while Tamsin is seeing Ms Silverton, the child psychologist. Parky and Phillip have managed to persuade me to put Tamsin through this.

Waiting, watching the world go by. Patients and their carers come and go. So many patients. So many problems. I close my eyes. Please, Ms Silverton. Please help my girl.

106

Faye

Is worry like pain? One bigger worry pushes all smaller worries away? All I do is think about Tamsin. The spectre of Jonah has faded. I have stopped even looking out for his car. Phillip trusts me. Phillip believes me. I can tell by his eyes. His face.

107

Erica

Mouse is here. Taking me in his arms again and hugging me. It feels so right. So comforting. So reassuring. We are allowed a hug at the start of our visits, but no physical contact after that. He smells good. A mixture of sandalwood and patchouli oil. The woollen sweater that his dad's girlfriend knitted for him is warm and comforting against my skin.

We part and sit across a grey plastic table, and I want to hug him again, so much.

'Are you feeling a bit better? Have you stopped crying all the time?' he asks.

'I am feeling a bit better thanks.'

He frowns and nods his head. There is a pause. 'I miss you, Erica,' he says.

'I miss you too, Mouse.' I look out of the window behind him at the grey day. 'However did you manage to get here? It's drizzling.'

He shrugs. 'Because I miss you, Erica. I put myself out.'

His grey-brown eyes hold mine. 'Why did you do it?' he asks.

'If you knew about my childhood you'd understand.' I stir in the uncomfortable plastic chair.

His eyes flatten. 'I'm sure I would. I just wish it hadn't happened. You've left me on my own.'

I lean across the table to take his hand in mine, before I remember I am not allowed to touch him.

'I'm sorry, Mouse. So sorry,' I reply. 'You do have your dad,' I continue, pulling my hand back.

Mouse's mouth is in a line. 'He doesn't play chess.' There is a pause. 'When's the trial? You didn't tell me that.'

'In a few weeks.'

He grins and leans forwards. 'And then are you coming home?'

His words pierce into me. 'No. I'll be found guilty and sent back here. There's no getting around the fact I abducted a child.'

'But I need you, Erica. What about me?' His words pierce more deeply.

'I'm sorry, Mouse – I didn't think properly. I got everything out of balance. A psychologist who visits me in here is helping me to get it back.'

Mouse's mouth falls open a little. I don't think he understands what I am saying.

'Is he?' he asks.

'He's a she.'

'OK then, well, how does she do that?'

'We'll talk together three times a week. About things.'

'Things?'

'Yes. Problem-focused, action-orientated. Or at least that's what it says in the brochure.'

Mouse nods his head in an attempt to look wise. 'Do you think it would help me?' he asks.

'You've already had lots of help. My problems are caused by my upbringing. I need help now.' Mouse continues to nod his head. I continue speaking. 'Your problem is under control. Mine has been very damaging recently.'

His brown eyes darken. 'I've got a good dad? You had a bad mother? Is that what you mean?'

'Something like that. Yes.'

108

Faye

A sharp, cold day. Children wrapped up warm after school. Arriving at the play park, I lift Georgia out of her buggy and carefully balance her little legs on the ground. She toddles off towards the slide, walking clumsily like a clockwork toy, waddling her body from side to side. Tamsin dashes to the roundabout. Too far apart for me to watch both of them.

'Tamsin. Come with me. Let's help Georgia on the slide first.'

I prepare for battle, but it doesn't commence. Tamsin is not being awkward today. She smiles and runs to the slide. She climbs up the chute, slipping and sliding, fighting gravity, and meets her sister at the top. I hover anxiously as they sit snuggled close to one another and come down together, smiling and laughing.

'Swing now,' Georgia demands.

'Swing now,' Tamsin repeats with a giggle.

Tamsin gives Georgia a piggyback to the swings. I follow them. They sit on adjacent seats, and I can push them both at the same time. I watch the rise and fall of their flying bodies. When I was young, I remember being on a swing and thinking I was flying across the top of the world. A feeling of hope and exhilaration. I watch them and wish for a second I was a child again. A child who never made mistakes. A child who wouldn't have grown up to let Jonah rub the base of her spine.

'The bad lady is gone,' Tamsin announces at the top of her

swing. 'She's never coming back.' There is a pause. 'Ms Silverton says I will never see her again.'

'Will I ever see her?' Georgia asks.

'Course not. She's in prison.'

I stand pushing them, wishing I was swinging with them, Tamsin's words singing in my head. The bad lady has gone and she's never coming back.

109

Erica

'Good morning. Have you been thinking about the issues we discussed?' Jessica asks.

I breathe in and out to relax, and lean back in my chair. 'I've been focusing on the fact that Faye is a good mother who needs to be with her family. Her daughter Tamsin needs to be with her.'

'That's good, very good,' Jessica says, voice strong and resonant. 'And how are you intending to follow through?'

'When I look at Faye, instead of focusing on her infidelity and irresponsible attitude towards men, I'm going to think about her family life.'

'Yes. Yes.' Jessica leans forwards. 'And how are you going to do that?'

'By visualising her family together, having a good time, looking out for one another, as pictures in my mind.'

I close my eyes.

'Tell me what you're seeing.'

'It's autumn. They are in my favourite part of the woods, in Bushy Park, where Faye did her ice-cream photoshoot. Phillip and Georgia, Tamsin and Faye, holding hands. Tromping through golden leaves, kicking into them and laughing.'

'Excellent – but now picture what happened when you had Tamsin. That will help consolidate.'

The vision changes. We are back in the Premier Inn. Tamsin

is edging across the bed, away from me. Sobbing and yowling. I try to touch her, to comfort her, but she changes from girl to demon, kicking out at me, thumping and punching me. I open my eyes. I know I have to let this vision go.

'You look upset,' Jessica says. 'What happened?'

'Tamsin doesn't want me. She wants her mother. I was remembering.'

'That's good. Every time you think of Tamsin remember how unhappy she was when you took her.'

Tears are streaming down my face. 'I will never forget. I will never behave like that again.'

110

Erica

My trial is not long off now. I'll be transported from here every day in one of those vans that makes me feel sick, so Perdita will wait for me at the entrance of the crown court, with water and Gaviscon. Perdita is such a brick.

111

Jonah

At home, in my drawing room, watching flames rise in the grate. I have been leaving you alone for a while, Faye. I know you need to concentrate on Tamsin at the moment, to make sure she is all right before we begin to plan our escape together.

As I wait I have been reliving the memory of my conversation with Phillip. The look on his face when I told him the truth about the way you seduced me. His eyes widened in astonishment. He didn't believe you would want me. He's known me such a long time, and I always thought he admired me, was even a little overwhelmed by my superiority. So, his surprise that you were interested in me really insulted me.

As the possibility that it might be true began to dawn on him, his face became immobile, and his eyes lost their spark. As I watched him clench his fist, I feared he was going to hit me. But he put his hands behind his back and the moment passed. He sat staring into space.

'I don't believe you. Please leave our home,' he said.

I did as he asked, stood up and left. I didn't thank him for dinner. Stepping out into a mild evening, young moon like a sliver of fingernail. Looking up at the sky, at the stars so far away, feeling invigorated by the power of the universe. Its endless possibility. And I knew that this was it. My moment. Our moment, Faye. Your marriage is over.

You will end up with me, Faye. I am waiting. I am being patient.

Tonight I have sprayed some of your perfume on a pair of silk knickers I stole from your room. You didn't lock the bedroom door when I came for dinner so I managed to get some of your perfume too. You are always just a few steps away from me. I sit inhaling your scent, remembering the feel of you, Faye. The look on your face the first time I met you. The way your eyes held mine when we were making love.

112

Erica

In court at last, sitting between Perdita and a guard. In the dock behind floor to ceiling glass. Looking at the courtroom from inside a square goldfish bowl with nowhere to hide.

Court officials pace. My duty solicitor arrives, black bags beneath her eyes. More exhausted than ever. She slips behind a table near the front of court and starts whipping through her notes. From behind, her shoulders look frail and brittle, like the carcass of a cooked chicken. I feel sorry for her because I can see that she is riddled with early osteoporosis.

My barrister strides in adjusting his wig, and smiles across at me. A smile that doesn't reach his eyes. I try to smile back but it doesn't work, and I nod my head instead. The prosecution barrister is here. A man who wants to destroy my life. A man who hates me and wants me to die. Young and foppish, with blond hair that he keeps pushing from his eyes. This man, so young his life has hardly begun, wants to take my life away. I close my eyes and think about my therapist, Jessica. Her voice floats towards me.

Focus. Focus. Change the dynamic in your mind.

Focus. Focus. Change the dynamic in your mind.

I open my eyes and I see him, sitting down, bat-wing gown wrapped around him. A young professional doing a job, that's all. Nothing more. Nothing less.

Mouse walks in, and my body lightens. The only real friend

I've ever had is giving me a high five across the courtroom. I want to feel his hand against mine like I used to, so much that I have to swallow to prevent tears. He smiles at me, and for a second he looks so handsome, like the man he might have been. Then his frown settles, and he is Mouse again.

He sits in the viewing gallery. I sit looking at him. He is wearing the leather jacket that his father bought him last year. The jacket he is so proud to own.

'Look at me,' he said, when his father gave it to him, 'I'm a real man about town.'

We both laughed.

'What exactly is a man about town?' I asked.

He shrugged his shoulders. 'I don't know.'

We laughed again.

One of the clerks strides out of court and returns with the jury. I try not to stare at them. I look at my feet. I look at the floor. But my eyes are like magnets. They can't keep away.

Three young women dressed in trendy clothes. Topshop, New Look sort of girls. A grandad figure with grey hair and cosy glasses, studiously reading the notes in front of him. A woman who looks as if she works in an office. A woman who is glossy. A pretty Asian girl with a stud in the side of her nose. A man with a black bushy beard. A man with designer stubble. A man with his hair in a ponytail. He is nice-looking. I like the ponytail. It's interesting. Maverick. Two dark-suited men with short hair and straight faces. Lawyers? Accountants? Maths teachers?

I feel sick as I sit watching them. All the DBT in the world isn't going to save me from their assassination. That's what they want to do. Assassinate me. The word reverberates in my mind. I need to take control. To stop this from happening. To make my thoughts slow down. Turn my reaction into a positive.

Panic sears into my stomach. I keep staring at the jury, watching their every move. As they turn to one another, eyes down, muttering a whispered comment. As they wriggle in their seats.

Should I pretend they are my friends, not my enemies? My nurses and doctors? My carers? Should I pretend they are the ones who are exposed? Sitting there cold and naked?

Judge Peterson arrives, and everybody stands. He sits down. Everybody sits down. Puppets, following the judge.

I look across at Mouse's familiar shoulders and tell myself: *Erica, you can cope. You can handle this.*

113

Phillip

I'm sitting in front of my computer screen. And despite all this worry with Tamsin, and Erica's trial, and you being so uptight – Jonah's words still hammer through my brain.

'I hate to tell you, Phillip, but she finds me attractive too.' 'Can't you see the pull between us?' 'Why did she seduce me?' I want to go back in time and shout, 'Of course she didn't seduce you, you stupid prick.'

I want to punch him so hard in the stomach that his spleen ruptures.

You and I dealt with it; spoke about it the next morning. 'What happened between you?' I asked.

'Nothing, I swear,' you replied, voice cracked. 'Jonah's a destructive monster.'

I held you against me, feeling the rushing beat of your heart, so wanting to believe you it hurt.

'He's a destructive monster who wants to ruin my life,' you continued. You began to cry. Gently at first. Bursting into racking, pitiful sobs.

Sobs and cries that built and built, increasing in anguish until they reached a crescendo and began to diminish. 'I love you so much, Phillip, that I can hardly bear it. I never want to lose you. Nothing must ever drive us apart.' I kissed you. As I touched your lips time stopped. 'I love you for ever,' you said. I hold on to that moment, on to those words, but still can't get an image out of my head, of you and him together naked in bed. My wife and my oldest friend.

114

Erica

Another day of the trial. Two weeks feel like two years. My DBT is on the back foot. Instead of confronting issues and turning them into positives I am dissociating myself. Pretending it is happening to someone else. How am I supposed to apply DBT to this? I don't know what is happening, how long I might spend in prison. How can I turn uncertainty into a positive? People need certainty to anchor them, and nothing is ever certain, except for the fact we will die. So we wrap ourselves in as much certainty as possible to cushion ourselves. At the moment I can't do that.

The barristers are arguing again. Their words twist in my mind. First I am a demon. Then an angel who has had a difficult life. How can the same person be so different? And neither of those people is me.

Mouse turns his head from his seat at the front of the public viewing gallery to look at me, eyes clouded and anxious. I smile at him to try to reassure him. I want to hug him and whisper, 'Please don't worry, Mouse.'

He doesn't smile back. He frowns. My heart quickens. Doesn't the judge understand how difficult this is for me? Doesn't he understand that I need to get out? I need to help Mouse's father look after Mouse.

115

Jonah

I am tired of waiting, Faye. I have been patient because of your problems with Tamsin, caused by that monster Erica. But my desire for you is rising uncontrollably, and I can no longer stem its force. When my breath has calmed I grab my phone and text you.

Phillip knows about us. Your marriage is over. We are free to escape.

116

Faye

My phone vibrates. I pick it up. A text from Jonah.

We are free to escape.

My body stiffens. I feel sick. I rush to the bathroom and vomit. I've denied everything. Told Jonah I don't want him. Surely he must realise it's time to move on? I'll have to try to speak to him again.

117

Erica

I sit in the dock waiting for judgement, body simmering with dread. Perdita is sitting next to me. Looking straight ahead, as worried as me. Mouth in a line. She senses me looking at her, and turns her head towards me. She reaches across and takes my hand in hers. I pull my eyes away from her, and look across to Mouse. He is staring straight in front of him and doesn't look around.

Waiting. Waiting. As if we will wait for ever. Time and movement stop in my mind. I close my eyes. Here but not here. Back in Mouse's shiny flat playing chess. Mouse has made a move and trapped me, eyes glistening with pleasure. I shrug my shoulders and laugh. Back watching Faye holding Tamsin's hand and pushing Georgia in the buggy, on the way to school. Back holding Mouse's hand.

'The rain won't hurt you, Mouse. I will never let anything hurt you.'

Back on the bed in the Premier Inn with Tamsin. She is kicking and screaming.

'I want to go home.'

The more I think about her spoilt behaviour the more I wish I had taken the opportunity and brought her under control.

No. No. No.

I stop myself. She doesn't belong to me. Not my responsibility. How can I have let my mind ramble like this?

Perdita is nudging me, pointy elbow digging into my ribs. I open my eyes. The jury are arriving, ambling in. I cannot bear to watch them, to try and second-guess what they are about to say. So I sit ignoring them, looking at the floor in front of me. Wooden planking. Old and cracked. Perdita nudges me again. The judge is arriving and everybody stands. The judge sits down and we follow.

'Have you come to a decision on the charge of abduction?' the judge asks the jury.

The foreman stands. He is the grandad figure with grey hair and cosy glasses. He looks as if he should be at home wearing slippers and sitting in a rocking chair.

'Yes,' he replies.

'Is it the opinion of you all?'

'Yes.'

'Please inform us.'

'We find the defendant guilty.'

Guilty.

My heart sinks like a stone. I knew this was coming, but hearing it out loud in court makes me feel so bad. Guilty of what? Trying to save the life of a child? Stealing a bit of money to help me do it? I feel sick.

'I sentence the defendant, Erica Sullivan, to twelve months in prison,' the judge announces.

Twelve months.

Mind and fingers trembling I try to focus. Twelve months. My solicitor has told me that my sentence is likely to be halved for good behaviour. I've already been in for two. Possibly only four months to go. Four months. Not long. I want to sing for joy. To dance on the ceiling. My heart is racing. I want to laugh. To cry with happiness. I look across at Mouse and smile. This time he smiles back and his smile lights my world. His eyes are shining.

'I have sentenced at the bottom end of the sentencing guide-lines,' the judge continues, 'because I am particularly struck by

216

the defendant's excellent response to DBT therapy. She is full
of remorse. There is a very low risk of re-offending. However I
am granting the prosecution the restraining order requested.'

My spirits dip again.

118

Faye

'Twelve months, for abducting my child – and she's already served two?' I shriek down the telephone. 'She'll be out in four months' time. What wanker came up with that?'

I hear Phillip breathing down the phone line. I hear him swallow.

'You're too worked up, Faye. I'm coming home. Right now.'

119

Phillip

I drive home, body trembling. Breathe. Breathe. I need to contain my anger to help you. But I am as angry, if not more angry, than you. My anger towards Erica unleashes my anger about Jonah into a tsunami, about to crash and break up our relationship. The car moves on automatic pilot. Why does Jonah of all people, someone I thought was a friend, want to destroy what I have? To save it I need to trust you, Faye. Can I do that?

I pull into the drive and my normal world begins to come into focus. Our neat little town house, garage in the basement, brick steps to the front door. Pansies in a pot. Brass door knocker.

My head is aching. It feels as if it is about to explode. Breathe. Breathe. Slowly, slowly, in and out. Listening to my tape of white noise. Ten minutes is all it usually takes. But ten minutes is not enough today. Twenty minutes later I step out of the car rubbing my temples, head still throbbing. Walking up the steps to our front door.

But before I have even begun to rummage for my keys, the door has opened and you are standing in front of me.

'What were you doing sitting in the car for so long?' you ask, voice clipped and brittle.

'Listening to my tape.'

'What about me?' you shriek.

'Calm down, Faye. You sound like . . .'

'Sound like what?'

You move towards me and pummel my chest with punches. You let out a feral scream. I put my arms around you, and your punches begin to lose their intensity. Your body softens and folds into mine. You are crying now, tears streaming down your face.

'I'm sorry. So sorry,' you whisper.

Tangled together we move into our sitting room and sit curled up on the sofa. Your tears are still falling.

'Faye, please, please, don't worry. The restraining order was granted. She can't come near us. We're safe.'

120

Faye

In the changing room at the Anytime Leisure Club, getting ready for boxercise. I smile at familiar faces, as I stuff my clothes and phone into my locker and fill up my water bottle from the fountain in the corner.

Into the exercise room, I find a space at the back, where there is more room to be in my own zone. The music begins. A slow warm-up. Leisurely muscular movement, pushing my mind back to freedom and peace. Back to when I was younger, in another life. Imagining I would grow up to live in a perfect world without worry.

The music quickens. Now we work in pairs. My partner is a girl with strawberry blonde hair, wearing navy blue Lycra. I hold the guard and she punches first. Sweat drips from her forehead.

The music changes. It is my turn now. Punching my partner's pads to the rhythm of the music. I tighten my fingers inside the glove and go for it. Take that, Erica. Erica, get the hell out of our lives. I see Tamsin's and Georgia's eyes, Tamsin's so like mine, Georgia's like Phillip's, widening as they talk about the bad lady. In their minds she has been minimised by therapy, by careful handling, to a pantomime character, far away and distant, whom the world will protect them from.

But to me she is real. A threat, a menace. Take that, Erica. I punch so hard, so repeatedly, I see my partner tighten her lips and wince. Her face becomes Erica's. I tighten my whole body and swing my right arm, faster, further. Take that, Erica. I up the ante. My partner's cushion vibrates. She steps back. She raises her arm.

'Calm it. Cool it.'

I am breathing so rapidly, I cannot reply. My heart pumps blood against my eardrums. I bend over double and slowly catch my breath. 'It's an exercise class, not a fight,' my partner says. She is standing, arms curved, boxing gloves resting on her hips.

'I got carried away. I'm sorry.'

'OK OK,' she says. 'Let's go. But be gentle this time.' There is a pause. 'And I'll start if you don't mind.'

I nod my head, step back and stand, guard up. She taps her foot to the beat of the music, then gently begins to punch. Her face becomes Erica's again, and every punch, however insipid and gentle, is eating me up. Erica's face is pushing towards me laughing. 'You can't look after your children,' she is saying. 'I will take them away from you.' Panic rises like a wave of electricity inside me. I step back, raise my arm and shake my head.

'I'm sorry. I'm not feeling well today. I can't do this.'

I leave my gloves and guards in the box by the door and walk back to the changing room, without waiting for her to reply.

The changing room is peaceful. I do not like it when it is full of other women. They chat so much. Boasting about their children. Their A level results. Their top university applications. They spread their toiletries and underwear all over the communal bench. I keep as far away from them as possible, in the corner by the door. If they look my way I nod and smile politely. If they ask me a question I give a closed answer. I never encourage them by asking one back.

I am so pleased to be escaping early, as I do not want to have a post mortem with the sweaty strawberry blonde. I open my locker, throw my coat over my gym kit and walk briskly to pick Georgia up from the crèche. I have to be patient. Lively after

222

her nap, she is busy climbing and sliding into the elaborate bright blue and orange plastic ball pit in the centre of the children's area.

She eventually runs towards me red-faced and grinning, opening her arms. I bend down. We wrap our arms around one another, clamping together like ivy.

'Mummy, Mummy you're early. I've not even had a drink and biscuits.'

'Well then, let's go to McDonald's for a treat.'

She pulls away from me and jumps up and down, squealing with pleasure. I have never been sure what it is about burgers, ketchup and chips looking and tasting like cardboard that causes this reaction. But with the promise of such delicacies ahead I manage to rush her into the buggy and strap her in with ease. Being Georgia, vacillating so effortlessly between liveliness and exhaustion, she immediately falls asleep.

As I step out of the lobby into the car park, I see a lilac Jaguar with a man sitting in it hovering outside. Jonah. The tremor I was suppressing in my fingers increases as I hold my head high and walk towards him. Just as I am level with the car he winds the window down and grins at me.

'Get in. We need to talk.'

'I don't want to talk to you ever again.'

121

Phillip

'Thanks for supper, Faye.'

I lean across the table and kiss you.

'I'll just go and check on the children and then shall we have a glass of wine?'

'Thanks,' you say, attempting a grin, which doesn't quite work. You widen your lips a little and the skin around your eyes crinkles.

I pad upstairs, past all our photographs on the landing, taken in happier days. Into Tamsin's bedroom. She is fast asleep, lying curled up on her side, thumb in her mouth, surrounded by an overdose of pink. Pink pillow. Pink duvet. Sickly candyfloss pink. So vulnerable. So innocent. How could that woman have thought it was all right to take her away from us? No wonder you are in such a state, Faye. I lean across the bed to give Tamsin a kiss. A soft gentle kiss on the top of her head so as not to wake her. Her hair feels like silk.

Slowly, on tiptoe, I creep out of her room to see Georgia. Georgia is lying flat on her back, chubby arms stretched above her head, mouth open, duvet falling off. I pull it back over her, and kiss her forehead. She doesn't stir.

Back downstairs. You have cleared up. I open a bottle of Merlot and pour us each a glass. I flick the Sonos on. Beethoven. The composer Jonah and I always used to listen to at university. The composer we still both love. My anger towards Jonah isn't going to stop me listening to my favourite music.

'I hate Beethoven,' you snap.

My body tightens. 'What's going on, Faye? You always enjoyed it when I put it on in the past.'

'I've gone off it.'

'Since when?' I ask.

'Since recently. I'm pig sick of it. So repetitive and boring.'

'OK OK, sorry. What do you fancy then?'

'Ed Sheeran.'

'Ed Sheeran it is.'

I press a button and 'Galway Girl' springs into the living room. We sit on the sofa sipping our wine. 'How are you feeling, Faye?' I ask after a while. 'I want to know whether you're OK?'

'Of course I'm OK.'

I take your hand in mine and squeeze it.

'There's no *of course* about it.' I pause. 'We're allowed not to feel OK. We've had a major trauma. Our daughter was abducted. Tamsin has needed counselling. Perhaps you do too?'

'No. I'm coping.' There is a pause. You pick your wine up from the table and take a sip. 'But I can't understand why Erica chose to hound me. Why she homed in on our child. And I also can't get over why your oldest friend is trying to damage our relationship. That's the worst of all.' Tears well in your eyes. 'Has he, do you think?'

I put my arm around your shoulders.

'No one will ever be allowed to damage our relationship.' I caress your back.

Tears begin to tumble down your cheeks. 'I'm begging you, please cancel the building work. If we don't have that I will have no contact with him.'

'But . . . But . . .' I stutter. 'We've paid a large sum up front.'

You pause to wipe your tears. 'You know I've been trying my best to cope with what's happened, and I've managed quite well.' You lean forwards and put your head in your hands.

225

'Please, please believe me, I really can't cope with Jonah any more.'

The more you can't cope with an old friend you claim you've done nothing with, the more I suspect you, Faye.

122

Erica

No longer on remand. A fully fledged prisoner now. Walking towards the north wing with a prison officer, carrying my clothes and toiletries in a plastic bag. About to share a cell. The corridors wind and wind. Like a maze. Will I ever learn to find my way around alone?

At last the prison officer stops, and presses a code on a door lock. The door opens slowly and together we step inside. It locks behind him. A woman is sitting with her back to us, watching TV. She must be very deaf as the volume is so loud.

'Hello, Sylvia,' the prison officer shouts above the TV. 'This is your new cell-mate, Erica Sullivan.'

She doesn't turn around. Maybe she hasn't heard him.

'This is Sylvia Smith,' the officer explains, gesticulating towards her.

He looks from side to side nervously and coughs. 'I'll be off then. Leave you two to get to know one another. Any problems, press the buzzer.'

He unlocks the door and leaves. I hear the electronic whirr as he locks it behind him again. I place my plastic bag on the floor, wondering what to do with myself. Still my cell-mate doesn't turn around. I move towards her and tap her on the shoulder.

She turns around. A knife-like pain lacerates my cheek and my head snaps back. She has punched me in the face. I hold my hand to my cheek as blood seeps through my fingers.

'Don't you dare touch me again,' my cell-mate yells.

The room is spinning around me, moving in and out of focus.

'Let's get a few things straight,' she shouts. I look in her direction but my vision is blurred, and I can't really see her. 'You are sleeping on the bottom bunk. You can keep your clothes on the floor beneath the bed – I have taken all the drawer and cupboard space. I'm in charge of the TV. You're not allowed to touch it without my permission.'

Her face begins to come into focus. She is slim and neat-featured with shiny blonde hair.

'OK OK, that's fine,' I manage. 'What are you in here for?' I ask with a tremor in my voice.

'Child abduction,' she snaps.

'Me too.'

'I know all about you,' she says menacingly. 'You are a low-life, taking someone else's child.' There is a pause. 'I took my own child. I don't deserve to be locked up for that.'

123

Phillip

I ring Jonah's doorbell. I'm sure he's in. Lights are blazing from every window of the house, classical music belting out. But there is no reply. So I ring the bell again.

The door opens. He stands in front of me, dapper in a silk paisley dressing gown. Nothing on beneath it; bronzed muscles peep out, blond body hair nuzzles its way down his chest.

'Long time no see.' There is a pause. 'To what do I owe this pleasure?' he asks with a mocking smile.

'I just want to talk.'

'Come in,' he says, waving his arm towards the house flamboyantly. Smooth and creamy. Too smooth. Too creamy. Why did I ever trust him?

He leads me into his drawing room. Gold upon gold. Damask curtains. Regency sofa. Dripping with antiques.

'About Faye?'

'Yes. I wanted to apologise about the way I asked you to leave my home several months ago. Rather ungenerous of me when I had invited you round to thank you for saving my daughter's life. And I've bought you a present,' I say, handing him a striped bottle bag, containing a bottle of Glenmorangie that has set me back fifty quid.

'Why thanks, mate.'

I squirm inside at his use of the word 'mate'. His use of such colloquial language has never suited his image or accent. It annoys me more than ever this evening. He opens the bag and pulls the orange and black designer bottle out.

'Thanks, mate,' he says again. What a joke. He is not my mate. There is a pause. 'But I do understand. I had given you rather a shock,' he continues.

I smile half a smile. 'I'll cope with it. I know you were lying.'

He raises his eyebrows. 'Do you?' He grins wholeheartedly. 'Do sit down. Would you like a tipple?'

'I'll just have a beer if you don't mind.'

He disappears for a while. I sit in his living room, looking at expensive antiques. A walnut cabinet. A marble statuette of a nude lady. An oil painting of the sea. When he returns, he slips me a cold beer and hands me a photograph.

'Have a look at this,' he says with a crocodile grin.

I lift it closer to my face and try and work out what I am seeing. When I realise my insides explode. It is of you, Faye, and Jonah lying together naked on the carpet in this room. I cannot believe it. It looks as if Jonah is taking you from behind. The air around me feels thin. My breathing quickens. I force myself to keep looking at the photograph. At your face, Faye; lips slightly parted, eyes closed. Body contorted with pleasure. My heart is racing. A fist is grabbing my chest as if I am having a heart attack.

124

Erica

Jessica Bell looks crisp today; white linen, gold accessories.

'How's it going?' she asks.

I sit opposite her and pull a face.

'Not good then?' she continues.

I take a sip of water from the plastic cup in front of me. The cool water soothes me. 'I lost track of my DBT during the trial.'

'Why do you think that happened?' Jessica asks, holding my eyes in hers.

I feel my bottom lip trembling. 'I felt insecure. I had nothing solid to latch on to.'

Jessica takes a deep breath. 'But you are here; you got through it.'

I shrug my shoulders. 'Only because time passes. Not because I felt in control.'

Jessica's body stiffens. 'Coping with a trial is difficult. It is over now. Let's just draw a line under it and move forwards.'

I watch her draw a thick line in pen straight through her notes. She looks up at me, eyes shining with determination.

'I would like to do that,' I reply. 'If things go well I shouldn't be in here too long. So I really think I need to do that.'

'You are learning so much, Erica.' There is a pause. 'What are your plans for the next few months?'

I clasp my hands together on my knee. 'It's simple. I am going to continue to exercise and lose weight – and continue to confront my issues.'

Jessica crosses her legs and leans forwards. 'I'm so impressed. You are a very intelligent, responsive patient.'

'Intelligent? Me?'

I feel choked. My eyes are misting. No one has ever said anything like that to me before.

'Yes, Erica. You are. And you will move forward from this.'

I shake my head. 'But I have a new problem now. A difficult cell–mate.'

Jessica frowns as she contemplates this. 'You need to try and understand her then. There are three rules when you have a problem with someone else. Communicate. Communicate. Communicate.'

'I'll try, Jessica, but the last time I tried to communicate with her, she punched me in the face.'

Jessica's eyes darken and her face hardens. 'Then she should be reported to the prison governor, immediately.'

'No. No.' I shake my head. 'She has violent connections outside. You have to be very careful not to dob on her.'

'Who told you that?'

'I heard it whispered in the canteen.'

Jessica's pale face becomes paler. 'Keep your head down then. Try to understand what she might be going through. If anything else happens let me know.' She pauses. 'Despite all our best efforts, in prison sometimes things can be difficult. Be careful, Erica. You're right to be pragmatic. Whatever happens, promise me, you'll look after yourself.'

125

Phillip

I leave Jonah's house, temples throbbing, feeling dead inside. I walk home in a daze, not sure exactly where I am at any moment. On automatic pilot I turn the key in the lock, open the front door, and burst inside. The house is quiet. The children must be in bed; when they are awake, noise percolates. I find you tidying our galley kitchen, a Joe Wicks recipe book on the stand by the cooker.

'What on earth's the matter?' you ask.

'Jonah has shown me a photograph.'

Real time dissolves. Everything transposes into slow-mo.

'What of?'

Your voice sounds contorted as if you are speaking to me from inside a giant bubble. I reply from what feels like the far distance. As if it isn't me who is speaking, but someone else.

'Of you and Jonah lying together naked on the carpet in his drawing room. To put it delicately it looks as if he is inside you.'

Here but not here. Speaking to you from another world.

Slowly, slowly, I watch your face turn ashen. Slowly, slowly, I watch your shoulders rise. 'He must have fabricated it.'

My fist clenches, and through this contorted fug of time and distance, for the first time in my life, I want to hit you. To pummel the truth from you. But I restrain myself.

'Why would he do that?' I ask through clenched teeth.

You lift your shoulders higher, like a cat about to jump. 'I've told you before. He's jealous. He's trying to split us up.'

126

Faye

'He's jealous. He has always been full of envy. Can you really not see that, Phillip?'

Panic boils inside me. I feel like a volcano about to erupt.

127

Erica

Prison gym. Feet pounding on the running machine. Repeatedly slapping against the moving plastic mat. The mat is moving faster and faster. I am challenging myself so hard today, I can only just keep up. The machine is pushing me backwards so that I'm about to fall off. I tighten my mind and my body. I inhale and exhale deeply, take longer strides and pull my body towards the front. Forty minutes on eighteen kilometres per hour. Thirty minutes gone. Thirty minutes that seem to have taken for ever. The gym is heavily subscribed but I manage a session three times a week.

Thirty-five minutes gone on the running machine. I look ahead at the wall to try and distract myself from the pain. Creamy grey wall with a crack in the paint. A small spider. A brownish stain. My chest is being pricked by needles. Not enough oxygen going to my tissues. This feat at this speed is a big ask.

I need to run like this every day. I try to keep fit during association. But it is so cramped in the yard. Last week when I was attempting to jog between the throng of chatting prisoners, I nudged the shoulder of a woman called Sharon, as I passed her.

'Watch it you fucking freak,' she shouted.

I carried on around the yard, dodging other inmates. The next time I passed her she grabbed me from behind. I turned to face her. She punched me so hard in my stomach that I fell to the ground winded. She put her head back and laughed. 'Sylvia's told me all about you, you bitch.'

I lay in agony. Sharon and her entourage walked on. Everyone continued to walk past me. After a while an officer noticed me lying cradling my stomach and escorted me to the medical room. The doctor, a wrinkled artificial blonde of a certain age, examined me.

'You're lucky you've not got a ruptured spleen.' There was a pause. 'I wouldn't jog in association — there are a lot of inmates you wouldn't want to tangle with.'

'But . . . But . . . I need to keep fit,' I spluttered.

'Keep fit, or stay alive? Your choice.'

Thirty-eight minutes down, two to go. I inhale deeply to catch my breath.

128

Jonah

Phillip is playing it cool. Pretending not to believe me. But I know beneath his calm exterior I am ruffling his feathers, like a cat hunting; biding my time, waiting to pounce. Soon I will come in for the kill and Phillip will be reduced to blood and guts.

And you, Faye, you must be missing me so much. He is like a gaoler, never allowing you close to me. At the moment I only ever see you from a distance. Every time I go to your house to check on the building work, he is there, and you are nowhere to be seen. You are practically living at the sports club. Members only, with eagle-eyed security. And even though I can't follow you inside there, I watch you walking to class every day.

Don't worry, I'll find a way to be with you soon. I still love you, Faye.

129

Faye

The girls are at school and nursery, so normally the house would be quiet but the building work has started and it is teeming. Phillip is in charge – working from home, in the middle of the dining area downstairs, watching everyone come and go. Every second of our lives interrupted by drilling or banging from upstairs. Today it is banging.

I am hiding in our bedroom trying to snatch a bit of time alone. My hand trembles as I reach for my laptop. I settle myself on our bed, back propped up with all four pillows, open it up and start a Google search.

Fake photography.

How to manipulate an image.

An hour later I pad down the stairs to show you, Phillip. You are bent over your laptop; engrossed. I put my hand on your shoulder. You turn around, and when you realise it is me your face hardens.

'Please just look at this,' I beg, leaving my open laptop displaying the best results from my search, next to yours.

Your eyes flick across the screen. They turn towards me.

'Oh, Faye, I so want to believe you that it hurts.'

130

Erica

Three rules. Communicate. Communicate. Communicate. The words pound in my head as I lie on the bottom bunk of my cell trying to ignore the pounding in my head from Sylvia's overloud TV.

Communicate. Communicate. Communicate. What a joke. If I try to speak to Sylvia, her face stiffens and she looks the other way.

Maybe I am being too complacent. Maybe I need to be more assertive. Mark my own territory. She is watching TV. I want to do some exercise. I step out of bed and put my trainers on. I creep behind her, to the far side of the cell, by the entrance to the bathroom. I grab a towel and lie on it. I begin to do my stomach crunches.

'What the fuck do you think you're doing?' Sylvia shouts, above the shouting that is now emanating from *EastEnders*.

'Keeping up with my exercise,' I reply.

'Stop it,' she yells.

I continue.

I see her in my peripheral vision, standing up and stamping towards me, head high, shoulders back. A tinge of fear pulsates through me, but I continue to do my stomach routine. She is standing over me, face red, eyes spitting. She is sitting on top of me, her full weight pressing on my stomach.

'What the fuck do you think you are doing?' she repeats.

I do not reply. I lie still beneath her, transfixed by her anger.

'You think you're better than me, don't you?' she hisses.

I shake my head. 'No.'

'You do. I've come across women like you in here before. You think you are less of a criminal than me, just because you have a shorter sentence.' There is a pause. 'You are full of your own importance.'

'I hardly know you. How can I judge you?'

She laughs. 'You do. It's obvious. I see it in your eyes. In the turn of your head.'

'I don't mean to communicate that. It's not what I think.'

'What do you think of me then?'

My mind freezes. I do not know what to say. She begins to laugh again, louder this time.

'You have nothing to say. You think nothing of me. That I am a nobody.' Her laugh is harsh and sharp. It sears into my brain. 'I'll show you what I do to people who think I am a nobody,' she continues.

She pushes her face so close to mine that our breath is intermingled. She weighs my chest down with hers and suddenly tugs on my left arm. Pain as sharp as electricity lacerates my shoulder. I think she must have pulled my shoulder out of its socket. I yelp and try to breathe deeply to control my anguish.

'Apologise!' she shrieks.

'Sorry,' I splutter.

She pulls on my arm again and pushes my shoulder back into its socket. The pain immediately begins to diminish.

'Any more from you and next time you'll have to get the hospital wing to sort it out.'

131

Phillip

Today, Jonah is standing on our doorstep in front of me. Overdressed as usual. Wearing a double-breasted suit and an alarmingly wide grin, tapping his foot impatiently, eager to come in.

'Good morning,' I say as nonchalantly as possible. 'Not much progress made yet. Nothing for you to check on.'

'I really don't mind coming even though it's only just started.'

He steps towards the door. I broaden my shoulders and cross my arms to block him. 'After the way you've behaved, I don't want you in my house right now.'

His eyes darken. 'It wasn't just me.'

'Oh yes it was. I know all about doctoring photographic images.'

He grins, a mocking grin; broad and flamboyant. 'Do you now?'

'Yes.'

There is a pause. He holds my gaze. 'I need to come in because the builder has asked to see me.'

'What about?' I demand.

'The drainage.'

'For fuck's sake, Jonah. That's not your area of expertise is it?'

He puts his head on one side and grins again. 'I'm not just your architect. I'm your project manager, remember.'

'Yep. But I only needed you to keep a rough eye on things in the first place, so I'm keeping an eye on things myself now.'

'So I've noticed,' he replies with a shrug.

I sigh inside with relief as I watch him walk away. He was once my friend but now I can't bear to have him anywhere near me. Or anywhere near you, Faye. I keep looking back at all the time the three of us have spent together. Did you really used to flirt with him? Was this all your fault?

132

Erica

Another week. Another battle with the treadmill. But it is becoming easier all the time. Twelve minutes down, eight to go, pumping my legs, thinking about how much I hate Sylvia, what a bitch she is. Pumping, pumping, the spectre of Sylvia disappearing from my mind. She says I am a low-life, but I know it is the other way around. Six minutes left. Worrying about Faye. Is she looking after Tamsin and Georgia? Is she still shagging Jonah? What is wrong with the woman? Doesn't she believe in the sanctity of family life? I breathe deeply. I continue running. Running away from Faye, into my own life.

I look at the digital display in front of me. Five minutes in. Pain diminished, legs like air now, I close my eyes and think of Mouse: playing chess, making beans on toast, tidying his flat. His image moves towards me. His strong face. His thick head of brown hair. I know I will see him soon. He is visiting me in two days.

Four. Three. Two. One. The rubber mat slows and stops. My legs buckle with relief. I bend over double, nursing a stitch that feels like a metal staple inside me. I reach for my water and gulp it down like nectar. The best drink in the world. Sweeter today than the finest champagne. And now the moment of truth. Legs wobbling I step from the treadmill and walk towards the scales. I remove my trainers, take a deep breath and step on.

I've reached my target weight.

133

Faye

Georgia has started at nursery school now, so I have five mornings a week to myself. Although I am feeling despondent after what happened with Tamsin, and frightened by the permanent threat of Jonah and Phillip's arguments, I know I'm looking good. Preened and polished. I spend so much of the day out of the house trying to avoid Jonah that there is no end to the amount of pampering I have been lavishing upon myself.

But still I am emotionally fragile. Frightened of the world. Blaming myself for what happened. Blaming myself for everything. Today I am going to be brave and pop into the agency. I haven't heard from Mimi since just after Tamsin was abducted. She knew I was having a break. I haven't contacted her. But life must go on. I must get back in the swing. So, I am walking along Twickenham high street, towards Serendipity Model Agency. Past charity shops and nail bars. I drag up the stairs to the agency and knock on the glass door.

'Come in,' Mimi shouts.

I open the door, make my entrance and smile broadly.

'Hello,' I say as enthusiastically as possible, elongating my syllables. I have been watching a motivational TED talk.

Mimi stands up and walks across her office to greet me. Her hair is bright green today. It doesn't suit her pale colouring. It makes her look seasick. As if she is about to vomit.

'Faye, how lovely to see you.'

She hugs me, holding me tight against her. As if I am a long-lost lover. Then she steps back.

'You're looking good,' she continues. 'Really good. How have you coped? I've been worrying about you.'

Worrying about me so much, she hasn't even contacted me. Mimi has always had a loose way with words.

'Do sit down,' she instructs.

I do as I am asked. 'Just thought I'd pop in and see how things are going.'

I sit back in the hard chair and widen my shoulders to try and look as relaxed as possible.

'You won't believe this, I was just about to ring you.'

I silently agree with her. It is hard to believe.

'Don't look like that, Faye. It's true. It's true. I've got some exciting news.' Mimi runs her fingers through her bright green hair. 'Mrs Matterson has changed her mind. She wants to use your photographs from the photoshoot.'

'Mrs Matterson. The horse riding job?'

'Yes.'

'But . . . But . . . What's happened? Why?' I stutter.

'She tried two other models and even though they were better riders than you, the photographs came out rather flat.' She pauses to fiddle with one of the studs in her right ear cartilage. I wince as she turns it around. 'After she rejected their photographs, Sandy finally persuaded her to look at yours properly. She had initially refused, because your riding wasn't technically good enough.'

Mimi is running her words together quickly, with excitement. I have never seen her like this. 'She said your photographs were vibrant. Full of energy. She sends you her apologies.'

My body is tingling. Am I dreaming this?

I leave the agency feeling as if I am floating. But from the corner of my eye as I step outside, I see Jonah's car cruising slowly past, and my heart turns to cement.

134

Jonah

I will get in and see you this time. It is 8:15. So early you can't have left yet. I stand on your top step by your pot of pansies and ring the doorbell. You answer. My luck is in. You are dressed in a short black velvet dressing gown, which shows off your legs. No make-up. You look good. So natural and delicious. I want to sweep you up and eat you.

But as soon as you see me your face collapses into a frown.

'What are you doing here?' you rasp.

'I need to check the property urgently, as the building inspectorate are making an urgent inspection. They only let us know last night,' I say loudly. I pause. I step towards you and inhale your scent of mint and lavender. Your hair is still slightly damp. You have just showered and cleaned your teeth.

'I needed to see you,' I whisper.

Your body stiffens. I am disappointed, Faye.

You step through the hallway, into the dining room, and I follow you. Phillip is sitting at the dining table, reading the news on his iPad. He looks up and when he sees me his face contorts.

'Why are you here, again?'

I decide not to tell him I just need to get close to you. To feel your heat, to inhale your scent. So I repeat the lie I just told you. You smile at him and shrug your shoulders. I don't like the way you are both communicating across me. It makes me feel excluded. I will be talking to you about that, Faye.

'OK, OK,' you say with a sigh. 'Come with me.'

You begin to climb the stairs. I follow your perfect legs, your sumptuous velvet, your fresh scent, and my erection pulsates. I grab your arm on the landing to stop you disappearing into your bedroom. You turn towards me.

'If you don't tell him soon that you are running off with me – he is going to be given some more proof that we have made love,' I continue.

Your eyes flicker now. Your face tenses. Your lips curl downwards. 'Fuck off, Jonah. He didn't believe you about your stupid photograph, why should he believe you about anything else?'

You pull away from me. You step into your bedroom and lock the door. Oh, Faye, you will regret pushing me away. It will not get you very far. I hear voices chatting. You are in there with your children. Why have you locked yourself and them away from me? We need to bond. I will be responsible for you all one day.

I pad up to the loft area. The smell of drying plaster burns into my nostrils. I move a few tools around to make it look as if I am doing something, and then stand looking out of the window on this soft spring day, blossom blowing in the wind like confetti. Is that an omen? Not long to go until our wedding, Faye.

I wait ten minutes, thinking of you, dreaming of you. Of the way you stood in front of me in my drawing room, ripping your clothes off. Of the sight of your washboard torso. Your red silk underwear. The way you let me remove it. My erection pumps as I start to walk downstairs. I arrive at your bedroom door and turn the handle. Still locked. Still excluding me. Well I warned you, didn't I, Faye?

I pad downstairs to the living area where Phillip is eating his breakfast now: muesli with raspberry and avocado. His eyes snarl into mine.

'Was it all OK?'

'Yes. Tidied up a few things.'

'What time is the inspector coming?'

'He just cancelled.'

Snarling eyes. Snarling eyebrows. 'Very unreliable these inspectors, aren't they?'

''Fraid so, yes.'

Softly, quietly, I lean towards him. 'You still don't believe I've slept with her, do you?' I almost whisper.

He smiles, a steady slow smile. 'You know I don't believe you. Why bother asking?'

'Just so you know, I love the mole on her inner left thigh. So small and cute. Shaped like a butterfly. So dangerously close to the mound of her buttocks, and her labia.'

135

Phillip

So the manipulative bastard I used to call a friend knows you have a butterfly-shaped mole on your inner thigh. I'm going to really, really hurt him now. I'm going to do everything to protect my life, to protect my family.

136

Jonah

Phillip wants to meet in his favourite pub to discuss our situation. I am glad I am getting beneath his skin, worrying him. So here I am waiting, weighing up his choice of destination. His selection of public house is very much as I would expect. Both the food, and the interior design, mediocre. The whisky selection poor. I manage to order a cheap whisky, and head to a table in the corner. The table is wobbly. The chair I am sitting in, uncomfortable.

Phillip is five minutes late. He eventually ambles through the door, too casually dressed as usual. Jeans. Holed T-shirt (snagged, not designer). Dark eyes flash towards me as he approaches.

'Good evening.'

'Hello there,' I reply.

'Can I get you a drink?' he asks.

'Another whisky. The best they can manage. Thanks.'

He walks to the bar. I watch his lean gangly body from behind as he chats to the barmaid. There is something too insipid, too insubstantial about him. You need *me*, Faye; a man with bite. When I compare myself to him I win on every level. Better educated – a better college at Cambridge. Better dressed – Hugo Boss and Brooks Brothers. Wealthier. More successful. Harder-edged personality. And judging from the way you climaxed with me, it's obvious I'm better in bed. The question is not whether you will get rid of him, but when?

He returns from the bar, cradling a pint of ale and a large shot of whisky, balancing the menu beneath his arm. He sits down, places the drinks on the table, and hands the menu to me.

'What do you fancy?'

I open the faux-leather plastic menu splattered with fat and beer stains. One quick look. Everything is deep-fried and served with chips, except the cauliflower curry, the vegetarian option. I put on a brave smile. 'Scampi please.'

He returns to the bar to order. Then he is back, smiling at me half-heartedly. 'Come on, mate, spill the beans. What did you want to see me about?' I ask.

'Let's have a few drinks before we talk properly,' he says, sipping his pint.

I know I've riled him, talking about your mole. He's outraged. Pretending to be friendly. But I sip my whisky and play the game. He says let's talk but he doesn't start a conversation. He just sits watching me as he drinks.

After a while he frowns. 'Have you seen *Once upon a Time*, on Netflix, an amalgam of present time and fairy tales? My favourite character is Rumpelstiltskin.'

Yawn. Yawn. No wonder you are bored of him, Faye. Fortunately we are interrupted by the arrival of our deep-fried lunch. The barmaid places them in front of us, and stands, hand on hip.

'Can I get you anything else? Salt and pepper? Sauces?'

'Tartar sauce and cruet please.'

'Cruet?' she asks with a frown.

'Salt and pepper,' I snap.

'Ketchup please,' Phillip says.

By the time the barmaid eventually returns with the cruet and a bowl of plastic sachets, my food has gone cold. I lace my grease and cardboard with salt and plastic sauce, and take a bite.

'Delicious,' I lie.

'Good, isn't it?' Phillip replies, nodding his head.

Doesn't my old friend understand sarcasm?

'Let's order some dessert. This place is famous for its sticky toffee pudding,' Phillip suggests when we have finished our main course.

Famous? Get real, Phillip. But trying to be amenable, Faye, to your soon to be ex, I nod my head. We sit in silence. I hear the murmur of the barmaid chatting to her colleague in the distance. The sound of passing traffic. The clatter of our cutlery on the oversized pottery pub plates. The waitress pads over to take our empty plates. Phillip orders the special dessert for both of us.

'You're in for a treat,' he says.

137

Phillip

The waitress places the sticky toffee puddings in front of us. The toffee-caramel aroma rises in my nostrils and emboldens me.

'Why don't you order us a couple of coffees to have after dessert?' I ask Jonah, and when he goes to the bar, I finger the vial of powder in my pocket. I lean across his pudding so that no one at the bar can see, then I tip the powder from the vial into his custard. I stir it with my spoon, and wipe my spoon on my serviette. I look up. Just in time. He is returning, carrying a tray with two coffees on. I smile at him as he sets them down.

138

Jonah

I place the coffees on the table, sit down and start to eat my pudding. A weird combination of flavours, pudding too sweet, custard too bitter. Phillip devours his and takes a sip of coffee. He leans towards me.

'I invited you for lunch today because I feel sorry for you. You are living in a fantasy world, where you think you are in, or have had, a relationship with Faye.' He pauses. He puts his right elbow on the table. 'She doesn't love you.' He bangs his fist on the table. 'She never went to bed with you.' Another volcanic thud of his fist. 'You need to get help.'

I want to get hold of that fist and ram it down his throat until he chokes. But I take it easy and smile. Staying calm will rile him most.

139

Erica

Sylvia is watching *The One Show*. Still playing power games. Still refusing to let me choose anything on TV. Her programme choice bores me. So I am lying on the bottom bunk reading. Across the dulcet tones of Matt Baker, I hear the electronic cell door buzzing open. A prison officer steps inside. The door closes behind her. She is of an indeterminate age, somewhere between middle-aged and elderly. She has rheumy eyes and pockmarked skin, and is standing in the middle of the cell. Shoulders wide, hands on hips.

'Erica Sullivan, you have been summoned to see the governor at free-flow tomorrow morning. Please wait outside her office at 9:30. Is that understood?'

My stomach quivers. 'Yes.'

I know my release date is only a few weeks away. It was set at trial. Is something wrong? Is everything OK?

She leaves, accompanied by more electronic buzzing.

'What've you been up to?' Sylvia asks turning her head from the TV and narrowing her eyes at me.

'Nothing.'

'That's what they all say isn't it? Nothing, Gov? Dark horse, ain't you? If you're up to something, don't get me involved.'

I close my eyes for a second. DBT. Think of my DBT. How do I turn Sylvia's attitude towards me into a positive? Communicate, communicate, communicate, I whisper in my head. I take a deep breath and open my eyes.

'I can assure you I'm not up to anything,' I reply.

'Nothing? Taking someone else's child?'

Her eyes are blazing. Spoiling for a fight. I inhale deeply again and turn my mind in on itself to concentrate.

'I took Tamsin to try to help her. I suppose I felt responsible for her, as if she was my child.'

Sylvia's face is frozen, immobile with anger.

'What happened to you?' I continue. 'Did you think your child was in danger? That you needed to have him to yourself?'

'Sexist are you? My baby is a girl,' she spits. 'Yes. I did need to take her. I didn't just *think* she was in danger, I knew it, but no one would believe me.' Her eyes are shining. She is almost in tears. 'And now she's in care; and I am locked up in here.'

Aggressive, difficult, but now she has told me her story I feel sorry for her.

Unsure what to say, I whisper, 'I was in care, but I'm all right now. I've survived.'

'Depends what you mean by all right,' she says, jaw tightening. 'If you are all right now, how the fuck did you end up in here?'

140

Faye

'Look,' Mimi says. 'Let me show you. Don't the photographs look good?'

She pulls a file out from the cabinet behind her, and opens it across her desk.

Large airbrushed photographs of me spill across her desk. Close-ups of my face, hair tumbling out from beneath a riding helmet. Speed photographs of me, open-mouthed as I cling to the horse's neck, wide-eyed and exhilarated, pearls of sweat on my upper lip.

'They're going in the local magazine, and maybe a national magazine too. The clients are considering forking out for more press coverage.' Mimi's words are running together; she is almost breathless with exhilaration.

Her hair today is monotone. Stiff and blue.

'I'll send your money when it arrives – minus my commission of course. Five thousand quid. Better than a kick up the arse.'

She puts her head back and laughs.

'I'm getting lots of enquiries about you. I think it's because of the photographer – Sandy. After this shoot, he keeps telling people how photogenic you are when you are stimulated; scared suits you.' There is a pause. 'Soon you will be inundated with work.'

Sandy. Putting in a good word for me. For a moment I am back at the end of the photoshoot, smelling the faint aroma of nicotine on his breath, trying to suppress my tears, as he told me they needed to reshoot with a model who could ride. Funny sometimes how bad turns to good, and good to bad. Sandy putting in a word for me when I thought I had let him down is quite a surprise.

141

Erica

Next morning at free-flow, I walk along the corridor with all the other prisoners on the way to their jobs. Today I will be late for mine. I help to clean the gym. Occasionally that guarantees me an extra session. I deliberately left my cell a few minutes before Sylvia so that I didn't have to walk along the corridor with her. I wouldn't have minded an empathetic cellmate. Some people seem to find them. Some love each other so much they walk along together, arm in arm, in pairs, claiming to be soulmates. But I don't need a prison girlfriend, I have Perdita, Jessica Bell, and my visits from Mouse.

I sit outside the governor's office, stomach churning. Has something happened? Are they keeping me in? The 9:30 bell for jobs trills. The governor opens the door.

'Erica Sullivan?'

'Yes.'

'Step inside.'

The governor and a prison officer. She sits behind her desk. The officer at my side. Her office looks like two empty prison cells, poorly decorated, inadequate light. Sparsely furnished: a desk, a chair for her, two chairs for visitors and four filing cabinets. Nothing luxurious to confirm her status. She looks too young to have such a senior position. Mid-thirties. A similar age to me. A pretty woman, with neat cheekbones, which even her large statement glasses don't detract the eye from. She sits studying some paperwork, mine presumably, forehead folded in concentration.

I sit back straight, stomach churning more heavily than before, feeling as if I am about to vomit.

She looks up.

'Erica Sullivan, I just wanted to talk to you. As you know, your release date is fast approaching. In view of the positive statements the therapist has made about you, I wanted to ask whether you feel your time with us has been beneficial?'

My stomach stops churning. My shoulders widen with relief, and for the first time in hours I can breathe without thinking.

'I do indeed. I have found the DBT most helpful.'

'I also wanted to ask you whether you would consider writing a profile statement for our files, for when we are next inspected, describing the benefits of your time here?'

'It would be my pleasure.'

She takes off her glasses and wipes them with a cloth, which she pulls from a drawer in the desk in front of her. Without her statement glasses, her eyes look smaller and her face seems bare. She puts them back on and catches my eyes in hers.

'I also want to remind you of your release conditions.'

Release conditions. I have been trying not to think about them.

'As you know you cannot return to Twickenham,' she continues. 'The Bakers applied for a restraining order, and it was granted. You must live at least ten miles away. You are to have no contact with Faye, or her family, and must not travel within ten miles of Twickenham, at any time.' She pauses. 'I hope you realise that if you breach these conditions you will be straight back in here. You could serve up to five years for breaching this order. I needed to speak to you to ensure there is no misunderstanding about this.'

'I do understand. I have the written order I was handed in court. When I get out I am going to live in Weybridge, ten miles away from my old home.' I pause. 'But Twickenham was my life, so I'm worried about it.'

'It's the Bakers' life too, and under the circumstances they have priority.'

I nod my head and try to look understanding. But just the thought of not going home to be near Mouse makes me feel raw inside. I have been coping by not thinking about it. Every time I have imagined getting out, I have imagined going home to my flat with Mouse living just above me. Being near Mouse was what kept me going.

142

Faye

Phillip has insisted that we sit down and talk to Jonah. All three of us, openly. As far as I am concerned it will be a disaster. But on the surface I had no rational reason not to agree. So I am sitting in our living room waiting for him to arrive, while Phillip paces up and down our galley kitchen. I hear his shoes pounding on our Amtico tiles.

We have declared a no-alcohol rule. Alcohol will inflame the situation. I have been taking St John's Wort for several weeks now to try and help me feel calmer. So far it hasn't started to work. But friendly advice from the internet assures me it will. I close my eyes. Inhale. Exhale.

143

Phillip

Pacing towards the kitchen window, I watch Jonah walking towards our house. Sterile and smart. Old man's jacket, with wide lapels. No one of our age wears jackets like that any more. He sees me and waves. A cheery wave; as if we were meeting to plan a holiday.

Jonah is in our hallway.

'Hello, mate.'

Mate. Once we were mates. Drinking together in pubs in Cambridge. Languorous evenings spent sitting by the river at The White Swan in Twickenham, on hot summer nights. How did we all end up in Twickenham? Was it just a coincidence? A twist of fate to prolong our friendship? For many years now he has been trying to drown me with his superiority. His knowledge of facts so obscure I cannot challenge. Expertise on wine I can't afford. Condescension towards my choice of reading material.

Is trying to steal my wife his final show of dominance? A final show that he is not going to get away with. He thinks I am a wimp, but I am not. I am a stag, and stags fight.

144

Jonah

I sit on one sofa. You sit holding Phillip's hand on the sofa opposite. You do not need to hold his hand. Are you doing this to provoke me?

'It was so kind of you to be concerned about me in the pub, saying I need help because I'm delusional,' I start, 'and to insist we have this meeting.' I take a deep breath and stand up. 'But I need to clarify the situation. Faye and I made love. Come on, Faye. This is your big opportunity to come clean about it.'

Slowly, slowly your eyes widen, and you shake your head. 'You've always been besotted with me. You've got emotional problems. You're the one who's lying.'

Phillip stands up and walks towards me. 'You need therapy, Jonah.' There is a pause. 'And you need to find a real relationship.'

I turn to leave. He follows me and stands with me on the doorstep, eyes spitting into mine.

'I have found a real relationship. You're both in denial because of your family,' I tell him, voice and eyes calm. 'You need to confront the situation as soon as possible.'

145

Phillip

It's not just the words, it's the look on his face that makes me lose it. So confident. So sanctimonious. So believable?

I am not sure about that, and yet I close my eyes and see you lying naked on your back, thighs open, waiting for him. I see him moving towards you, erect and naked. I watch him put his hands on your thighs and open your legs further. He moves his head slowly down between your legs and kisses your butterfly mole. So gently.

And something inside me explodes, as he stands on our doorstep about to leave. Body and mind pumping. With pulsating blood. With electricity. I have never felt this angry before. Anger flashes inside me like hot metal. I do not know what I am doing. A higher being has stepped inside me and taken over. My fist clenches, so tight that it is no longer a fist but a ball of metal. I pull my ball of metal back, I swing it forwards and I smash it into Jonah's face. Blood spurts. My ball of metal becomes a fist again, and I step back covered in blood, nursing knuckles that ache.

146

Jonah

Phillip hits me in the face and steps back. But he is such a big wuss, I hardly feel it. Blood drips from my nose to the ground, but I know it's just a scratch. I have had enough of him now. He needs dealing with. I have been putting up with his nonsense for too long. I don't know why you are still putting up with him, Faye. He's boring. He's overprotective. He doesn't give you the lifestyle you deserve. He needs to learn a lesson, starting a fight with me. I'll show him. He is such a fool to mess with me. I know exactly how to do this.

I clench my fist and sock him one of my best. Doesn't he remember I boxed to an almost professional standard when I was at Cambridge? He is just a jerk, who throws a punch like an insipid football hooligan. I catch him unaware as he is stepping back, shaking his fist to relieve the pain in his knuckles. On the side of the jaw – a perfect sideswipe. His head snaps to the side. He slumps to the ground.

147

Phillip

I am lying in bed on stiff white cotton sheets. On a pillow so hard it makes my neck ache. I move my head a little and it feels as if it is full of lead weights, pulling on threads running through my brain, making pain reverberate. Pain upon pain.

I open my eyes. I cannot see at first. Then a blur of machines next to my bed begin to separate and come into focus. I am in hospital. I must be. But what has happened? Why? Have I been in a car accident? I turn my head. The balls of lead in my head clash together and pain overwhelms me in a flash of white heat. You are here, Faye. Moving towards me. I cannot see the detail of your face. I see your silky black hair, your piercing violet eyes, and I smell your perfume. Your heady perfume of vanilla and ginger envelops me and comforts me, for a second. But then panic overwhelms me.

'Where am I? Are you OK, Faye? Have we been in a car accident? Where are the children?'

You hold my hand. I feel your fingers brushing against mine. You lean across and softly, gently, kiss me on the forehead. I feel your heat. Your love.

'We're all fine. Nothing has happened to us.'

My fist aches, as you squeeze my hand. My body stiffens. Then I remember what happened. I hit the bastard first.

148

Faye

It tears my heart in two to see you like this, beaten up by my one-night stand. My body and mind tremble as I stand looking at you, struggling to move your head. You are thin and lanky, kind and non-competitive. No match for a conniving, treacherous bastard like Jonah. And it's all my fault.

I kiss your forehead. I hold your hand. I tell you that I love you, with tears streaming down my face. For the hundred millionth time I wish I hadn't behaved as I did. If only I could roll back the clock.

The doctor is here. A young man, wearing a pink polo shirt, with a stethoscope around his neck. He checks the machines monitoring you. He reads the notes at the end of the bed.

'How are you feeling?' he asks you.

'Been better,' you reply.

'You soon *will* feel better, but we are keeping you in for observation for a few days.'

He turns around to me and smiles.

'Mrs Baker, please don't worry, all his vital signs are fine. After someone has been knocked unconscious it is just routine to keep a careful eye on them, and hospitalise them for a while. He has had a brain scan, which showed only mild swelling. I have every reason to believe that you will have a healthy husband back home before too long.'

'Thank you.'

I try to smile back but my lips don't move. I hear his shoes tapping confidently along the ward as he leaves. I look at my watch: 9 p.m. I need to go and pick the girls up from Ashmolean's house. Her mother picked them up from school and has been looking after them for me this evening. I hardly know her. But I had to ask. When I think about not being there for the girls, worry simmers inside me. After what happened. After Erica. Panic begins to press against me. Now I know you are all right I need to get home, to get back to them.

I move towards you and kiss you on the forehead. 'Take care. See you in the morning, my love.'

But you do not hear me. You have fallen asleep again. I turn and walk along the ward to leave. Past other patients I avoid looking at. Trying not to invade their privacy, when they are so vulnerable. But my eyes slide inadvertently. I see pale worried faces, eyes riddled with pain. Hospitals depress me. I need to get out of here as quickly as possible.

I reach the nurses' station. Your nurse, a blonde curvy young woman, with a pale face and large round eyes, is busy with paperwork. I nod and smile.

'Thanks. I'm off home now. See you in the morning.'

'Mrs Baker, isn't it?'

'Yes.'

'The police are here. They've just gone to check on casualty and they'll be back in a few minutes. Would you mind waiting? They asked for a quick word with you.'

My stomach tightens. Police. Of course. I knew they'd get involved in the end. Do we press charges against Jonah? Has he pressed charges against you? I hover by the nurses' station, pacing. Watching the nurse filling in forms. Listening to bleepers sounding. Too many bleepers. Too many forms. At last I hear footsteps resonating down the corridor. I stand still and wait. Two police officers appear around the corner, and move towards the nurses' station. A man and a woman. Young. I guess they're still in their twenties. The man has a heavy face. Mournful and severe. The nurse looks up from her paperwork. She gesticulates towards me.

'Mrs Baker is waiting to talk to you.'

'Thank you,' the woman says, in a light frothy voice.

They turn and walk towards me. 'Let's go to the waiting area at the end of the corridor,' the policewoman suggests.

'Fine,' I mutter.

'How's your husband doing?' she asks as we stride along the corridor.

'Not too bad,' I reply.

Into the waiting area. Two blue brushed nylon settees. A water machine. A coffee machine. They sit down on one sofa. I sit opposite. Two pairs of eyes burn into me. One pair grey. The other brown.

'What do you want to talk about?' I ask.

'We just wanted to tell you that Jonah Mathews has decided not to press charges against your husband.'

'Charges?'

'Yes. Jonah informed us, and it was corroborated by one of your neighbours, who was walking past, that Phillip started the fight.'

'But . . . but,' I splutter. 'Jonah pulverised my husband.'

'So do you think your husband might want to press charges?'

'I don't know. He has been so confused that I was worried he had a brain injury. We hadn't got round to thinking about pressing charges. He hasn't been well enough to think about anything.' I pause. 'I'm not sure he even remembers what happened.'

The policewoman's brown eyes soften. She leans across to put her hand on my arm. 'Are you OK?' she asks.

'I think so. As OK as you can be when your husband's been beaten up.'

'But, Mrs Baker,' the male officer says, 'do you know why

they were fighting? Were you involved in any way?' He pauses. 'Do you feel safe?'

The word *safe* cuts into me.

'Yes,' I lie, keeping my trembling fingers behind my back.

The policewoman takes her hand from my arm. She reaches into her pocket and pulls out her card. She hands it to me, smiling with her eyes. 'Please come to see us if you are worried. If anything else happens.' There is a pause. 'If you are worried about anything at all, ring the number on this card. You can talk to us anytime.'

149

Erica

I'm getting out of prison. Release shouts in my mind as I arrive at my job in the gym. As I wipe down treadmills, bicycles and rowing machines with antibacterial liquid. As I vacuum the floor. As I shine the tap of the water fountain. As I lunch in the canteen, feasting on overcooked meat and stringy vegetables. As I try to exercise during association. Release. And anger that I cannot go back to Twickenham.

By evening lock-down I am lying on my bunk in a state of hyper-excitement, planning exactly what I am going to do when I get out. How I am going to manage exclusion from my old home. How I am going to settle into Weybridge as best I can, inviting Mouse to come and stay with me as often as possible, learning to play chess with him properly – not just pretend.

How I'm going to get a job and keep it. At that thought electricity pulses through me. That would be a pinnacle for me. I got the job as a dinner lady, didn't I? The prison governor gave me a leaflet about Nacro, an organisation that helps people coming out of prison sign up for benefits and advises on job applications. I'd been on benefits for so long, until I got the dinner lady job. A job is what I am going to strive for at last. I look down at my new svelte figure. Looking better will help.

And somehow I'm going to find a way to check on you, Faye. Just once, so I know that you are all right, after what I did to you. And then I'll leave you alone. For ever.

I lie on my bunk trying to ignore the sound of Sylvia's TV show. But she turns the volume up. A problem session, with a celebrity TV host. A woman is sitting on the couch with the celebrity, discussing the fact that her husband has cheated on her with her best friend. She wants to know whether she should forgive – him, or her, or both of them.

I wish I couldn't hear it. Why can't she sort it out for herself? When I think of all the problems I have had to cope with, completely by myself, I grit my teeth. Not long now. Soon I'll be able to watch whatever I like. *Crazy Ex-Girlfriend*. *The Walking Dead*. *Game of Thrones*. Anything I like.

I hear the electronic whirr of the cell door opening. Two male prison guards step inside; one skinny, one burly.

'Stand still. Hands up. Random search,' one of them shouts. I am so shocked I am not sure which.

My insides coagulate. My heart stops. My worst fear has been unleashed. Sylvia must have planted some drugs on me.

'Keep your hands up. Both of you. Move across to the door,' the officer whose stomach is so large he looks as if he is nine months pregnant instructs.

Sylvia and I stand in front of the cell door. He stands eyeballing us, feet apart, hand on his truncheon, while the other officer, the skinny one, searches our cell. He lifts our mattresses, pummels our pillows. Ransacks our drawers. He checks through every item and leaves them on the floor.

'All clear,' the slim one eventually announces, with a snarl, as if he has had a tip-off and is disappointed. 'Tidy your cell please,' he barks.

They leave. The electronic whirr of the door follows their exit, and Sylvia and I are locked in together, alone once more. Sylvia switches the TV off. The unusual silence jolts me. She stands in front of me and pushes her eyes into mine.

'You got away with it that time. You won't the next.' Her eyes are like marble. 'Your release might not happen you know. A lot can go wrong in two weeks. I'd watch out if I were you.' There is a pause. 'You took someone else's child. You don't deserve to get out before me.'

150

Faye

Walking through the hospital car park, feeling shaky after being interviewed by the police, when I feel a hand on my shoulder. I turn around.

Jonah.

Blond hair gleaming in the moonlight. Brown eyes shining into mine.

'What do you want?' I ask.

'You. Come with me now, or I'll press charges against Phillip,' he says as he lunges at me, grabs my shoulders and pulls me towards him. 'Stop resisting me, Faye. Let me have just one kiss.'

I struggle against him, anger emboldening me, making me bigger, braver. I lift my knee and pierce it straight into his groin. He yelps in pain. He is holding my shoulders, squeezing me against him in an attempt to stop me. But I have a good angle. I pull my knee back and kick him again. Higher. Harder. The tissue of his groin collapses against the bone of my knee. I pull my knee back and crush his groin again and again.

151

Erica

So far, so good.

I'm getting out. As long as Sylvia doesn't set me up first. When I am settled in I am going to really look after my home in Weybridge, so that Mouse is happy to come and stay. My anger at having to leave Twickenham is diminishing. I am trying to think positively. Having a change of scene will help him to gain confidence, to be more flexible. I am still determined to get a job. I'll do anything: cleaning, admin, standing outside giving out advertising leaflets that nobody reads.

So far, so good.

I walk along the corridor after an anaemic evening meal of coley fish, and new potatoes that tasted like plasticine.

So far, so good.

I step into our cell for lock-down. Sylvia is already here, sitting in her pyjamas, watching TV with the volume turned up full-blast. She doesn't acknowledge my presence. I flop onto my bunk with a sigh. Tonight I am going to try and read. I roll onto my stomach and fumble beneath my pillow to find my book – *Under Milk Wood* by Dylan Thomas. I borrowed it a few days ago from the library. I never expected to like poetry, but when I began to read it I loved the sound of the words in my head.

As I reach for my book I feel something hard and square, tucked inside my pillowcase. My fingers clasp around it. Cannabis wrapped in plastic. Must be.

My mind and body freeze. This is it. The set-up. I roll onto my side, back towards Sylvia. I pull the package out and look at it. A greeny brown cube, wrapped in plastic. The size of a sugar cube. I hide it in my right hand, hold my book with my other hand and pretend to read it.

I slip onto my back now. I do not look across at her. I do not dare. I sense the movement of her head. She keeps looking across at me. I am going to dump this shit down the drain tomorrow. In the shower block in the morning. No one will ever link it to me.

The electronic cell doors whirr. I sit bolt upright in bed. Two officers. Same as before. Quick as a flash I put my hand to my mouth and swallow the cube. It sticks in my throat. I swallow and swallow. As it lumbers down my gullet, I pray to the god I don't believe in, that the plastic doesn't burst.

'Random inspection,' the chubby officer shouts.

'Stand up, by the door, arms above your heads,' the skinny officer shouts. 'Move quickly.'

We move quickly. The skinny officer stands in front of us, hand hovering over his truncheon.

'Don't move an inch,' he instructs.

The chubby man searches our cell. He struggles for breath and his face turns red, as he lifts my mattress and pummels my pillow half-heartedly. He groans in exasperation as he stretches to the top bunk to inspect Sylvia's bed. Panic simmers inside me as he rummages through our clothing drawers. Has Sylvia planted something else?

'Nothing here,' he announces.

My body almost collapses with relief, but I hold it together and remain standing up straight.

'Swallow it did you?' Sylvia hisses as soon as the officers leave, pinning me against the cell wall. She stabs her fist into my stomach so hard I cannot think, I cannot breathe. 'Good luck to you. I hope that makes it burst.'

152

Jonah

I am limping as I walk to Anna's house. My groin is swollen. A kaleidoscope of dark iridescent colour. Black and purple of all shades, a little green thrown in too. I have been beaten up by a woman. Not just any woman, but you, Faye. The woman I love. What is the matter with you? Have you spent too much time with my ex-best friend who socked me in the face to start a fight? He is such a bad influence on you; you need to get away from him as soon as possible.

A tinge of pain shoots down my leg as I walk, and makes me wince. All the hours spent nursing my groin with ice packs and all the ibuprofen I have swallowed haven't helped. I push through the pain to walk up the path and ring the doorbell.

Anna answers the door.

'Is she ready?' I ask, as I step inside.

'Yes,' Anna replies without looking me in the eye.

I walk through the hallway. I knock on Sally's door.

'Come in,' she invites.

I walk into her bedroom. It is warm, over-heated. The sweet smell of her cheap perfume chokes me. She is waiting for me, lying on her back, arms and legs splayed, hands and feet tied to the four corners of the bed. Naked except for the dark wig and blue contacts I bought her.

She smiles at me. Nerves or pity? Do not pity me. Women do not dominate me.

'Did Anna explain to you what I want?'

She nods her head.

'Do not nod, speak,' I snap.

'Yes, she told me. I consent.'

I take a sip of Glenmorangie from the flask in my pocket. It burns the back of my throat. Another sip. Larger this time. More of a three-swallow gulp. I stand looking out of the window at Anna's small, neat garden, all lawn and bushes, no colour. I'm still drinking, waiting for the liquor to hit. When I feel as if it has softened me, made the world a little easier, I turn around to face my victim.

'Are you sorry for hurting me, Faye?' I ask.

'Yes, very sorry.'

I walk towards the bed. I stand above her and give her a Chinese burn on her right arm. She yelps in pain. I twist my hands tighter.

'Say it again.'

'I'm sorry. So sorry, Jonah, I will never hurt you again.'

I straddle across her and smash my knee into her pubic bone as hard as I can manage.

'Apologise again, you bitch.'

153

Erica

On heightened alert. Checking my bed and my pillow, my clothes, before I leave our cell in the morning, and as soon as I return at night. Checking the bathroom. Checking and praying, all the time. Hovering so that I always leave the cell after Sylvia, watching her every second.

The cannabis cube passed this morning. It didn't even hurt. So Sylvia, shame on you, it didn't burst. I shoved an excess of paper into the toilet to weigh it down, and flushed it away. Your unpleasant plot didn't succeed.

And now I am walking along the corridor at free-flow, on my way to work.

An officer taps me on the shoulder.

'The governor wants to see you immediately. Report to her office straight away, please.'

My stomach aches. I feel sick. What has Sylvia managed to do now? I walk towards the governor's office, heart and legs like lead. After so much hope of freedom, how can I cope with staying here? I move along, shoulder to shoulder with other prisoners, until I eventually arrive.

I knock on her door with trembling hands. 'Come in,' she shouts.

I open the door and step inside. She smiles at me. A good or a bad sign? Her smile fades quickly leaving her face sad and serious. The sickness rising in my stomach pulses towards my mouth, and I swallow to hold it back.

'Do sit down,' she says.

Silence presses against me, ringing in my ears, as I wait for her to speak.

She adjusts her glasses and leans forward. 'I wanted to ask you, whether after you have been out six months, you'd consider coming back to give a talk to the prisoners about how you are coping with life on the outside?'

I exhale in relief. 'Yes of course.' I beam.

154

Faye

Georgia and Tamsin are skipping along the hospital corridor in front of me, so excited about picking up Daddy. I am too. I can't wait to have him home. Whenever he isn't around, after so much difficulty, I feel panicked. As if my whole life is a time bomb waiting to explode, and that something is about to go wrong at any minute. We turn the corner into the ward and are stopped by a sign telling us we need to sterilise our hands.

'Come on, girls,' I shout. 'Come and clean your hands.'

They skip towards me holding hands. I show them how to use the pump. They disentangle themselves from one another and rub antibacterial foam into their skin.

Phillip is waiting for us, fully dressed, in his bedside chair, mini-suitcase at his side. I bend down to kiss him. The girls scramble onto his knee, and hug him so hard that he can hardly breathe. He still looks pale. So pale and weak. The side of his face is a kaleidoscope of colours, faded now from the initial shades of dark purple and sage green, to pastel streaks of violet and khaki, interspersed with pale yellow. At least the swelling has gone down, his face is a normal shape again. A few days ago he looked like a boxing monster, with slits for eyes.

He lifts the girls up into the air as he stands up, and swings them to the ground. Giggling, they hover next to him, then cling to his legs like tendrils of ivy. I pull his torso towards me and hug him.

'Faye,' he whispers in my ear. 'I'm coming home to really, really look after you now.'

155

Phillip

Back home, feeling mixed. Head still aching. Working from home. I do that most of the time now – I need to be here to protect my family. The doorbell rings. Jonah. I am expecting him. I open the door. He stands in front of me looking as overdressed as usual, in white chinos and a pale green shirt embroidered with miniature parrots – bright and unnerving.

'Thanks for coming,' I say with a smile.

'What's with all the sudden friendliness?' he asks.

'I invited you here to tell you I've decided not to press charges. And I hope you feel the same.'

'Yes. I think we need to work together, not against one another.'

'Yes. Yes. Of course.' I pause. 'So we could say it's a truce then?'

He runs his fingers through his thick blond hair. 'Yes.'

'Do sit down,' I say gesticulating to our living area, which just so happens to be tidy today.

'Thanks.' He sinks into one of our sofas.

'Would you like a coffee?' I ask.

'Yes please.'

I step away from him, into the kitchen and put the kettle on. I spoon Nescafé into two mugs; and put some powder from the vial in my pocket into Jonah's. I know it tastes bitter so I add a bit of sugar as well. The kettle boils. I make our drinks, place them on a tray with a plate of shortbreads, and carry them through to the living room.

Jonah is sitting in the middle of the sofa, looking across at the photograph of you, Faye. The one he always stares at. Watching him looking at you I want to punch him all over again.

'Here you are,' I say, handing him his mug of coffee. 'Would you like a shortbread?'

'Yes, please.'

What a relief. The sugar in the shortbread will mask the taste of his coffee. He looks up and smiles slowly.

'I don't know why you're being so friendly. It's time you faced facts: your wife's not in love with you. She's in love with me.'

I keep calm and smile inside. Thank God the stupid bastard doesn't realise that I only enticed him over to poison his coffee.

156

Erica

A final inspection before I leave prison. My heart is in my mouth as the prison officer appointed to release me frisks my room. A brisk young woman with long blonde hair tied back in a ponytail. It flicks across her shoulders as she inspects. As she lifts my mattress and Sylvia's. As she pulls the pillowcases off and shakes them. As she pats the pillows. As she walks across them with stocking feet. She checks every item in the suitcase I have been given. Every item Sylvia is left with.

'All clear.'

So nearly out of prison. I walk along the corridor with her. People know I am leaving. People are staring. I am careful to avoid physical contact. I do not want anyone planting anything on me at the last moment. We arrive at the holding area and are locked in. Almost out. So nearly there. The last hurdle. I sit on a scratchy sofa and a randomly allocated inmate fetches me a cup of tea. I smile at her.

'Thanks.'

The perky ponytailed officer disappears and a timid prison officer with bucked teeth and frizzy hair hands me my possessions: my coat and handbag. Everything they took from me when I came in. My mobile phone. She sidles off and returns with a pile of paperwork. I sign a plethora of release papers. I am given even more forms to sign for life outside. Overwhelmed by forms, I decide to read them tomorrow. I am trembling now with the desire to get out; a final prison claustrophobia closing in on me.

Finally I am released. I step out of the prison and blink in the bright April sunshine. I haven't felt the sun in such a long time. The yard we were allowed to walk around during association was always in the shade because of the prison blocks that surrounded it. My eyes will need to get used to the sun again. I inhale deeply. The air smells so fresh and clean, blowing away the scent of antiseptic and sweat that pervades the prison. I tighten the collar of my coat as a sharp wind is blowing, and march solidly along the footpath towards the car park where Mouse has promised to wait.

A horn honks loudly. I follow its direction to see Mouse at the driver's seat of the bright red Mini Cooper his father bought him, waving frantically at me. My heart jumps. I smile and wave back, running towards the car. He leans across and opens the passenger door. I slip into the passenger seat.

'Mouse.'

'Erica.'

I lean across and hug him. He smells so sweet. I recognise his Hugo Boss Orange aftershave. He is wearing his favourite woollen jumper. It feels so comforting when he holds me against him. But he pulls away, frowning.

'Where do you think you are going, Erica?'

'To a B & B in Weybridge. Just for one night. Until I sort myself out.'

Mouse's eyes light up with pleasure. He shakes his head. 'No, no, no. Dad owns a cottage there. He is letting it to you, and you can have it free of charge for the first few weeks, just until you sort yourself out. I wanted you to have a wonderful surprise.' There is a pause. 'It's because Dad has investments there that I suggested Weybridge in the first place.'

'Your dad is wonderful, Mouse. The most wonderful dad in the world. And you are wonderful too.'

Mouse smiles a high-wattage smile. 'Good to see you, Erica.'

'Good to see you, Mouse.'

I lean across to the driver's seat and hug him once again. After a while he pulls away from my embrace.

'High five.'

'High five.'

Our fingers touch and make static electricity.

Mouse starts the car engine. We set off towards Weybridge. My stomach is quivering with excitement. A cottage instead of my damp flat. I can't believe my luck. I've never had luck before. There must be some catch. I look across at Mouse, frowning as he drives, staring intently at the road ahead. To Mouse, driving is the biggest responsibility in the world. The biggest responsibility that he ever has. He takes it very seriously.

I sit looking out of the car window at all the other cars, each one a time capsule, containing a family, a relationship, an individual on the road to somewhere. After so long incarcerated, it seems surreal to be watching people moving freely, able to go wherever they want. The electronic buzzing of doors closing behind me will haunt me for ever. These people I am watching are going wherever they want, but I have to go in the opposite direction thanks to Faye and Phillip, when I was only trying to help.

Mouse pulls into Weybridge. It looks like a very posh town. Large houses set back from the road. Wide leafy streets. A green. A war memorial. A long high street.

'It looks all right, doesn't it, Erica?'

'Yes, Mouse.'

The strident tones of Mouse's satnav tell us where to go, and soon we are parked outside my new home. My heart catches as we step into the living room of the most perfect little cottage I have ever seen. A cosy floral sofa and two chairs facing the fireplace with a large flat-screen TV above it. An Indian rug. A wood burner. Oak beams. Mouse and his dad have moved all my possessions here. The photograph of Mouse and me, on our day trip to the seaside last year, laughing and leaning towards the camera. My teapot. My pack of cards.

'It's fantastic, Mouse. I'll have to thank your dad. And I'm going to get a job and pay back every penny.'

'I know. He knows. We believe in you, Erica.'

My eyes fill with tears and I step towards Mouse and hug him. He hugs me back. 'It's almost perfect. I just wish I was nearer to you.'

I swallow to stop my tears from falling.

'But, Erica,' Mouse says putting his arm around me. 'It's not far on the train. I promise I'll come and see you every single week.'

157

Faye

I've dropped Tamsin at school and Georgia at nursery whilst panicking inside. Erica has been released from prison and even though she is subject to a restraining order it doesn't appease me. She could be anywhere. As far as I am concerned she deserves to be locked up for ever.

And ever since I knew she was released, yesterday morning, my heart has been racing, my hands trembling. My joints pulsate with a strange electricity that at the same time as pumping me up makes me feel tired. Sudden noises frighten me. People standing too close to me. People talking too loudly in crowded spaces.

I'm walking to see Mimi but I feel so frightened and strange. I stop to pop a Valium. I have a few in my jacket pocket that Phillip gave me. He has become a whizz kid at buying stuff from the internet. I'm still taking St John's Wort but I think it's the Valium that is keeping me calm. I swig it down with a sip from the small water bottle in my handbag, and carry on walking towards Serendipity Model Agency. I am skipping my exercise class this morning. My heart rate is in overdrive – I mustn't stimulate it even more.

Past McDonald's, Costa Coffee, NatWest Bank. Still too early for frying; no fish and chips yet today. I climb the stairs to go and see Mimi.

Her hair is growing out. It is black. Too black to be natural, like a goth's. What is the matter with her? Over forty years old. Will her rebellious stage ever end? Not if you judge by the number of piercings. I think she has an extra one in her nose. A dumbbell in each nostril as well as the safety pin now. Surely that must be tricky when she has a cold?

'Faye, sit down. We need to talk,' she says, waving her arms in the air, gesticulating towards the chair opposite her desk. She has a silver ring on every finger, as well as her thumb rings that look so strange and clumsy. Six thin silver bangles on each arm. Today she is wearing a floral skirt instead of ripped jeans. She looks like a modern gypsy.

I sit down.

'You're needed for two new jobs.'

My stomach rotates.

'Hands and legs,' Mimi snaps.

Hands and legs. Disappointment skitters.

'Don't look like that. One is for the local nail bar.'

I growl inside. The local nail bar. Hardly high-profile.

She smiles a mischievous smile. 'The other is Dior tights. They love your legs.'

'Dior tights? Pity it isn't Dior make-up. Pity they don't want my face.'

Mimi leans into the fridge behind her and pulls out a bottle of champagne, and two glasses from the shelf behind her.

'Fucking *Dior*, darling,' she says. 'They pay well. Don't complain.'

158

Phillip

Faye, who is frightening you most? Is it Erica? Is it Jonah? I would have to toss a coin to guess. I don't suppose I will ever know. But Jonah is my nemesis. The one I would like to eliminate. I have been watching him. Watching his house. I am standing outside it right now. A statement house. The sort of house that likes to tell you how much it is worth. With the shape of its floor to ceiling Georgian windows, luxurious material peeping around their edges. The shiny front door. The highly polished brass door knocker. Understated elegance that everyone knows is expensive. And he only has it because his family suddenly inherited money from a Swiss trust account; held on to since the Second World War. He hasn't earnt enough money designing extensions to live in a place like this. Dirty money of some sort if you ask me.

Tuesday night. He always goes out for two hours from 8 p.m. until 10 p.m. on Tuesday nights. I don't know why. He goes to a Victorian house a few roads away. Maybe he goes to play bridge or something suitable for an uptight fart like him.

I have everything I need. Brick. Rubber gloves. Bleach. Rubber slips for my shoes. A bag for my booty. I walk up the Portland stone path past the front door, and enter the back garden from the side gate. It unfolds before me. South-facing. Perfectly landscaped. Even the plants in it must be worth a fortune, never mind the bronze sculpture of a nude woman, the stone pots and the basket-weave furniture. What an idiot to keep the side gate unlocked.

Standing by a tumbling Acer plant, which is just coming into leaf, I pull the plastic slips I have brought with me over my shoes, and the gloves over my hands. I take the brick from my bag and brace myself. Quickly. Quickly. I smash it through the side kitchen window. Then I hide behind the lilac tree, to wait and check that no one has heard. That no helpful neighbour will come to investigate when they hear an alarm. No alarm. I look at my watch. I give it five minutes. No one comes. Sometimes the privilege of privacy has its disadvantages, doesn't it, Jonah?

I step across the springy lawn, and climb through the broken window, slowly, carefully, to make sure I don't cut myself, landing on the granite kitchen counter and jumping down onto thousands of pounds' worth of travertine. The sort of stone I wish I could afford at home. Why do some bastards have all the luck financially?

Jonah's kitchen is sterile and perfect. No dishes left on the side. No crumbs on the counter. No childish fridge magnets or hastily scribbled notes for a partner to find. I grab the toaster and slip it into my bag. And the small TV at the end of the kitchen counter. That's it. That's enough to make it look like a petty crime.

Now for the main business. I open the cupboard next to his shiny designer kettle. He is so anal. Boxes of tea in straight lines. Alphabetically arranged. Jonah this is a kitchen, not a library. And the Gold Blend in a jar at the front. That figures. He likes his Gold Blend. That is what he always drinks when he is at ours. I pluck the jar of Gold Blend from the cupboard and open it. I take the vial from my pocket and pour its contents into the coffee. My secret concoction. Powder ordered specially for Jonah from the dark net and the perfect amount of darkened sugar to disguise its bitter taste. I stir it together with the plastic straw I brought with me. Slowly, carefully, I put the lid back on the jar, and place it back in the cupboard at exactly the angle I found it. Jonah Mathews, a gift for you. Drink it as often as you like.

I look at my watch. Eight-thirty. An hour and a half before he is home. I am going to look around his house, to see whether there are any clues as to what he's been up to lately. I step from the kitchen into his dining area with its crystal chandelier and white marble fireplace, when I hear the front door opening.

He must have forgotten something, and come back home. I race back into the kitchen, pick up my bag. Heart pounding, I scramble up onto the counter, slide through the broken window, and run as fast as I can to hide behind the lilac tree again. I peer around it to see what is happening.

Jonah is there. Standing in the middle of the kitchen. Looking at the broken window. Frowning. Mobile phone pressed to his ear. He must be phoning the police. I am lucky I have got this far. But I need to disappear immediately. My body and mind vibrate with panic. If I go around the front he will see me. I am stuck in a six-foot-high walled garden where a maniac who used to be a friend lives, and the maniac has called the police.

I look around. A garden shed by the back wall. I sigh with relief. Bag slung across my body, I slip towards it, hiding behind trees and bushes. The garden shed is behind a big tree. It cannot be seen from the house. I throw my heavy bag on top of it, pull my shoe slips off, put them in my pocket and edging my hands and feet around the wooden slats of the shed, manage to climb onto its roof. I roll across the roof, grab my bag and then swing my body over the wall, landing heavily on the pavement at the back of the house. As soon as I land I whip off my plastic gloves.

Heart still pounding in overdrive, I walk away. Trying to look as calm as possible as I listen to police sirens wailing in the distance. I turn left at the end of the road behind his house. Left again and end up back on the main road. There is a skip on the corner. I throw my bag in there. And slowly, calmly, walk home.

159

Faye

The loft extension is finished. Phillip and I are celebrating over a bottle of Pol Roger. We are sitting on the bed in our new guest room, sipping from wedding-present crystal, trying to admire our own good taste. Dorma bedding. Hand-made pottery bedside lamps. State-of-the-art wet room. Automatic halogens.

The children are in bed. That is when our life together begins these days. We clink glasses. Now we have a proper family home, big enough for guests to stay whenever we like. But at what cost? Jonah using it as an excuse to try and see me whenever he wanted. Thank God it's finished. Now he will never have an excuse to come into our home again. I am trembling just thinking about him.

'I'm so pleased with your news from Mimi,' Phillip says.

Phillip. Wide reassuring shoulders. Wide reassuring face. The man I always wanted to meet. The man I do not want to lose.

'Yes, I'm quite pleased,' I reply. 'Wish they wanted my face though.' I shrug my shoulders.

'You're very competitive aren't you? Boundaries always changing. There was a time when you would have been thrilled to get anything from Dior.'

As he leans across to top up my glass, my eyes begin to fill with tears. The news about Erica engulfs me once again. The heavy sense of guilt that I am so familiar with washes over me again. I didn't look after Tamsin properly. I allowed another woman to take her. I am her mother. It is my fault. I shouldn't have been late for the pickup. Now the woman who took my daughter is out of prison. I feel a panic attack coming on. I am breathing too quickly. Phillip has stopped sipping his champagne. He is staring at me, eyes riddled with concern.

He puts his arm around me. 'Are you thinking about Erica again?'

'I'm always thinking about her, about what she did. I can't push her from my brain.'

I feel the intake of Phillip's breath pull across my face. The sigh as he exhales. 'Faye, you know the restraining order has been granted. Even if she wanted to, she can't come anywhere near us.'

He pulls me towards him and wraps me in his arms. I melt into his warmth. His muscular chest.

'What if she breaches it?'

'She won't. She'd go back to prison.'

My breathing speed increases. Pins and needles shoot up my arm.

'And what about Jonah?' I ask.

'There's no need to worry about Jonah. Leave it to me. I'll take care of him.'

160

Jonah

I have been feeling tired, so very tired lately. Going to bed at 10 p.m., hardly able to rouse myself when my alarm goes off. Dropping off to sleep at work, slouching over my designs. Is it because I am low, as you are pushing me away? Maybe I should go to the doctor and have a blood test. Faye, you are still in denial. I am trying to keep going by taking my pleasure elsewhere. Not that it is real pleasure. You are the woman I love. Sex with anyone else is a poor substitute.

Last Tuesday, after my violence, Anna had to get me a new girl. And everything went wrong. The new girl was nothing like as good as Sally, and a shadow of you. She was lying naked on the bed, waiting for me. First I filled up on whisky. The Glenmorangie Phillip gave me. I tossed back the last fingerful from my glass and left it on the dressing table. I began to unzip my pants. She sat up on the bed and moved towards me to help me.

'Stay down. Lie back,' I barked.

Even though I don't really want anyone else to touch me, Faye, and I am saving myself for you, I usually get an erection at the thought of dominating someone new. But something wasn't right. My erection wasn't stirring. I looked down. My penis was like a pink caterpillar, curled up and sleeping. I couldn't believe what was happening to me. It only happens to people who are really old, or people on the wrong kind of antidepressants. Not to virile men like me. But then I have been sleeping so much lately. Perhaps I'm not well. Perhaps I am anaemic and need a blood test. Then I pinch myself. No.

It must have been the girl's fault – she was so unenthusiastic. Not attractive enough. If I had the energy I would travel into central London, go somewhere really upmarket. But instead I'll just have a word with Anna, ask her to get someone more expensive, until the day I have you to myself.

So, as things hadn't worked out, I didn't stay at Anna's as long as usual. And when I got back home some fucking bastard had broken into my house.

161

Faye

Another day, another photoshoot. I've done the legs and the nails. A hairdresser is blow-drying my hair, teasing it with a large curling brush, and blasting it with the hairdryer. I watch her in the mirror and try to relax. Relaxing is hard these days. I took two Valium on the way here, but they didn't seem to help.

So tense and out of sorts just when my career is beginning to take off. Be careful what you wish for, and I wished for this so much. I used to think that telling people I was a model would be everything to me, but everything is nothing if you're worried about your family. I walk around cradling panic in my stomach.

'All done,' the hairdresser announces, holding up a mirror and reflecting it in the mirror in front of me, to show me the back of my head.

'Very nice, thank you,' I say, smiling at her like an automaton.

'Off you go. Time for make-up,' she instructs.

Make-up. Never my favourite part of the modelling business. Still reeling after super excited Daisy and her reference to my crevices. The usual. Moisturiser, followed by layer after layer of pancake foundation. Eyelids scraped. Eyebrows tweaked. The make-up artist is the silent type today. At least she's not intrusive. Intrusive does not suit my mood.

I have no need to change clothes for this photoshoot. It is just head shots. Nothing too extravagant or complicated.

Sandy arrives. 'Bit less exciting than Dior and horse riding,' he says.

'I hope so,' I reply. 'I'm ready for a rest.'

Two hours of tossing my hair and smiling, of brushing my hair and tossing it again. Finally, I step out of the salon, still feeling uneasy as I begin to walk home. Stomach tightening as someone puts their hand on my arm. Turning around.

Jonah.

Eyes stabbing into me.

'What are you doing here?' I ask.

His hand clasps my arm. 'Wouldn't hello Jonah be more civil?'

'Do I have to be civil to a man I don't want to know?'

His mouth twists downwards. 'I'm not sure your attitude is advisable, Faye.'

His fingers are forming a tight band of pain around my arm. 'You're hurting me.'

Fingers tightening. Pain increasing.

'I need you to listen. I want to speak to you, Faye.'

I shake my arm and try to prise his fingers away, but I cannot manage.

'I've got a film of us together,' he says in a stage whisper so that people passing can hear. 'And I want to show it to you.'

Blood is rushing to my cheeks. I know I am blushing. I stop struggling and stand, eyes trapped in his. 'How did you manage that?'

'I set up a selfie to record us on my iPhone while we were making love. I can send it to Phillip if you like?'

'I don't believe you. You wouldn't have been able to.'

'How would you know? You were very drunk.'

Still holding my arm so tightly it feels as if he is cutting off my circulation, he leads me into the tiny café we were standing outside. To a table at the back. It is a small, bare café, with wooden floorboards and six wooden tables. The waitress smiles at us. I do not manage to smile back. Late morning. No one else there.

'What can I get you?' she asks as we sit down.

He is still holding my arm. 'Nothing for me thanks.'

'Whisky please. Make it a double.'

She shakes her head. 'We don't have an alcohol licence.'

'Make it an Americano then with hot milk,' he snarls.

'So now,' he says. 'Two friends? Two lovers? Or a beautiful woman having coffee with her architect? Which do you want it to be?'

I don't reply. He loosens the grip on my arm. I shake it in relief and the circulation begins to flow back.

'Let me see the film then, Jonah?'

He taps into his phone, starts the film and hands it to me. I sit watching myself undressing and pulling Jonah towards me, I am beginning to tear off his clothes. I cannot bear to watch any more. Still holding the phone, I stand up and run to the toilet as fast as I can. Pushing past the waitress who is walking towards our table with Jonah's coffee.

I burst into the single cubicle, locking the door behind me. Hands trembling, I throw his iPhone down the toilet, and flush it. I sit on top of the seat and wait for my heart to slow. I hear a fracas outside. Jonah is banging on the door of the cubicle, yelling at me to come out. The waitress tells him to back off. I look down. Somehow I managed to bring my handbag with me. The frosted window of the toilet cubicle is open a crack. It looks out onto the road. I push it wide open and manage to scramble through. I run around the corner to my car, heart pounding, and drive home, still feeling the pressure of Jonah's fingers pushing into my arm. His shouting resonating in my ears. The movie he showed me plays in my mind, on constant rewind. I cannot make it stop.

162

Erica

Alone in my cosy cottage. Not so cosy when Mouse isn't here. Weybridge is prettier than Twickenham. Posher, I'd say. Larger houses with football-pitch-sized gardens. Wider, leafier streets. Double the number of thriving shops.

It's raining today. I feel like a caged animal pacing up and down my sitting room, thinking about Mouse. About how he braved the drizzle to come and visit me in prison. About how I always used to play chess with him to distract him when it rained. He visits me once a week like he promised, but when you're used to seeing someone every day, once a week is not the same.

The rain is falling harder now. Bullets pelting against the pavement. A rumble of thunder in the distance. The sky explodes with light. Mouse will be cowering beneath his bed covers crying. I cry inside.

I continue pacing to calm myself. Through the sitting room into the bathroom. I glance in the mirror. All the jogging I have been doing in the woods by the station has really paid off. A woman who I don't recognise looks back at me. A skinny woman with long, shiny hair. Svelte and sophisticated. Not someone who ended up in a children's home because her foster parents couldn't cope with her. A woman who is not a caged animal. A woman who is brave enough to go wherever she wants.

Faye

Jobs seem to be 'pouring in' now, at least compared to my career so far. I am beginning to contribute towards the family finances again, as I did when I got my lucky break with Accessorize and M&S Foods. That only lasted a few months. Let's hope the steady build-up so far will give me some traction now.

This time I am several miles from home, modelling some pieces for the most stylish dress shop in Richmond. Silky and elegant. Top-end sophisticated. Pale pinks and purple from Italy, looking good with my eyes and hair. Usual routine. I sit back while the make-up artist covers me with grease. But I am distracted. Even though I haven't seen Jonah for weeks. The film he showed me plays continually through my mind. When he shows it to Phillip my world will explode.

164

Jonah

An organic café, Hill Rise Richmond, two doors down from the dress shop where your make-up is being applied, sitting at an outside table on the pavement, waiting for you to come out. I'm so good at this. You don't know I'm here do you, Faye?

You made a mistake damaging my iPhone and running away. Did you really think I wouldn't have the film backed up? You haven't apologised. I'm losing my patience, Faye.

165

Phillip

You are sitting at our dining table opposite me, face still slightly bronzed, an aftermath of the heavy make-up you've been wearing today. We are eating early with the children. Fish fingers and salad for you. Fish fingers and chips for the rest of us. So many fads and dislikes with the children, finding something we all like is a challenge. But we've almost managed it today.

'My friend Ashmolean says models are vain,' Tamsin chirrups, fork in hand.

'Well,' you reply with a smile, 'we do need to look after our looks, so I suppose we can come across that way.'

'If someone is vain their looks are more important to them than anything else,' I say, as I put more salt on my chips. 'And with your mother that most definitely isn't the case.'

You look across at Tamsin, eyes shining with love. 'Yes. That's right. I love you, Georgia, and Daddy, more than anything else.'

'Would you look like a pig to protect us?' Tamsin asks, with a snort and a giggle.

You smile as you push your salad around your plate.

'Yes,' you reply. 'Or even a warthog, and warthogs are even uglier than pigs.'

Our daughters are both giggling, small milky teeth pressed together, lips wide and stretched.

'What about you, Daddy?' Georgia asks, turning to me, eyes wide and inquisitive. 'What would you do to protect us?'

I do not reply. I keep my secrets to myself.

Phillip

I dial Jonah's work number from a cheap new temporary phone I bought at Tesco. I have to use a phone number he won't recognise. He picks up. I put on my best, drawled-out West Country accent. The one I've always been so good at.

'Good morning. Noel Thoroughgood here, from the Consumer Research Association. You have been randomly selected to answer a few questions about your eating habits. Would you be willing to help us?'

Silence down the phone line. Silence so loud it presses against my eardrums. Then, 'How long will it take?' Jonah snaps.

'Less than one minute.'

'OK,' he says reluctantly.

'It's very simple. We just want to know your top five favourite cakes and biscuits, in order of priority.'

'That's easy,' he says. 'My favourite is a simple Victoria sponge with lashings of strawberry jam, and icing sugar on top.'

'Good. Good. And the second?'

'Chocolate brownie.'

'And then?'

'Lemon tart, millionaire's shortbread and apple strudel.' There is a pause. 'Is that all you need to know?'

'Yes. Thank you very much. And we'll put you in the free draw for a luxury version of your favourite confectionery.'

Faye

We have run out of milk. I pop to the newsagent around the corner to fetch a few pints. My body stiffens as I see Jonah's car pull up in front of me. He springs out, slams the door, and walks towards me. Before I can step away he clasps his arms around me, in a pseudo bear hug that feels more like a wrestling hold. I can hardly move. I can hardly breathe.

'How lovely to bump into you again, Faye. How are you?' he almost shouts.

My heart thumps against my ribcage. He presses against me.

'Let me go. You're hurting me.'

'You're coming into my car for a chat.'

'No I'm not,' I say struggling to pull away from him, but he overpowers me and bundles me into the passenger seat of his car and locks the door.

My whole body trembles. He walks around the car, uses his key fob to unlock the driver's door only, and slides into the car next to me.

His eyes burn into mine. 'We need to talk. I am prepared to overlook the way you have been treating me lately, injuring me, running away, damaging my property. I need to explain how we are going to move forwards. You are going to leave Phillip and come to live with me. I will forgive you for having children with another man. I will treat them as if they are my own.'

'If you don't stop threatening me, I will go to the police.'

He laughs. 'Then they will find out what you have done. Everyone will know. Did you really think I wouldn't have copies of that film?'

I take a deep breath. Give a light shrug. 'Phillip already knows. He's cool with it,' I lie.

'Phillip's not cool with anything. Don't make the wrong choice, Faye.'

'Do whatever you want. I can take the fallout.'

He is smiling and shaking his head, letting me know with his eyes and his mouth that he doesn't believe me.

'I don't love you, I hate you. Whatever you do or say I'm not leaving Phillip.'

168

Jonah

'Whatever you say or do I'm not leaving Phillip.'

Your words burn into me. I look into your beautiful face contorted by rage, and something inside me snaps. I have loved you so much for so long, begged you so many times to be with me. I had come to terms with the fact you weren't interested in me, but then when we finally made love, hope soared again.

But your attitude today is devastating. It is over between us. You are a heartless siren; attracting me, playing with me, dumping me.

That was your last chance to come with me voluntarily, Faye.

169

Faye

He lunges across the gear stick, pulls my body roughly against his and attempts to kiss me. I close my mouth; he snogs my skin. I can hardly breathe. At last he pulls away. He presses a tab on the steering wheel and the passenger door clicks to unlock. Relief floods through me so quickly my body feels empty. I open the door and begin to slide out of the car.

'One week, Faye. I'll give you one more week.'

170

Erica

The doorbell rings. I open the door of my cottage to my supervising officer.

'Come in.' I beam cheerfully.

She enters my home, eyeballs sliding up and down my body. Round and round my cottage. Radar eyes. Eyes that do not respect my privacy. I scrubbed, cleaned and tidied before she arrived. She cannot fault my home-maker skills.

'Do sit down. Can I get you a cup of tea?' I ask.

'No thanks, I'm fine.'

I sit down opposite her. She is young and snappish. Dressed in grey and black.

'How are you settling into Weybridge?' she asks.

'I love it. I much prefer it to Twickenham,' I lie enthusiastically.

Her eyebrows quiver. 'That's unusual. Most criminals prefer their hometown.'

The word criminal sears into me. I like to think of myself as a person, not a criminal. I have done my time now.

'Why do you prefer it here?' she asks.

'It's prettier. The architecture is more characterful.' I frown a little as I think. 'Also it's bigger. There's more stuff to do.' I shrug my shoulders. 'It's an opportunity for a fresh start.'

'Is that what you needed? A fresh start?'

'I think so. Most of us *criminals* do.'

She leans forwards. Her eyes burn into mine too intently. 'Are you looking for a job?' she asks.

'I will be soon.'

Her eyes keep burning. 'Why not yet?'

'I'm just settling in first. Learning to keep my head above water, out of gaol. Learning to keep my cottage nice.'

'You're certainly doing well at that.'

She smiles, but her smile is condescending. It doesn't reach her eyes.

Middle-class stupid. Degree, but no brain. I'll get a job when I know Faye and Mouse are safe.

'Claiming benefits, are you?'

'I've managed that yes.'

She stands up, still pretending to smile. 'Well as everything seems to be in order here, I'll be off. Thanks for letting me in, Erica.'

Phillip

Jonah has won a Victoria sponge, from a local celebrity baker's. He's a lucky, lucky man. I have laced it with lashings of the finest strawberry jam, and sieved a splash of icing sugar across the top. Trimipramine from the dark net is mixed in with the jam. A double dose in fact. The strongest dose that I have fed him yet.

172

Jonah

I have been feeling so tired. Sleeping twelve hours a night, dragging myself out of bed in the morning. Soon we will feel tired together, Faye. Together for ever.

Erica

The svelte young woman who I hardly know has been busy shopping. She has managed to find timer switches at the local pound shop. Now she is moving routinely through her whole flat, plugging in appliances. The TV is set to come on from 9 p.m. until 11. Radio 2 from 7 to 9 a.m. in the morning. Blinds down. Bedroom curtains drawn. No one will know whether she is away or at home. Everything is set up. Her next meeting with her supervising officer is over a month away, so she can have some freedom for a while. But she has to come back here to sign on. Until she gets a job she really needs her benefits. So the unrecognisable, svelte young woman can leave Weybridge, but not for very long.

174

Jonah

Beethoven's Fifth Symphony is pounding out of my Sonos system, resonating around my house. So positive and vibrant, filling me with energy, reminding me of the special time when we made love. Faye, soon you will be with me for ever.

My hands tremble with excitement as I rummage through my bedside drawers. Diazepam. Fluoxetine. Zopiclone. Tranquilliser, antidepressant, sleeping tablet; the strongest on the planet. The stockpile of my prescription drugs that I have not taken for over a year, except for zopiclone, which is an addiction for me; I have to take it all the time. I couldn't stockpile so I lied. Pretended I left my tablets behind when I went abroad on holiday, so my doctor was fooled into prescribing them for me again.

I scoop the drugs into a carrier bag and take them downstairs, into my kitchen. First I crush the diazepam tablets with a pestle and mortar, pulverising them into powder. I weigh the powder carefully and divide it in two. Half each. We will share everything from now on.

Then I break the fluoxetine capsules open with a knife, one at a time, and then once again weigh the powder and divide. Zopiclone last. Zopiclone is my favourite, a powerful finishing touch.

175

Erica

Checking my reflection in the mirror before I set off to the railway station, I hardly recognise myself. A different woman from the one who went to prison. Mulberry handbag. Size 10 Hugo Boss trouser suit. Both rescued from a local charity shop. The charity shops in Weybridge are a treasure trove.

I set off down the side passage at the back of my cottage, turning onto the wood-lined main road. The woods where I jog every morning. Nothing much to look at except for passing cars and trees. I'm the only person on the pavement. Walking isn't very popular around here. At last I arrive at the roundabout by the station, walk through the car park and down the steps to the station.

I have practised this moment so many times. The moment I am pretending to be a normal person; a person who is allowed to step on a train heading towards Twickenham. It is mid-morning. Not too many other people around. I mustn't do anything to draw attention to myself. I buy a ticket from a machine, not the kiosk. I find out that the train I need leaves from platform one. I do so from the screen, not by asking anyone for help.

Ten minutes to wait. I stand halfway down the platform, watching the other passengers from beneath my hat. An elderly couple with too much luggage, rearranging it on the platform. A young woman wearing mascara so heavy it looks like spider's legs. A middle-aged man in a blue North Face jacket and a bobble hat. A woman with a baby.

The woman with the baby is holding it against her chest in a sling. She is looking at it, transfixed. I can only see the top of the baby's head. She stretches her neck to lean forward and kiss it. So softly, so gently, such tenderness in her eyes. And, for a second, I want to die. The enormity of what I did to Faye hits me. The cruelty of taking away someone she loved so much. I cannot bear to watch. I walk to the furthest end of the platform.

The train I am prohibited from boarding arrives. My limbs feel heavy as I walk towards it. The judge's voice shouts in my head. I hear the buzz of electronic locks closing behind me. My legs weigh a ton. I can hardly walk. The guard blows a whistle and I have to push my heavy legs through mercury to run. One foot on the train. The doors start to close. I raise my other leg from the platform, and step forwards. The doors slice shut. I am on the train. It starts to move and I feel jubilant. I have done it. I am on my way to Twickenham.

176

Jonah

Faye, you don't recognise my new car do you? A grey VW Polo. So many of them around, like chewing gum splatters on the pavement. No one notices what I drive now.

Faye, I know you hide the spare set of keys to your house, under the rock beneath the Choisya. I borrowed them and had my own set cut.

177

Faye

I turn the key to the front door, glad to be home, laden with shopping. Rushing around after my exercise class, looking forward to a break. To sitting down for ten minutes and having a cup of coffee.

Since Georgia started at nursery school, after thinking life would be easier, I have been busier than ever. But busy is good. It almost takes my mind off Jonah. Sometimes the film of us together stops rolling through my mind. Sometimes I stop feeling his hands pressing into my skin and hurting me. Sometimes I forget the claustrophobia of his greedy kiss. He threatened me with a week. What is he planning? What can he do? Nothing. If the situation gets any worse I will have to come clean with Phillip and we will both have to go to the police. I tremble at that thought as I dump my shopping bags by the door, and step past the cloakroom, towards the kitchen.

A footstep behind me. I turn around, surprised. Is Phillip home? No one. I continue walking. Steps behind me again. Arms from behind, pressing like bands of steel, across my chest, across my throat.

'Don't fight it, Faye,' Jonah's voice says.

I lower my chin, sink my teeth into his arms and bite. I taste the salt of his blood.

'Stop it, bitch,' he shrieks and removes his arm from my throat to pull my head back with my hair.

Pain sears through my scalp, and my teeth release his flesh. Pain again. A thud to the back of my head. Dots in front of my eyes. The world turns black.

A room is coming into focus around me. A room with apricot walls, and a painting of golden sunlit mountains. Its familiarity engulfs me. My dining room. My home. My mouth is dry. The back of my head aches. I try to run my hand across my scalp, but I cannot move my arm. Rope is cutting into my wrists. Binding my chest to a chair. Swathed around my ankles. Then I remember Jonah's voice from behind me, and fear simmers through me.

Jonah is pulling out a chair and sitting across from me at the dining table. A bottle of champagne and two glasses in front of him. I frown, but frowning causes the pain in the back of my head to explode, so I smooth my forehead, again.

'What do you want?' I ask.

'You know what I want, Faye.'

I wriggle to try and make myself more comfortable but pain cascades throughout my body.

'You can't have me. I belong to Phillip.'

He taps his fingers on the dining table and smiles. 'I am going to have you, Faye.'

My heart pounds up towards my throat, pushing the air from my lungs. The pain intensifies.

'Untie me, Jonah. You don't want the police involved in what happened between us, do you?'

He lifts his shoulders, and his eyebrows. 'As long as we're together, Faye, I don't care who's involved.'

'Phillip will be home soon.'

Another smile. 'Nice try. Did you really think I hadn't checked? He's away at a digital marketing conference. He won't be back until late.'

178

Erica

At Virginia Water, I find a seat next to a lady of about sixty with grey hair. She is nursing a large, well-worn leather handbag on her knee, and wearing comfortable shoes. A double seat facing backwards. She is the only person who can really see much of me, and she is nonchalant; looking out of the window. Staring at the horizon and daydreaming.

Good. I can relax. I can breathe. The leaden feeling in my limbs begins to lighten. The train journey is only twenty minutes. No one will recognise me. No one can stop me. I flick through the free magazine someone left on the platform, half ignoring the words, half concentrating. Nothing very interesting. A theatre review. Sports teams. The adverts at the back. People selling junk. Threadbare sofas and broken lawn mowers. Out to make a quick buck from things they no longer want.

I turn the page. That's when I see it. Your face in a large colour advert. That is when my ache to be as attractive as you, which has been dimming, intensifies again. I haven't seen you for so long I'd forgotten how large your eyes are. Their intense colour of violet had softened in my mind. I'd forgotten how sharp your cheekbones are, how full your lips.

I close the magazine and sit with my head in my hands. I try and pull back to the success of my DBT when I was in prison. I tell myself that life is not a competition. It doesn't matter that

I will never be as attractive as you. Now I have lost weight I am attractive enough, and I'm healthy. I'm on my way to see Mouse. And to check you are OK.

I hear the brakes of the train begin to scrape along the tracks. The train slows down and stops.

The intercom buzzes.

'Ladies and gentlemen, we are being held at a red light because of a signalling problem. The engineers are working on it. Sorry for the inconvenience. We will let you know what is happening as soon as possible.'

I sigh inside. Just when the journey was going so well.

'This is a nuisance, isn't it? Are you in a hurry?' the woman sitting next to me asks.

I give her half a smile. Only half, so as not to encourage her to talk to me. 'No. No problem. It's fine,' I say trying to push away the knots in my stomach.

The train is hot and stuffy. I begin to feel mildly sick. I flick through the magazine again, trying to find an article that I actually want to read. Five minutes pass. Ten. I end up staring at the picture of you once again. The woman in the next seat looks across at your photo.

'Pretty isn't she? Do you know her?' she asks.

'No. Do you?'

'No. I don't have any children, so I only know people my age.'

Her eyes shine into mine, brimming with loneliness. So she is talking to me to be friendly, not because she is suspicious of me. I know what loneliness used to feel like. I pity her and relax a little.

'Do you have plans?' I ask.

The train begins to move again.

'I'm just going home. No one is waiting for me.'

She begins to talk. About the last general election. About the weather. As the train continues to pull towards Twickenham.

Slowing now, brakes squealing as we pass familiar lines of terraced cottages, on the last few hundred yards before the station.

'Lovely to meet you, dear. What is your name?' she asks me. A name comes to me out of the blue. 'Jennifer Bugle,' I lie.

179

Faye

Breathe, breathe. Keep him talking. Like they do in films.

'Jonah, if we went off together where would we go? To the Caribbean? To the Philippines?' I ask through the fug of pain.

His eyes are glassy, staring straight ahead. 'That's right, Faye. We're going somewhere special together, that's why I've brought the champagne.'

'Where, Jonah? Where are you taking me?'

He turns to look at me, eyes sharpening. 'We were perfect together. You enjoyed my body so much.'

'Yes I did. So very, very much.'

'Don't worry, Faye. You will never need to sleep without me again.'

180

Erica

As soon as the train arrives in Twickenham, I am the first to open the heavy door and jump off it. Relieved to have escaped from the other passenger's loneliness, which is still clawing at me, pulling me down; making me realise how lucky I am to have Mouse. I think that so many times a day now.

I need to walk from the station to your house. I need to know that you are OK. Loneliness has never been your problem, has it, Faye?

Through the centre of town, past NatWest Bank and Iceland. Turning left at the traffic lights and striding along Cross Deep. Right towards Strawberry Hill, the leafier side of town. Wider pavements. Detached houses. Past Range Rovers. Audis, Volvos and BMWs, neatly parked and shiny.

Into your road. Into your development. Buggy folded at the top of your steps. Around the back to find the gate to the back garden unlocked as usual. I push it open and close it behind me. Slowly, slowly, creeping and lowering my body to hide behind bushes, I step towards the patio windows, keeping to the edge of the garden so that you can't see me. Hiding my body behind the wall, leaning in to the edge of the window, to take a glimpse.

181

Faye

I scream as loud as I can, air bellowing from the bottom of my chest. A curdled, twisted scream. It pierces the air and makes me feel stronger. Makes me feel there is hope.

But my strength cannot last. He is behind me, hand tightening across my mouth.

'Shut up,' he hisses.

I feel the snake of his breath across my cheek, hand so tight I can hardly breathe. His hand slips away. I scream again. This time it takes longer for the sound to build. Rumbling through my throat, slow to reach full throttle. Stopping as he pushes a gag into my mouth so roughly that I begin to choke. Choking and choking. He slaps me on the back.

'Enough of that,' he snarls.

The gag loosens. My throat relaxes, as he puts tape across my mouth.

He paces up and down, in front of our patio windows. Restless like a caged polar bear, eyes burning and dangerous. I cannot think. I cannot move. He turns and walks towards me. He sits at the table opposite me again, pulls a gun from his pocket and points it at me. I am numb now. I can't believe this. I have only ever seen guns on the TV. A hand pistol, with a silencer on it.

Phillip. Tamsin, Georgia. My body aches to talk to you. To hold you. To tell you that I'm sorry. I close my eyes and see you moving towards me, taking my hand in yours. 'Have courage, Faye. Have courage.'

Your image fades. I see Jonah placing the gun on the table and opening the champagne. He pours it into the glasses, which I now see have some sort of powder in them. He pulls a spoon from his pocket and stirs the concoction.

'Our champagne cocktail. A very special drink,' he announces.

Champagne fizzing in the glasses, he picks up the gun. I tremble inside. He steps around the table and kneels behind me. He clamps his left arm around my breasts and thrusts the tip of the gun into the soft flesh of my neck, behind the jawbone. Then he raises his left arm and pulls the plaster from my mouth.

'If you scream again I'll shoot.'

The tip of the gun pushes harder. He removes the gag, and brings one of the glasses.

'What are we celebrating?' I ask, voice blistered and cracked.

'Our suicide pact.'

His words sear into my heart; his gun pierces into my windpipe. He pulls my hair to hold my head back and forces the liquid into my mouth. I hold it in my mouth for as long as possible.

'Swallow it or I'll shoot.'

I swallow it. It tastes bitter. Tears are streaming down my face.

'If I can't have you, Faye,' he whispers in my ear, 'no one will.'

182

Erica

I am watching, Faye. I see what he is doing to you. Don't worry. I am here now. I will run for help.

183

Jonah

You look so beautiful. Deathly pale and fragile. Already fast asleep. I untie your bindings and carry you upstairs. Gently I lay your precious body on the bed. I arrange your body so carefully. I brush your hair until it shines. I wash your face to remove the mascara that your tears have smudged around your face. I wish I could have made love to you one last time, but I have been feeling tired. So very tired. We will both be at peace now.

I sit next to you on the bed and hold your hand. 'For richer, for poorer, in sickness and in health. Congratulations, Faye, we will be together for ever, my love.'

I lift my champagne cocktail to my mouth and gulp it down. For a second its bitterness makes me wince, but I lie next to you on the bed and hold you in my arms. Your breathing is heavy, rhythmic. I hold you. I love you. I close my eyes and drift towards sleep. I love you so much. My treasure.

184

Erica

I creep back through the garden, slowly, carefully, camouflaged behind bushes. I push the gate open and run. Running for your life, Faye. Running for mine. If you die, Faye, I will never forgive myself.

Running. Feet pounding on the pavement. Heartbeat pounding in my ears, in my brain. Breathing slowly trying to stop panic rising. Back to the phone box I passed on the way. I dial 999. Police. Ambulance. Emergency services, quickly, quickly, please help. I sigh inside with relief that I managed not to give in to the urge to use my mobile. Using it to report a crime would have aroused police interest in my identity. My location would have been obvious and I would have been sent back to prison for a very long time. But police, ambulance, emergency services, after the delay of me running to the phone box, please, please, I beg you, don't waste any more time.

185

Faye

I open my eyes, half awake, half asleep, fear slivering through my body. The fear is sharp-edged, tinged with electricity. I know I am in my bedroom. I see the photograph of Phillip, the girls and me at Thorpe Park, on my dressing table in front of me. We are all laughing, arms around each other, leaning towards the camera. I remember that day so well. We were high on summer sunshine, and artificial entertainment. I put my arm across the bed to feel for you, Phillip. I want you to hold my body against yours to help combat the fear.

Your body feels wrong. Rigid. Solid. I roll over and as I roll my body aches. The fear is burning now. It isn't you. It is Jonah. My heart seems to stop beating. One look at his face and I know he is dead. Eyes glazed and staring.

Why is he here? What has happened? Why is he lying dead in my bed? I push and push to try and remember, but I cannot. I can't remember seeing Jonah in my house. I cannot remember getting into bed with him. Where are the girls? Where are you, Phillip? Is this a dream? Is it real?

I try to roll my body away from Jonah's. I want to reach out and ring for help. For the police. For you. But my body is stiffening too. I cannot roll. I cannot move. The air is closing in around me, becoming solid, pressing against me. Burying me. My eyelids are heavy, so heavy. I cannot think, I cannot move. I can only close my eyes and let sleep engulf me. The sweet, sweet release of sleep.

Faye

I cannot move. I cannot speak. I know Jonah is here when I want you, Phillip. I want your warmth. I only feel coldness. I hear sirens. Whispering in the distance to begin with, pulsing in my brain, then wailing and insistent. Surrounding me. Sound and people surrounding me. Lifting my body onto a stretcher. Lifting me out of my bedroom.

Where are you, Phillip? Where is Tamsin? Georgia? I need you, my family. I am lying in a metal casket, surrounded by machines and men in uniform. The sirens are wailing again and still I cannot see you. Still I cannot speak.

Phillip

In a seminar, when my mobile vibrates. I step outside to pick up.

'Twickenham Police here, is that Mr Baker?'

'Yes,' I reply, stomach coagulating.

'I am ringing to inform you that your wife is on the way to the West Middlesex Hospital in an ambulance. It would be a good idea if you got there as soon as possible.'

The world stops.

'What's happened?' I ask, grabbing my coat and walking through the door.

'She's been found unconscious.'

Empty. Sickness rising.

'Where? Has there been an accident?' I ask.

'We can talk about the circumstances when you arrive.'

Too shocked to drive, I call an Uber. It seems to take for ever to get to the hospital. Traffic almost at a standstill through St Margarets and Isleworth. The driver tries to talk to me, but I am too worried to make conversation. Forty-five minutes later, I arrive at the A&E Department and race inside. A queue at reception. I cannot cope with this. I push straight to the front, heart racing.

'My wife has been brought in, in an ambulance. The police rang me. I need to see her immediately.'

'Name?'

'Faye Baker.'

Glossy nails are tapped onto a keyboard. Grey eyes pierce into mine. 'She's in critical care. Go to the entrance of critical care and a nurse will take you straight there.'

Critical care.

Dying inside, I walk to the entrance to find a nurse in a blue uniform waiting for me, holding the door open for me to walk through.

'Mr Baker?'

I nod.

'Come with me,' she instructs, mouth and shoulders in a line.

'How's my wife? What's happened?'

'I'm sorry, Mr Baker, I don't know. I haven't been with her on the ward, I am just here to take you to her.'

We walk past cubicles containing suffering people. I can hardly bear to look as I worry about what has happened to you. Through A&E, into critical care. The nurse leads me to your bedside.

I cannot believe what I see. You are unconscious. Intubated. Attached to a cacophony of machines. You who were so beautiful, so full of life this morning. I pull up a chair and sit next to you. Your face is so still. A puppet being kept alive by machines. Your eyelids flicker and my heart quickens. Are you somewhere inside there, Faye? This cannot be happening. This is a nightmare. I will wake up in a moment. I bite my tongue to see if I am really here. It hurts. It is real.

I cannot take your hand in mine as your arm is attached to too many wires. I lean across and stroke an unencumbered part of you. 'I love you, Faye,' I tell you. 'More than you will ever know.'

Footsteps behind me. I turn around. The doctor is here. He isn't wearing a uniform but he has a stethoscope dangling from his neck. Tall and thin with a roman nose. Fine head of wavy hair.

'Can I have a word, Mr Baker?'

'Of course.'

'She is stable at the moment. We have washed her stomach out. But most of the drugs have already been absorbed. It's symptomatic treatment from now on.'

'What on earth happened? Did she take an overdose?'

'Have you talked to the police yet?'

I shake my head.

'They will talk to you about what happened.'

'But . . . but . . . surely you can tell me. What happened must affect her condition?'

'It's just speculation at the moment and . . .'

'Tell me, will my wife live?' I interrupt. My voice resonates around the ward, plaintive and desperate.

'The next few hours are crucial.' There is a pause. 'We still don't know what she took. The lab are testing the contents of her stomach at the moment, and will get back to us as soon as possible.'

'What she took? Are you saying she took an overdose?'

'It's complicated. As I said, wait for the police to explain.' He puts his hand on my arm. 'Try to calm down, Mr Baker. We are doing everything we can for your wife.'

Calm down.

I feel like grabbing hold of him and shaking him until he tells me what he thinks happened. But I manage to contain myself and allow him to walk away. I sit watching the lines on your machines, body pumping with anxiety. A nurse arrives to check your vital signs, adding information to the notes at the end of your bed. She doesn't speak to me, just nods as she passes.

After what seems like for ever a detective inspector marches into the ward.

He holds his hand out in greeting. 'DI Jones.' There is a pause. 'Shall we step away from her bedside?' he suggests.

He leads me to a small seated area at the side of the ward.

336

He sits opposite me and leans forwards. He is about my age. Dark and swarthy.

'Do you have any idea what happened?' I ask.

'We suspect that Jonah Mathews attempted to murder your wife. He left a suicide note claiming they had a pact to die together, to take a concoction of drugs. But we found evidence to suggest she was restrained. Bound and gagged. Her fingerprints were not on the note.'

His words stab into me.

'Where?' I ask.

'In your home.' He pauses and takes a deep breath. 'By the time we arrived he was already dead.'

188

Faye

Phillip, you are here. I feel you, but I cannot see you. Your scent. Your heat. I am running towards you, away from Jonah. Running away from Jonah in my mind, but my legs and my feet won't move. My body is stuck solid; only my mind is fluid. My mind is tumbling like a waterfall.

189

Erica

Pacing up and down Mouse's flat. It used to be the other way around, especially when it rained. He'd pace. I'd watch.

'It's the not knowing I can't stand.'

Mouse is sitting in the middle of his trendy IKEA sofa, cradling a cup of tea in a white china mug.

'If she was dead it would have made the local news,' he says to try and reassure me.

'How can you be so sure about that?' I snap.

He raises his right hand in protestation. 'Well Jonah's death did.'

'I need to know, Mouse. I need to know whether she's all right.'

Mouse places his tea on the coffee table in front of him and walks across to me. He stops me pacing by standing in front of me and putting his hands on my shoulders. His eyes hold mine.

'You must be careful, Erica; even though you look so very different now. So much slimmer, so glamorous, completely different hairstyle. You are not supposed to be here. I do not want you to be recognised. I do not want to lose you again.'

My stomach rotates. Mouse thinks I look glamorous. I never thought I would hear anyone say that. 'I don't want to lose you either, Mouse.'

'Come on, Erica. Try to forget about her for a while. Shall we watch TV?'

I sigh inside. 'OK, Mouse.'

He takes his hands from my shoulders and sits down again. He flicks the remote at the TV and Netflix explodes across the screen. 'What about the *Santa Clarita Diet*?' he suggests.

'That always makes me feel sick.'

'The new series of *Stranger Things*?'

'Fine with me,' I say unenthusiastically.

The theme music for *Stranger Things* blasts around the living room. I try to melt into the moment but I keep seeing him holding your head back with your hair, and ramming liquid down your throat. I keep seeing his hand holding the gun.

'She must be in the West Mid,' I shout over the music. 'They must have taken her there. A woman in a critical condition, the local news reported a few hours ago. I just can't get it out of my mind. She must be in the critical care ward at the West Mid.'

Mouse pauses Netflix.

'I'm going to go there and find out,' I continue. 'Pretend I'm someone else. No one will recognise me. No one will be able to guess who I am.'

Mouse sidles next to me on the sofa, and takes my hands in his. 'I beg you not to go, Erica. Please stay here with me.'

190

Faye

Half awake. Half asleep. Lying in a comfortable bed, surrounded by stiff white sheets. A hotel or a hospital. I know I'm not at home. Phillip is here. Sitting at my bedside, leaning towards me. I see his dark hair. His broad cheekbones. So familiar. So comforting. His features are sharpening. Eyes glistening.

'Faye, Faye, can you hear me?' he keeps asking.

I smile, to tell him I love him and know he is by my side. I feel as if I am in the middle of a kaleidoscope, the world slowly spinning around me, in a fragmented pattern. It slows. A hospital room comes into focus, standing still, surrounding me. A world of white walls, wires and machines.

'Faye, Faye, talk to me. Can you speak?' Phillip begs.

He is stroking my arm, my forehead, my cheeks. I feel his touch. The warmth of his breath on my cheeks.

'Phillip,' my voice croaks at last. 'What happened?' I ask.

'We're all waiting for you to tell us that.'

I squeeze his hand and drift back to sleep.

191

Phillip

You are growing stronger every day. Every morning and every evening when I visit you I see differences. You are awake for longer. More able to remember facts. About the children. About life, arrangements, plans.

Today when I arrive you pull yourself as far away from your machines as your wires will allow you and cling to me more tightly than ever.

'He so nearly killed me,' you whisper, tears streaming down your face. 'Who called the ambulance?' you ask. 'A passer-by?' There is a pause. 'How would a passer-by know what was happening?'

'Don't complicate things, Faye. Maybe someone saw him breaking in?'

'I thought you said he had a key?'

'Maybe someone saw him opening the front door and realised he shouldn't have been. Come on, Faye, it's over. Let's not worry about every detail.'

Your lips find mine and we kiss. There is a desperation in your kiss that never used to be there.

'I love you, Phillip, so much.'

Your voice is needy. It clings to my skin. I know what you did. I know I need to forgive you, Faye. I prise your body from mine. I need to get away from your intensity.

Age-old excuse. 'Off to the bathroom,' I tell you.

I pad to the communal toilets at the end of the ward, splash my face with cold water, and then lock the door behind me in a private cubicle. I put the toilet lid down and sit on it. I take my laptop from my bag, open it and plug in the memory stick Jonah posted to me the day he died.

I must stop looking at it, or it will send me demented. I watch it for what I promise to myself will be the last time. The most awful sight, every second of it sending pain lacerating through me. You strip off in front of him and pull him towards you. You caress him and tear off his clothes. Then, there is a close-up of him entering you, followed by a close-up of your face. Spaced out. What did he do to you? He must have spiked your drink. Your long silky hair is tousled, wet with sweat. Your lips are slightly parted, your dyed eyelashes long and feathery. And then a close-up of him grinning, like a demonic gargoyle, triumphant and sinister.

My body stiffens. My heart is leaden. To send this to me thinking you would be dead by the time I received it. What kind of a monster was he? I wish I could send him a film of you, still alive in my bed. I would like to torment him in hell.

I know I need to forgive you, Faye. I will try as hard as I can, because I love you. I have always wanted our relationship to work. I should have killed him, long before he tried to kill you. In time I know I can forgive you. But I will never be able to trust you. When you come home, from now on, I will never let you out of my sight.

192

Faye

I am sitting up in bed, wire-free. Able to move my arms whenever I like. The girls are here. Sitting on the bed, cuddling up to me. Phillip, you are sitting in the armchair opposite. Looking dear. Looking familiar.

I close my eyes and the ghost of Jonah flits across my mind. I feel the heat of his breath as he stands too close to me. At the school gates. In the supermarket. His intensity as he thrusts me against the wall in our dining area.

I remember sitting on the sofa with him at the party, allowing his hand to massage the base of my spine. The feel of my party dress as it slipped across my skin to the floor at his house. The moment I woke up, mouth parched, head throbbing, clamped in his arms. His gun piercing into my windpipe. The pain as he pulled my head back with my hair, forcing the liquid into my gullet. His words: 'Swallow it or I'll shoot. If I can't have you, no one will.'

I open my eyes and look into your solid face, Phillip. Your features contort, and for a second you are staring at me too intensely. For a second I am confused. Are you Phillip or are you Jonah? Then your face softens and you are Phillip again.

193

Phillip

The doorbell rings, slicing unexpectedly into my day. I pad to the door to open it. DI Jones is standing on my doorstep, grinning at me. A boyish grin. Dimples on both cheeks.

'Now that your wife's recovering so well, do you mind if I come in? I just want to keep you informed.'

'Of course. Sounds good. Please do.'

He follows me. Into the hallway. Into the sitting room. Stepping over a sea of soft toys and Duplo.

'Sorry about the mess. Only just got the girls to bed. Bit chaotic when I'm on my own.'

'Of course. How are you managing?'

'Well, I'm working from home, most of the time, at the moment.' I pause. 'Do sit down.'

DI Jones moves a teddy along the sofa and finds a place to sit.

'Can I get you anything? Tea, coffee?'

'No thanks I'm fine.' He leans back and crosses his legs. 'We've had the autopsy results on Jonah Mathews.'

Electricity pulsates through me. 'And . . .?'

'It seems he had taken slightly different drugs to the ones he administered to your wife. Trimipramine, a tricyclic antidepressant, was found in his system as well. That wasn't detected in your wife's samples.' There is a pause. 'Unlike the rest of the drugs he used, trimipramine wasn't one he had been prescribed.

It is a powerful antidepressant, and interacted with his overdose of sleeping tablets.'

'So you think the trimipramine finished him off?'

'Maybe that's why he died so quickly. If he hadn't taken that as well by the time we arrived we could have saved both of them.'

His dark eyes pierce into mine. 'Do you know any reason why anyone would have wanted to harm him?'

'No, Inspector.' I shake my head slowly and frown a little.

'I've got to ask you because of what happened between you.'

My body tightens. 'The fight?' I ask.

'Yes. You started it, I believe?'

'I'm not going to deny it, although I had been friends with him for many years, he had started to annoy me. He had a thing about Faye. Maybe looking back he always had – I just hadn't noticed. We did have a few arguments about her. He said he had slept with her. She denied it. I believed her not him, but occasionally I allowed his baiting to rile me. That's what happened the day I lost it and punched him.' I raise my shoulders and arms in the air. 'But what would I have gained from poisoning him? How could I possibly have even managed it?' I pause for breath, and shrug. 'Anyway you can check up on my movements. I was in a seminar at the Shaftesbury Hotel.'

'We already have. Your alibi is solid.'

Solid alibi. His words punch into me. Panic rises. Language like that makes their suspicion sound serious, more than just a few idle questions in passing. I watch the inspector's eyes darken.

'Do you know who telephoned the emergency services?' he asks. 'They hung up without identifying themselves.'

I shake my head. 'No idea. None of it makes sense to me. I'm a digital marketing manager. You're the detective.'

The inspector laughs. A short dry laugh. Half a smile. Not showing me his dimple this time. 'Thank you for your time, Mr Baker. We'll be in touch.'

346

194

Erica

I stand up.

'Where are you going?' Mouse asks.

'You know where I need to go, Mouse.'

He walks across the room and stands in front of me, blocking my passage to the door. Feet apart. Shoulders wide. 'No I don't.' There is a pause. 'Or at least I don't understand it.'

'Who said we always need to understand one another, as long as we show respect?' Too much for Mouse. He frowns, and wipes his fringe back from his eyes. 'I want you to accept me for what I am,' I continue.

His frown is deepening. 'I do accept you, Erica. But I like to have you around, and as far as I can see your actions are breaking rules. Breaking rules has consequences. I always stick to rules.'

I put my hand on his arm. 'I know you do, Mouse. But I am different to you.'

He takes my hand in his. His eyes hold mine. They are shiny and sad. 'I'm frightened, Erica. I will suffer if you go away again.'

I lean forward and kiss him gently on the cheek. 'Don't be frightened, Mouse. This is the last time I am going to consider her, and then I'm going to sort our lives out.'

195

Faye

Sitting in my hospital armchair, by the side of the bed, waiting for Phillip and the children to collect me. All hospital discharge papers signed. Fully dressed. Bag packed. Still a bit weak. Still a bit dizzy. But I didn't tell the doctor who signed my discharge papers that.

I hear giggling in the corridor. Tamsin. Georgia. They are here. Running into my arms. Well, Tamsin runs, Georgia kangaroo hops.

'Mummy, Mummy, Mummy,' they both shout.

They sit on my knee. They entangle themselves, around my waist, my arms. Phillip appears around the corner, a smile plastered across his face. He bends down to my chair, managing to find a gap between the children, to reach my lips and kiss me. Surrounding me with the familiar scent of his sandalwood aftershave.

'Ready?' he asks. I nod my head. 'Let's get you out of here.' He pauses. 'Come on, girls. Get off your mother for one second, so that she can stand up.'

They slide off my lap and stand watching as Phillip holds my arm and helps to pull me up. As soon as I am upright they nestle against my legs, wrapping themselves around me like ivy. Phillip scoops up my suitcase and my discharge notes and begins to lead the way out. Entangled with my girls, I follow.

The doctors and nurses at the nursing station look up as we

pass. Phillip and I have already thanked them so many times, but we beam at them, and thank them again. I will never be able to thank them enough.

Out of the ward. Into the corridor. Down in the lift. Corridor after corridor. Snaking around the hospital. Off-white walls. Off-white floors. The lingering scent of antiseptic and pain assaulting my nostrils. The occasional piece of chunky artwork provided by local schools to brighten the environment. Impressionist mock-ups. Colourful and clumsy.

We wind our way until we are eventually ejected into the hospital lobby, wide like a river mouth. Unlike the corridors we have just meandered along, the lobby is commercial and shiny. Like a mainline railway station or an airport terminal.

The girls are holding my hands, skipping through the lobby as if we are going on holiday. Holiday. Perhaps we should do that to celebrate. Book a fancy holiday.

We walk past Costa Coffee, WHSmith, a hairdresser's and a florist. Through glass revolving doors. Fresh air hits my face. I inhale it like nectar.

A woman is walking slowly past. A woman with long, dark, shiny hair, a bit like mine. A skinny woman with a strong face carrying a blazing bouquet of flowers. One of the biggest bouquets of flowers I have ever seen. Purple and orange. Bold and striking. Orchids. Lilies. Daisies. Irises. Bell flowers. Verbena. Freesias. A woman who looks familiar, but I can't place her.

Our eyes meet. A smile erupts around her face. A smile so bright it competes with the bouquet. She stretches the flowers towards me and for a split second I wonder whether she is about to give them to me. Then I pinch myself. Chastise myself for being silly. Why would she want to give flowers to me? I pinch myself again. Do I know this woman?

'Good morning,' she says.

'Yes,' I reply. 'It is.'

Her eyes hold mine for a few seconds too long.

196

Erica

You are being discharged from hospital. My heart sings because I know you are all right now. These flowers, so bright and special, were meant for you. I was going to ask a nurse to pass them to you. But it is too late. You are already leaving the hospital, so I couldn't give them to you directly. I couldn't risk you recognising me. I have just walked right past you clinging on to my gift. Someone else will have them now.

I continue through the glass revolving doors into the hospital lobby. Straight to reception.

'Please could you tell me how to get to the geriatric ward?' I ask, still feeling light with relief.

'It's really simple, follow the yellow line,' the receptionist tells me.

I frown. 'Yellow line? Where does it start?'

'Through the doors at the back of the lobby.'

'Thanks.'

Through the doors at the back of the lobby, people smiling at me, admiring the flowers. Following the yellow line, past cardiology, radiography, paediatrics, the canteen, the pharmacy. I take a deep breath and enter. I stop at the nurses' station. A young nurse with Goldilocks curls is sitting inputting notes into a computer screen. I stand in front of her and watch. After a few minutes she looks up, surprised.

'Sorry,' she says. 'I was engrossed. Didn't notice you. Can I help?'

'I'm from the local florist. I've got a free bunch of flowers to give to someone who would appreciate them. Is there anyone on this ward who's a bit lonely?'

'How thoughtful. How kind,' the nurse says. 'Mrs Kennedy is nearly always alone. First on the right.'

'Thank you.'

I turn around. I enter the ward and move towards a lady with soft white hair, framing an oval face. She is sitting up in bed, wearing a pink cardigan over her hospital gown. Her eyes light up as I approach.

'What beautiful flowers,' she says.

'I've brought them for you.'

She frowns. 'But I don't know you, do I?'

'No. I just had some flowers to give away, and wondered whether you'd like them?'

'We're not allowed to keep them on the ward. The nurses let us keep them in the TV lounge, but I go in there a lot.' She sits looking at them, as I stand in front of the bed holding them. 'Thank you so much.'

'Would you like to touch them? To smell them?'

'Yes please, dear.'

I move to the side of her bed and place them on the bed tray in front of her. She buries her face in them, inhales their scent.

A random old lady. A new connection. My surrogate grandmother. I will visit her again.

197

Faye

Phillip is standing in the middle of our sitting room opening a bottle of wine. In the past we would have had champagne. But I will never drink champagne again. Not even at a wedding. He pours us a glass each. We clink glasses, and kiss.

'So good to have you home,' he whispers.

'Good to be here.'

He steps back from me a little, smiles and raises his glass again. 'To a new start. No looking back.'

I smile weakly without raising my glass. 'I can't manage that. I need to look back first.'

He frowns. 'How come?' he asks.

'I need to face what happened. To deal with my demons.'

'Your demons? Jonah and Erica. Which one of them haunts you more?'

'They both haunt me in different ways.' The wine glass trembles in my unsteady hand. I begin to cry. Tears stream down my face. I feel empty; panicked inside.

'At least Jonah is gone now. But Erica, she is coming back,' I continue. 'I even thought I saw her as we left the hospital. But it wasn't her. It was someone far slimmer, just with similar eyes.'

'She won't come back because of the restraining order.'

'She will. We need to warn the police. Tell them about her. The woman I saw is an omen.'

'No. No. Faye. You need to stop catastrophising right now.'

He pulls me towards him and holds me against his chest. So tight I can hardly breathe.

198

Phillip

'You need to stop catastrophising, right now.'

I take you in my arms and hold you against my chest. I kiss the top of your head. I hold your body more tightly against mine. I feel the warmth of your breath. Inhale your scent. Camomile and gardenia today.

'Please, Faye,' I beg. 'Try not to worry. Erica and Jonah will never affect you again.'

'They will always affect me,' you reply.

'Come on, let's get you into bed and then I'll clear up and take the recycling.'

You laugh a little. A dry contained laugh. 'Are you trying to drown me in domestic bliss?'

I coax you upstairs, into our bedroom, leaving you sitting at your dressing table in your powder pink negligee, removing your make-up. As promised I return downstairs to do my chores.

I flick the controller for the Sonos. The boisterous tones of Robbie Williams begin to bounce around our living room. 'I Love My Life' follows me as I clear the table and begin to stack the dishwasher. When the dining area is clear and the kitchen is tidy, I fill two carrier bags with bottles and paper, grab my coat, and set off to the recycling bins at the end of our road.

Full moon. Light so bright, like an old black and white film in daylight. The world I am walking through is surreal; hard-edged and sharp. It's 11 p.m. No one about. I clatter the bottles through the porthole in the recycle bin. They smash as they fall. Breaking glass explodes into the silence of late evening. Then I slip the old newspapers and magazines into the paper bank. Finally I take the bottle of trimipramine from my pocket, and throw the last few remaining tablets down the drain at the side of the road. The empty bottle goes into the recycle bin, straight into the right category: plastics.

No one will find it now.

199

Erica

It's raining in wire mesh sheets. The world is grey upon grey, low clouds like pan scrubs, almost touching the ground. But today Mouse isn't pacing. He is sitting at his dining table playing chess with me. Grey-brown hair falls across his eyes as he leans forwards in concentration.

I pretend to study the board too, but the movement of my pieces is a lottery. I look across at his wide frowning forehead, at his thick wavy hair, to contemplate what he might be thinking. I imagine a resonant, educated voice in his head advising him of his next move. Doesn't he know there is no need to concentrate to flummox me?

Slowly he leans forwards, and moves a knight. He leans back, looks up and pushes his eyes triumphantly into mine. My turn to concentrate now. But that is where I go wrong. I need to concentrate all the time. I begin to move my queen.

'No. No. Erica.'

I push the upturned palm of my hand towards him. 'Don't help me. Don't tell me.'

His shining face crumples. 'But . . . but . . . I don't want the game to be over too quickly. If you move the queen right now it's over.'

'How can that be?' I ask.

He sighs, a long low sigh. 'I'll explain.' There is a pause. 'Again.'

'Well thanks. But then it isn't a game now – it's a training session. So I'll go and put the kettle on to keep us going.'

He raises his hands in the air and smiles that smile. The one that makes him seem so handsome. 'Good. Good. I fancy a cuppa,' he says.

I stand up and move into his kitchen area. Shiny. Polished. IKEA trendy. As I fill the kettle I catch my reflection in it. I think Mouse is a bit OCD the way he keeps his flat so clean. He winces when I spill crumbs onto the counter as I slice bread. Or if I splash a little oil as I fry something.

Thankfully today he isn't watching as I rummage through the cupboard to find the teabags. As I throw them into two mugs and slop hot water on top of them, quickly pummelling them to release the flavour and then topping them with milk, spilling some on the counter. Usually he stands behind me with a cloth wiping my inevitable slops. Today he is concentrating on the chessboard.

I move back towards my lesson and hand him his tea.

'Thank you, Erica.'

'It's a pleasure, Mouse.'

He takes a sip and puts his mug down on his special mat on the dining table. Mouse never puts glasses or mugs down without a mat.

'If you have a few training sessions you'll soon get back into the game again properly.' There is a pause. 'You need to save the queen. To keep her best movements for the appropriate moment. You must never leave her vulnerable. She is the most important piece on the board. Lose her and you've lost the game. Watch this.' He picks my queen up with his thumb and forefinger, and moves her as I was intending. 'See. She would have only got two pieces, before being taken. She can move in any direction. She can do much better than that.'

I shrug my shoulders. 'I thought two was good.'

Mouse's eyes harden. 'Not good enough for a queen.' He pauses. 'Are you still worrying about Faye?'

'I haven't seen her doing the school run yet.'

'You've got to let her go. It's becoming a competition between us. A competition that Faye always wins.' He pauses again. 'I only win at chess.'

'No you don't, Mouse. You win on so many counts.'

200

Phillip

I worry about you, Faye, so vulnerable after what has happened. I watch you all the time. Dressing in the morning, pulling on your exercise Lycra, brushing your hair until it shines, tying it back to expose razorblade cheekbones and doe-like eyes.

I work from home, and watch your every movement. As you relax around the house; as you get back to normal doing household tasks. The way you hold your shoulders. The way you twist your neck. Every movement of your eyes, your face.

I have been looking after the children. You haven't left the house much yet. You haven't been to do the school run. You haven't been to the gym – you are working out to a video in our bedroom. You haven't visited Mimi. When you do I will follow.

What has happened has changed us both. I still love you. One day I may be able to forgive you. But I will never, ever trust you again, my darling Faye.

201

Faye

My first morning back to normal, taking both children to school, because Georgia has started there, part way through the summer term. A baking-hot day. Holding my daughters' hands, one on either side of me; both too grown up for the buggy now.

Sweat pools on my forehead and at the back of my neck. I shudder inside. The eyes that watch me all the time have turned into Erica's eyes. She is watching me now. Sweat begins to pool between my thighs and between my breasts. I look across to where the police told me she used to live and a stab of panic presses into me. I breathe in deeply. Breathe, breathe. I look up at the window of her old flat. The curtains move a little.

Slowly we walk. Past the space where Jonah used to wait for me in his Jaguar. Past the Lollipop lady. Past the yellow zigzags. Right into the school entrance. Across the school playground – past the School Gate Mafia. Eyes following me. Following me all the time.

My daughters pull away from my hands, skipping off to join their friends. I watch them joining in a game, racing around at the other side of the play area. Tamsin running at the front of the pack, head back, wind streaming through her fine hair. Georgia's little legs working overtime, so small, despite all her efforts she is coming last. But she doesn't care. So excited to be running around with the older girls, giggling and smiling.

I leave them and walk away, eyes burning into me and pressing against me as I walk across the playground. Eyes that will never go away.

202

Erica

So thrilled to see you doing the school run this morning. I watch you from Mouse's flat, scuttling past, moving your head from side to side, as if you are looking for someone. Not dressed in Lycra but with a backpack. Is your gym kit in there?

As beautiful as ever, hair blow-dried and buoyant. Make-up perfect. Just the right amount of blusher emphasising your cheek-bones. I like the outfit you are wearing today; very rock-chic. Grungy T-shirt, high-heeled sandals and denim skirt.

At a guess I'd say you have changed your exercise regime a little and you're off to see Mimi first. But you are still working out aren't you? Look at that neat waist, and those colt-like legs.

203

Erica

I am sitting by Mrs Kennedy's (Rose's) bed, in the West Mid hospital, feeling relieved that you are back to normal, Faye. The bouquet of lilies I have brought Rose are on her bedside table, waiting for the rather bossy nurse who is on duty today to whisk them away to the TV lounge. It seems hard to believe that something as beautiful as flowers causes respiratory problems in hospitals when they are such a natural occurrence in the wild. Life can be such a shit in so many ways.

'It's so lovely of you to come and see me again,' Rose says as she attempts to push herself further up the bed. But her shoulders and arms are so frail and thin. They do not have enough power in them to allow her to move. So I stand up, hold her gently by the torso and help her.

'Is that better?' I ask, as I fluff the pillow.

'Yes, thank you, dear.'

'Why did you come back?' she asks when she has settled herself.

'I just thought you could use some company.'

'That's certainly true.'

'How long have you been here?' I ask.

'Since last December. About five months I think.' She shakes her head. 'I fell in my kitchen.' Her voice falters. 'It was two days before anyone found me, and I wasn't very good.'

'How much longer will you be here?'

363

She shrugs her bird-like shoulders. 'I don't know. They're looking for somewhere for me to go. I can't look after myself. I'm not allowed back home.'

'Why are you on your own?' I ask.

She irradiates me with her large round eyes of cornflower blue. For a second I see the pretty young woman she once was. She shrugs.

'I was an only child. I never married. I'm ninety-one. My friends and family have all died.' There is a pause. Silence solidifies in the air between us. After a while Rose's voice pushes through it. 'I never thought I'd end up like this. I was so independent. This is such a lonely time.'

My heart rotates with pity. And suddenly as I look at her wafer-thin skin, riddled with age spots, I know what I want to do. Train to help old people. Get a job in a nursing home. I take a deep breath. But that would be a big, big step for a woman like me.

'What's your name, dear?' Rose asks.

'Jennifer Bugle,' I reply a little too quickly.

'That's an unusual name. Where are you from?'

I hesitate. 'I've lived all over.'

'Don't you have any roots?'

'I have a friend called Mouse.'

'Is Mouse a man or a woman?'

'A man.'

'Have you ever kissed him?'

'No. Not properly.'

'I think,' she says, looking at me intently with her large round eyes, 'you should go straight home and kiss Mouse properly.'

'It's not as simple as that.'

'There's nothing as simple as a kiss,' she says.

'Or nothing as complicated,' I reply with a smile.

Our eyes meet and we both laugh.

204

Faye

As I walk through Twickenham I know I am being watched. As I walk into the centre, past M&S Simply Food, past the fishmonger's. Past WHSmith and Poundland. Across at the traffic lights by Snappy Snaps. They recede as I step upstairs to Mimi's office.

Mimi's face lights up when she sees me. 'Thanks for coming in,' she says.

She is wearing pillar-box red. Her hair is pink. Pink and red clash don't they? But today, on Mimi, it works.

'How's my star client?' she asks as I settle in my usual position in the chair opposite her desk.

Star client. If I am her star client her business must be even worse than I thought.

'Good,' I reply as enthusiastically as possible and give her what I hope is a wry smile. 'How's tricks?' I ask.

'Everything's booming.'

'Really?'

'Well it is for you. Absence makes the heart grow stronger and all that.' She pauses. 'Don't look so surprised. Close your mouth. You look like a guppy. We are not modelling fish food, or at least not yet.' I try and readjust my expression. 'Yes, I've had so many enquiries about you while you've been in hospital. I told everyone you were away on a big modelling assignment.'

I laugh. 'Modelling hospital equipment?'

'I didn't specify.' She runs her hand along the side of her Mohican. 'Anyway they were all happy to wait and now you've got quite a programme for the next few months.'

I sit leaning forwards, hands clenched to the edge of my seat, waiting for the negative. What has Mimi got in store for me? Tampon adverts? A toilet paper demonstration? Incontinence pads?

'Super exciting,' I exclaim. 'What sort of things?' I ask, preparing myself for disappointment.

'First. A wedding fayre.'

Not too bad. Probably quite fun actually.

'They wanted some older models.'

Oh, Mimi.

'A fashion show in Bristol. And . . .' Mimi stands up and leans across her desk pushing her eyes into mine. 'Accessorize want you again, for a full-page colour magazine advert. Full face – advertising earrings.'

'That's fantastic.'

'Dead right it is. And Elizabeth Hurley Beach want you for swimming costumes. You'll have to have a fake tan.'

'That's amazing, Mimi.'

I stand up and hug her.

205

Phillip

You went to see Mimi didn't you, Faye? I saw you walking out of her office, smile playing across your lips. I know you have good news to tell me later when you come home after the school run. You are at the gym now. I followed you there, before I came back home to check the house again.

Ground floor first. Where he tied you up and stuck the gun in your gullet. All windows closed and locked. It is such a hot day but we can't take any risks. No one else will ever get in here again.

I climb our narrow staircase into Tamsin's room. I rattle the window locks. Fine. And all fine in Georgia's bedroom too.

Into our bedroom, where he lay next to you. Our bedroom, still full of the stench of his death. But I will not open the windows to release the smell. I use reed diffusers and scented candles. I check the windows, then pad upstairs, to the loft extension.

The loft extension that will always remind me of him, of what happened. I should have listened to you, Faye. I open the door and step inside. Sterile. Antiseptic. Unused. Unnecessary.

The doorbell rings. I look at my watch – 3:15. Too early for you. I pad downstairs expecting it is a door-to-door salesman to be shooed away. I open the door.

DI Jones. Standing in front of me, brandishing his smile. Brandishing his dimple.

'Can I come in?' he asks.

'Of course.'

I stand back, away from the door, to allow him access to our tiny hallway. He steps inside and follows me into our living area. He stands eyeing my computer.

'Working at home again?' he asks.

'Yes. Well, my job in digital marketing is fairly flexible.'

'Mr Baker, the thing is, I am afraid to say we're going to need your computer, your phone, your iPad, any electronic devices, for a few days – I have got a warrant.'

I stand frowning at him. 'Why's that?' I ask.

'There are just a few minor details we need to check.'

'Well how can I get on with my work then?'

His eyes darken. 'This is a police investigation. Your work will have to wait.'

'Am I allowed to ask what you want? What you're looking for?'

His shoulders rise and fall. 'It's nothing to worry about. We just want to clarify your computer and phone use. Check a few facts.'

I smile. A relaxed slow smile. 'I suppose you are always interested in a husband's actions when a man has been over-interested in his wife.'

'That's right, Mr Baker,' he replies, mouth in a line.

206

Faye

'What's going on, Phillip?' I ask rattling the bedroom window in an attempt to open it, realising that it is locked.

You stand behind me and hug me, so tight I can hardly breathe. You always hold me too tight these days.

'I'm keeping the windows locked so that no one can get in and hurt you again.'

I tremble inside at the memory, too tired to argue back right now. Despite being traumatised by what happened, I can't have this. I need to breathe fresh air. I'll find the key for the windows tomorrow. Turning my head, I kiss you on the lips and use the softening of your body to extricate myself and slide into bed. Already covered in a fine layer of sweat that feels slimy and oily against my body, I wipe the excess off with the handkerchief I keep under my pillow.

You use the bathroom and come and lie next to me, pulling me towards you and clinging to me like ivy. Heat and claustrophobia wrap around me and throb against me, solid and unnerving. I push you away, roll over and throw my covers off.

I slide into a restless sleep, and dream. The police are chasing us; you and me, and the children. I am holding Tamsin's hand. You are clinging on to Georgia. Running through a field of barley, wearing backpacks. My backpack is growing heavier and heavier. So is yours. Our knees begin to buckle as we run.

I hear the police officers' breath, as they pant behind us. It slides across the back of my neck. My rucksack feels like granite. Heavier and heavier, footsteps becoming impossible. I fall to the ground and let go of Tamsin's hand. You fall too. Tamsin takes Georgia's hand and they both run off through the stems of barley, which sway gently in the wind.

Police officers, heads covered by stockings – so we can't see their faces – surround us, pulling our possessions out of our rucksacks. Computers. iPhones. iPads. My make-up. Your wallet. The cufflinks I gave you for your thirtieth birthday. My engagement ring. As they steal my engagement ring I begin to scream. The screaming becomes louder and louder until I wake myself up, and find I am dripping in sweat, the bedroom like a sauna now.

I lie still in a pool of liquid as my body calms. Watching the rise and fall of your breath in the moonlight that curls around the curtain edges. Then I remember. The police have confiscated your electrical goods. Worry rises like bile in my throat. What are they suspicious of?

207

Faye

I am marching past Snappy Snaps and sandwich bars, on the way to the police station. Into the fine old stone building, which is cool inside. It smells of stale air and antiseptic. I shiver as I move towards the counter, which looks like a hatch, behind which a police officer is sitting dealing with enquiries. There is a queue. I join it.

Three people in front of me. I stand behind a tall, skinny man who looks as if he has been in a fight. Sling around his arm. Bandage on his head. As he turns around I see his left eye is decorated by an array of bruises. He nods at me and smiles. I nod back and stand behind him to wait my turn.

A woman with a loud voice is at the front of the queue, talking to the police officer. Her car has been stolen from the Waitrose car park. An Audi R8. I vaguely recognise her. Then I realise she is one of the School Gate Mafia. Her voice echoes around the police station, long-vowelled. Self-important.

'We've filed a report, Madam,' the police officer says. 'We'll get in touch if we hear anything. Sometimes it's just joy-riders and we get the cars back.'

The School Gate Mafia woman walks past me, heels clicking on the floor of the police station. Just as at the school gate, she doesn't notice me.

The next man only takes a few seconds as he is collecting lost property and then it is the man with the bruised face.

'Can I help you, Sir?' the police officer asks, as he steps forwards.

'Only if you catch the bastard who beat me up.'

A long, slow, graphic description of the fight follows.

At last it is my turn and I step forward feeling nervous. The police officer behind the desk is so young, he looks like a teenager. He hardly needs to shave. He still has acne on his neck. 'Good morning. Please may I speak to Clara Morgan?'

His face is solid. Disinterested. 'Would you mind telling me what you need to talk to her about?'

I show him the card she gave me, when Phillip was in hospital.

'She asked me to get in touch with her personally, if I had any problems.' I pause. 'I'd rather not go into details unless we are in private.'

A woman asking to speak to another woman in private presses the button: red light priority. His face jumps into action.

'OK OK, I'll buzz her – name please?'

I tell him. He dials his phone. 'Faye Baker in reception to see you.'

A velvety voice replies, 'I'll be straight out.'

I step aside to wait, while the teenager catches up on paperwork. Ten minutes later PC Morgan appears. Petite and curvaceous with blonde hair falling to her shoulders. She smiles and as she smiles her large brown eyes soften.

'Hello, Faye.'

Does she remember me? Or has she spent ten minutes looking at my files?

'Would you like to come to the interview room where we can talk in private?'

'Yes please.' My voice sounds soft and uncertain.

I follow her through the doorway by the hatch, into the core of the police station, along a white-painted corridor. Right and right again into the interview room. The interview room smells of another life. Of stale air. Of entrapment. We sit opposite one another across a grey plastic table.

'Can I get you a cuppa?' she asks.

I succumb. To her kind voice. To my sleepless night.

'That would be lovely, thanks.'

There is a phone on the table and she rings to order refreshments. Then she leans across the table towards me. 'Are you all right, Faye?'

'Yes.' I pause. 'I mean no. Not exactly.'

Her brown eyes darken. 'What's happened?' she asks.

'Two things. First. Your colleagues have taken my husband's electronic devices to investigate them.' My hands are trembling. 'I'm really worried. I'm having nightmares. What do you suspect him of?'

An officer arrives with a tray bearing two mugs of weak tea and a plate of digestive biscuits. I take a mug and begin to sip my tea.

'Faye, please don't worry. I am sure checking your husband's computer and phone is just routine. He will have everything back in a few days. We just have procedures we have to follow sometimes.'

'But . . . but . . .' I splutter. 'Life isn't a procedure.'

She takes a biscuit. I watch her bite into it. 'I can't discuss it with you. All I can say is that if we thought you were in any danger we would let you know.'

Danger. The word danger reverberates in my brain. Please, please, may I not be in any danger again. My stomach tightens.

'That's all you can tell me, is it?' She nods her head. 'Why did you give me your card and encourage me to come and talk to you if I was worried?'

She flicks her hair back from her eyes and puts her head on one side. 'I meant if Phillip was threatening you. After all he hit Jonah. Sometimes we find situations like this incendiary.'

'And I'm supposed to believe taking his computer is routine?'

'That's what I said, yes.'

I close my eyes and breathe in and out deeply. I need to keep calm. When I open my eyes PC Morgan is still watching me, head on one side.

'What else did you want to talk about, you said two things?' she asks.

I resign myself to the fact I will find out nothing more about Phillip. 'Erica Sullivan's broken her restraining order. I know she's back,' I announce.

PC Morgan leans forwards. 'Have you seen her?'

'I might have done.'

'What do you mean "might"?'

'I thought I saw her but I wasn't sure. But I did see the curtains to her old flat move as I walked past a few days ago. I feel as if her eyes are watching me all the time.'

'We'll check the flat. That's fine. And get back to you straight away. But just to reassure you, she has reported to her supervising officer whenever required, and her place in Weybridge appears to be occupied.' There is a pause. 'I know you've been through a tremendous amount. But please try to stop worrying. Everything's under control.'

208

Erica

A police car is pulling up outside. I close the curtains and continue to look through a tiny crack. Parking on the double-yellows outside our block of flats. Driver and passenger doors opening. Two police officers stepping out. Looking up. Looking up towards my old flat, and here I am just above it.

I need to run. I need to hide. Run or hide? My body won't move. My mind can't think. Run? Hide? Run? Hide? The police officers are young, one male, one female. Walking towards our block. Feet pounding on concrete. Determined expressions on their faces. Still my body won't move. I am locked to the window, watching them.

Closer. They are coming closer now. They must have a key. They are turning the lock and entering our building with ease. The landlord must have given them a key. I close my eyes. I feel them getting nearer. I stand still and wait. Wait for my life to be over. I do not even have the strength to call Mouse who is resting in his bedroom, to ask him to stand by my side. Someone must have told them I am here. Someone must have recognised me. And I thought I had been so clever to lose so much weight. So clever to look so different.

They are on the floor beneath us. I hear them banging on the door of my old flat. An eruption of banging and hammering.

'Police. Open up.'

More banging. More hammering. Once again: 'Police, open up.' There is a pause. 'We have a key. We're coming in.'

'Police, freeze.'

Please, I pray once more to a god I don't believe in, please don't come up here. Don't remember I was friendly with Mouse, one floor up. Don't remember he came to visit me in prison. Please, don't have checked him out. I hold my breath and wait. The world falls silent around me. A solid heavy silence that presses against me. Are they coming to get me? Are they coming up here? I feel my heart thudding against my ribcage. Blood pounding against my eardrums. Time stops.

After what feels like eternity but is probably about ten minutes, I see the police officers stepping out of our building, heads together in conference. Talking. Shrugging. Looking up at the building and pointing at the window of my old flat, one floor down. Talking into their radio-phones. Nodding. They open the doors to their police car. The male slides into the passenger seat, the blonde is the driver. They sit in the police car a while. Are they waiting for backup before they come for me? Still my heart thuds against my ribcage. Still blood pounds against my eardrums.

At last the engine of the police car begins to throb. At last the police car is driving off. My heart quietens. I breathe again.

Phillip

I look out of the kitchen window and see a police car pull up outside. They've found something on my computer and they are coming to arrest me. The doors open and a small curvy police officer steps out. My heart is palpitating. A vice-like grip tightens across my chest.

She walks up the steps to the front door and rings the bell. As I step towards the door I feel invisible; here but not here, watching what is happening to me from a distance, as if I am not part of it. I open the door.

'Do come in,' I hear myself mutter.

She steps inside and follows me, through our hallway and dining area, into our living room. She sits in the middle of the sofa. I sit on the sofa opposite.

'Can I get you anything? Tea, coffee?'

She shakes her head. 'No thanks. I won't keep you long. I was just driving past and I wanted to let you, and your wife, know that we checked Erica Sullivan's old apartment and as we suspected it's empty. She's definitely not in residence.'

My body softens with relief. A reprieve. A brief reprieve.

210

Faye

The police are lying to me. All of them. And so are you, Phillip. Eyes burn into me. I know someone is watching me.

Erica

You are walking past our block of flats again, more slowly than you used to, because you do not use the buggy any more. Two young ladies hold your hands now; young ladies who look more and more like you every day.

I sit by the window watching you, drinking in every detail. Electric blue trainers. Multicoloured skin-tight Lycra pants. Matching body. Hair scraped back to reveal those cheekbones.

I know you still train hard because your figure is still perfect, but I cannot follow you any more. It's too risky. I can't risk being found out. I want to stay here. I want to be with Mouse.

Mouse is standing behind me. Watching you too. I feel his hands resting lightly on my waist. His breath on my cheek.

'Pretty isn't she?' I say.

'Not as pretty as you, Erica.'

I smile inside. 'Don't be ridiculous, Mouse.'

Faye

Walking down the street hand in hand with my girls. Someone still watching me. Watching me every day. Jonah is dead. Erica's flat has been checked. She now lives ten miles away. But I still sense someone's presence. Someone's eyes burn into my flesh.

I see a car waiting past the yellow zigzags where Jonah used to wait. The car looks like our car. The driver looks like Phillip. But it cannot be Phillip. Our car is on our drive and he is in the library, using the computers.

'I've got ballet tonight, haven't I, Mummy?' Tamsin asks, dropping my hand, skipping a few steps and swinging her arms into an elegant curve above her head.

'I want to do ballet too,' Georgia announces, doing the same.

'I'll ask Mrs Massam if she has a space,' I reply watching the car that looks like ours drive off, and clamping their hands firmly in mine again.

A brown Volvo. Not a recent model. I breathe in and out deeply. Lots of dusty brown Volvos are driven to primary schools in the UK every day, aren't they? Phillip wouldn't follow me. He wouldn't come to school without telling me. I am really going mad. Unless . . . unless . . . My stomach tightens. Unless Phillip is worried because he also thinks someone else is watching me. Maybe he's been listening to me more than I think.

Phillip

Just home from the library, starting to chop vegetables for the girls' tea. Homemade vegetable lasagne. We need to introduce the girls to as many vegetables as possible at an early stage. So I chop aubergine, courgette, onions, peppers and mushrooms. I make a roux sauce, with ladles of cheese to disguise the taste of the vegetables as Tamsin hates mushrooms, and Georgia hates aubergines.

Just as I am bending to put the lasagne in the oven, a police car pulls up into our drive again. My heart palpitates. This time they must have finished analysing my computer. They are bringing it back. Or arresting me.

Two police officers step out of the car. Two. Must be arresting me, if they need to send two. I close the oven door and step to answer the doorbell. They are standing on our doorstep; DI Jones brandishing his dimple, and the tiny blonde woman who came last time frowning at me in soft sunlight.

I smile half a smile. 'Do come in.'

They step inside and follow me into the living room.

'Can I get you anything?' I ask.

'We're good thanks.'

They sit together on the sofa and I sit opposite them.

'Have you brought my electronics back?' I ask boldly, as I wait for them to cuff me.

'Yes. That's why we're here.'

My body sings with relief. DI Jones opens a bag he is carrying, pulls my electronics out and hands them back to me. 'Sorry we've kept them so long.' There is a pause. He smiles. His dimple deepens. 'All clear as you told us it would be. I hope you understand, we just have to check.'

'I know you do. Of course I understand. Thanks so much for bringing them back.'

All clear. All clear. I want to shout for joy. To dance on the table. All my dark net activities invisible. I always hoped I was clever enough. But now I know I am. I can use the dark net to obtain whatever I want. No one will get away with cuckolding me, ever again.

My stomach tightens. 'Just one question, Inspector, did you ever find out who called the police the night Jonah died?'

He crosses his legs and folds his arms. 'No. We assume it was a neighbour who saw Jonah entering your house and was suspicious. A neighbour who didn't want to be identified.' He shrugs. 'Some people are very wary of getting involved with criminal proceedings. You'd be surprised how wary people can be of the police.' He shakes his head. 'The emergency recording was very non-specific. A crackly line. We couldn't even tell if it was a man or a woman's voice. Just asking the emergency services to get there quickly. Nothing to ascertain the caller was involved or had inside information.'

'So what did you decide about the er . . . what is it called? Trimi . . . trimipramine?' I ask, trying to make my voice sound casual.

'Well.' He takes a deep breath. 'Jonah's computer is missing, so we can't analyse it, but we assume he obtained the drugs from the dark net.'

I suppress the laughter that bubbles deep inside me.

'Maybe he didn't want to kill Faye, just frighten her and finish himself off in her arms,' DI Jones continues. 'No sensible GP would have prescribed him more drugs so he must have got hold of them illegally.' He pauses for breath. 'Anyway, the case is closed. Ready to go to the coroner. Overwhelming evidence that he committed suicide, and attempted to murder Faye.'

I push the laughter down again.

214

Erica

Into the ward. This time I have chosen a bouquet of pink and white lilies. I walk past the nurses' station and around the corner. Someone else is in Rose's bed. A woman who is thinner than Rose, with longer hair. This is good news. They must have found a home for her. I picture her resplendent at last in a colourful bedroom, with photographs and ornaments all around her. A room with a view of all the flowers that she loves: roses, lilies, freesias.

I walk back to the nurses' station. Three nurses are having a doubtless much-deserved break, cradling cups of tea and chatting. I stand by the station and wait. After a while one of them turns around and smiles at me apologetically. A tall woman with a strong almost masculine face.

'Can I help you?' she asks.

'I came to visit Rose Kennedy. Please can you tell me where she is?'

The nurses exchange a glance. And as soon as they do that, I know. The tall one steps out from behind the nurses' station and walks towards me.

'Are you a friend?' she asks.

'Yes.'

Her face stiffens. She takes a deep breath. 'I'm very sorry to tell you that she died last week.' A pause. 'Her funeral was held at the crematorium, yesterday.'

My arms and legs feel hollow. Tears prickle in the corners of my eyes. 'What happened?' I ask.

'She had a heart attack. She died peacefully in her sleep.'

'What day did it happen?'

'Last Tuesday night.'

'I wish I had been able to say goodbye,' I mutter.

'Her ashes will be spread in the flower garden at the crematorium. So you will be able to visit.'

'Thanks.'

I turn away, tears in my eyes, wending my way through the hospital corridor towards the exit. I take the wrong turn and become trapped inside the hospital, winding and turning. Knots tighten in my stomach. At last I arrive at the shiny hospital foyer and manage to step outside. Cool evening air whispers across my face and calms me a little.

I do not want to visit the flower garden at the crematorium. Flowers growing in bodies burnt to ashes seems to me to signify the pointlessness of life, not its energy. I take the bus back to Twickenham. I walk through the centre of town, down Church Street. Past the Wren church and the museum, turning left to follow the tow path along the river, towards Richmond. The air is sharper here. I breathe more easily.

Walking and watching the river flowing gently soothes me. The river will be moving long after all our lives have passed. I stand beneath a weeping willow tree, throw the bouquet into the river and watch it float on. The river has energy and movement. Energy that will last for ever. Rose's voice and eyes shout into mine. You still have life. Mine is over. Everything gone, taken. Please enjoy what is left. And suddenly I realise that still having life, when Rose has none, gives me the responsibility to live. To really, really live.

215

Faye

I need to talk to Phillip. I slide out of bed and pace around the room, stretching my arms above my head to release the tension. I snap on the light. Phillip stirs. He sits up in bed, rubbing his eyes. I walk to his side of the bed and sit next to him. My eyes prickle with tears, which I push back by swallowing. Tears never help.

'I'm still being watched.'

He takes my hand and squeezes it. 'No. Faye. No.'

'Yes. Every time I take the children to school. Every time I pick them up. When I go to the agency. To a photoshoot. To the supermarket. Someone is always there, watching me.'

'Faye, you know that isn't true.'

'Don't patronise me.'

I look down at my trembling hands.

'The police checked the flat. Erica isn't there. Jonah is dead. No one is watching you.'

I look up into Phillip's dark eyes. 'You're lying. I thought I saw your car outside school the other day. You're worried too.'

'No, Faye, no.'

He leans towards me and pulls me into his arms. He holds me against his chest. 'You must go and see a GP, Faye. You really need help.'

216

Erica

I turn around. Mouse is standing in the kitchen area, by the kettle, waiting for it to boil.

'Coffee?' he asks, getting some mugs from the cupboard.

'Yes please.'

He reaches for the Nescafé. 'You aren't watching her for as long these days.'

'Well I didn't just come back for her. I came back to see you, Mouse.'

His eyes widen. 'Really, Erica?' he asks.

'Yes. When I was in prison, and when I was living in Weybridge, I missed you very much – and I miss you when I go back to sign on.'

He is standing, teaspoon hovering, over the coffee jar. 'Do you really, Erica?'

I smile. 'Of course I do, Mouse. I miss you very much.'

He puts the teaspoon on the counter and steps towards me. 'Then I need to talk to you about something. Something very, very, special.' He takes my hand. 'Come and stand in the middle of the sitting room.'

What is he doing now? Is it like the day he got the chess set? Has he bought something for us to share? Has he booked a holiday? His eyes are glistening. Lips slightly apart. He bends down on one knee, still holding my hand in his.

'Erica, I love you. Please will you marry me?'

I close my eyes. I can't have heard him right. Mouse, the closest friend I have ever had, has just asked me to marry him. We've only ever been friends. We have never even flirted with one another. Let alone kissed properly. Rose's words reverberate in my head. I open my eyes. He is looking at me intently, waiting for an answer.

'Do you really think our relationship could be like that?' I splutter.

'We are close friends already. I've read that's the hardest part.'

Close friends indeed. The closest friend I've ever had.

'We could try the other stuff, Erica, see how it goes? What do you think?'

His eyes shine.

'I think that's a good idea, Mouse.'

He stands up. His body moves closer. My stomach fills with dancing bubbles. It has never danced like this before. Slowly, carefully, as if I was made of Dresden china he puts his arms around my back and pulls me towards him. He is warm. Smelling of musk and vanilla. And mint. He kisses me. Softly, gently at first, and then as my body relaxes into his, his kisses become more urgent, more insistent. He puts his tongue in my mouth and my stomach rotates. I don't want him to stop. I want to kiss him for ever. But he pulls back.

'What do you think, Erica?' he asks.

'Not bad for starters,' I say with a jubilant laugh.

217

Phillip

You are in with Dr Hale, your GP, as I sit in the waiting room flicking through magazines. I am so worried about your mental health. You are looking good, getting modelling jobs, but your mind is not holding together well. I am keeping such a careful eye on you. You are my responsibility. I have never felt as responsible for you as I do right now sitting in the waiting room of our local surgery, waiting to drive you home. If only I had taken better care of you in the first place that bastard would not have been able to get anywhere near you. I am watching over you now.

218

Faye

I am sitting in the patient's chair opposite my GP, a thin, worried-looking woman who looks even more anxious than me. Her body language, legs crossed, shoulders rounded, hands together on her lap, looks defensive. How did Phillip persuade me to come and see her? He is sitting outside in the waiting room. Here to support me. Supporting me or following me?

She's a trained GP. A top academic. Of course she will be able to help. But someone is whispering in the corner of my mind: no one can help. You have no place to hide. No security. Anyone can stalk you. Any time. Any place.

The GP uncrosses her legs and leans forwards. Her body relaxes. Her shoulders widen. 'How can I help you?' she asks.

'I've had a few problems recently,' I say, eyes filling with tears.

'What sort of problems?' she asks.

I open my mouth and everything spills out. The way I ran into Jonah at that party. What he did. How he died. And Erica. How she hated me. And the eyes. The eyes that are following me.

She listens, looking transfixed, as if I am as interesting as a Netflix crime series.

'You've had a truly terrible time, you need to see a therapist,' she announces when I have finished my outpouring, 'to help you talk through this.' She leans forwards and takes my hand in hers. 'With the right help you'll soon feel better about yourself. About your life.'

219

Faye

I am standing in the hallway, about to leave for my first visit to my therapist, Martin Bayliss. You step out of the kitchen, car keys in hand.

'I'll drive you.'

I shake my head. 'No thanks. It's only by Strawberry Hill Station. It's a five-minute walk.'

Your eyes darken. 'It's no problem.'

There is a pause. 'I like to walk.'

'And I like to look out for you. Check you're OK.' You spin the car keys around on your right middle finger. 'I insist, Faye.'

We clamber into our dilapidated Volvo, and drive around three corners, coming to a halt outside Martin Bayliss's Edwardian house. I lean across to kiss you.

'See you later.'

'I'll wait for you.'

I feel heavy. Leaden. I never seem to go anywhere on my own these days.

'No need.'

'It's no problem.'

I shudder inside, slide out of the car and slam the door. I walk across the colourful Moroccan-style tiles that line the path to the house, and ring the bell. The door opens and blue eyes simmer into mine.

'Faye Baker?' a man about the same age as me asks. I nod my head. 'Please step inside.'

I do as instructed and enter a long, thin, beige-carpeted hallway. The walls are painted a warm peach and covered with local watercolours. Paintings of the river, Bushy Park, Ham House, Petersham Meadows.

'We're first on the right.'

Into his sitting room. Jazzy. Full of trinkets. Red walls. Funky tiled fireplace. The room smells musky; as if he is burning joss sticks, but I can't see any. Perhaps it is stale cannabis.

'Do sit down.'

I sink into the middle of a golden fabric sofa; it feels so soft. Soft as fairy dust. Just being in this strange, cluttered world makes me feel more relaxed. He sinks into the maroon velvet chair opposite and crosses his legs. I cannot help noticing his muscular thighs. They look as if they are about to burst out of his skin-tight jeans, but they don't so I guess the fabric is stretchy.

He grins at me, eyes holding mine, and my heart stops. Seriously handsome. Too good-looking. Embarrassed I pull my eyes away and pretend to concentrate on the carpet in front of him. But I'm not concentrating on anything; his physicality is filling my mind.

'So, Faye, what's going on? How are you coping?' he asks.

I lift my head and try to resist the pull of his eyes. I try to look at him nonchalantly from the distance of my thoughts. But even though I am trying not to be drawn in, I cannot help but admire his film-star looks. His strong nose. His perfect cheek-bones.

'I'm coping because my husband is my rock.'

My voice sounds thin and strained. Artificial.

'Isn't that a bit claustrophobic? Wouldn't you rather be coping by yourself?'

220

Phillip

Always sitting in the car waiting for you somewhere. Listening to Radio 2. Now I am waiting for you outside your therapist's house. I look at my watch. Three-fifteen. Your session has overrun by a quarter of an hour. What is happening? Why is it taking so long, Faye? Three more records. Ed Sheeran. Coldplay. Pink.

And the door is opening at last. A man is showing you out. You are looking into his face and smiling. A young Rob Lowe type. About our age. Piercing blue eyes. Designer stubble. I thought you were coming out; but no, the session is continuing on his doorstep. You stand eyes entwined talking through another record; 'One Kiss' by Dua Lipa. You put your hand on his arm. You step away, a smile playing on your lips, and walk back to the car, shoulders back. Just one session. More confident already.

You open the car door and slip into the passenger seat.

'How was it?' I ask.

You nod your head. 'Good. Good. I feel I really connect with him. He's booked me in for two more sessions next week.'

'Connect with him?'

'He listens. Really listens. And it helps.'

Your words sear into me. 'But I listen . . .' I splutter. 'And I'm always here for you.'

'I know you listen and you care. But we're so close. Sometimes it really helps if someone listens from a distance.'

'As long as it stays from a distance.'

A frown ripples across your brow. 'Why wouldn't it?' you ask.

Don't act the innocent, Faye. Haven't you realised that I know? You need to learn to be more careful about what you say.

221

Faye

The girls are in bed and I'm having supper with Phillip. He's cooked a risotto but I am not hungry, so I am just sitting and pushing it around my plate. I take a sip of Chardonnay.

He is staring across the table at me, a little too eagerly. Always so intense these days.

'Excuse me, I just need to pop to the toilet.'

'OK – don't be long or I'll need to heat up the risotto.'

'I'm sure it'll be all right.' I don't need to be told how long I can spend on the lavatory.

I stand up from the dining table and walk into the downstairs cloakroom, which is entered from our diminutive hallway. Our tiny cloakroom, walls plastered with photographs of the children, pinned to a large corkboard. I do not need to be here. I just needed a break from Phillip. From his staring eyes. His intensity. I sit on the lid of the toilet seat, put my head in my hands, and close my eyes. Martin's face appears in front of me. He is smiling at me. His smile smells of freedom. He's going travelling later in the year; to India and Nepal. Imagine if I could join him.

But then my heart lurches. I could never go away like that. I have the children. I feel heavy for a second but I know I wouldn't swap my girls for anything. I sit looking at their photographs. Holding hands, as they run across a beach together. Christening gowns. First steps. First shoes.

A knock on the cloakroom door. I jump.

'Are you all right, Faye?' Phillip asks. 'You've been in there seven minutes.'

I growl inside.

222

Erica

It is our wedding day. I have to keep pinching myself to be sure it isn't a dream, as I stand in the ladies' toilets at the registry office in Weybridge, looking in the mirror, checking my hair and my make-up. We are moving here. Mouse has sold his flat in Twickenham and his dad has bought us a large conversion flat in a Victorian house, in the nicest part of town. A characterful flat with high ceilings and cornices. And a shiny modern kitchen, with every IKEA utensil of my dreams. And, and, and, I have a job interview at a local care home, next week. I look at the perfectly made-up face, devoid of a double chin, that is staring back at me in the mirror. Is it really me – Erica Sullivan? I open my clutch bag, put on an extra layer of coral pink lipstick and smile back at myself.

I step out onto the staircase of the registry office, up a few steps into the holding area where Mouse, his father and his father's girlfriend Karen are waiting. Mouse steps towards me.

'Are you ready? Are you sure, Erica?'

'I've never been more sure of anything, but I am glad it's not raining.'

His father laughs as he steps towards me. He hugs me. Holding me against him. I smell the scent of his lemon aftershave. Then Karen hugs me.

'Always remember,' his father says, 'you are not just marrying Mouse; we are a family now too.'

A family. I have always wanted a family. For a second I see my mother's face clearly. She is young again. Looking like me. Smiling, eyes buried in mine. Wishing me luck. Wishing me continuity.

I am trembling: limbs, hands, lips. Mouse takes my hand. The couple before us are stepping out of the registry office. Smiles and confetti. A buzz of flashing cameras. We are surrounded by colourful clothes, people laughing and chatting. The registrar puts her head around the large wooden door and beckons us inside. She looks to be the opposite of the people she is marrying, trying to be as inconspicuous as possible, blending into the background, eyes and shoulders flashing downwards.

We step into a small but pretty room, with a white marble fireplace and wood-panelled walls. The registrar stands by the fireplace and we stand in a line, in front of her. Mouse's hand tightens over mine, and my trembling quietens.

The registrar begins the ceremony. The words fade in and out. All I see is Mouse's face. His eyes. His mouth. We declare we know of no legal impediment to our marriage. We contract to marry in front of our witnesses. We exchange rings. We kiss.

'I love you, Erica.'

'I love you, Mouse.'

Faye

'You're looking better than ever,' Mimi says.

'Thank you,' I reply.

I cannot say the same back. She is wearing her full regalia today. Piercings and studs in place. Hair white and red. Miniskirt. Fishnets with holes in. Doc Martens. Not a look I like.

'I've got another job for you,' she says.

'Good. Good.' Fresh out of a session with my counsellor, I am trying to mean that. 'What is it then?' I ask.

'A coffee ad for TV.'

I draw a sharp intake of breath. 'Wow, TV, that's fantastic. Do you know about Anthony Head? He did the Gold Blend adverts, and ended up in *Buffy the Vampire Slayer*.'

'One step at a time, Faye. It isn't Nescafé.' Mimi leans forward, eyes burning with concern. 'But it will increase your exposure considerably. I hope after everything that has happened you can cope with that?'

'Yes. Yes. I've been having regular therapy. I can cope with anything now.'

I think of Martin and my heart lurches. I think of Phillip waiting outside and it tightens again.

224
Erica

Our wedding night. Lying in bed with Mouse in our new flat in Weybridge. Mouse moves towards me beneath the covers and puts his arms around my naked body.

'We are about to consummate our marriage – are you nervous, Erica?'

'Don't ask questions. Just kiss me, Mouse.'

Faye

'Don't be late out today, we need to go to the supermarket before we pick up the girls from school,' Phillip barks.

'Well, if it's a problem, I could pick them up on my own. You could go to the supermarket alone. We don't need to do everything together.' I pause. 'And I don't like to rush my sessions with Martin.'

Your face darkens. 'So I've noticed.' Your jaw stiffens. 'I'll just wait here as usual, thanks.'

I sigh inside. I step out of the car, slam the door and march away. Just standing on the pavement, away from you for a few seconds I feel calmer. Jonah and Erica were bad enough, but you are like a tsunami, engulfing me. You are always here, hovering too close to me.

I walk up the path and ring Martin's bell. As soon as he opens the door, I am a teenager again. Heat permeates my skin by osmosis, and I know I must be blushing. My heart oscillates.

'Can I get you tea, vodka, anything?' he jokes, laughing blue eyes holding mine.

'Better not hit the vodka. We're going to the supermarket after this.'

'Life is full of fun and opportunity,' he says sarcastically as I follow him into the sitting room.

His clutter of treasures fascinate me. I see a piece of volcanic rock on the mantelpiece, nestled in a pile of dust. 'Where's this from?' I ask, picking it up.

'Mount Etna, Sicily.'

'I'd love to go there one day.'

'If you want to go there I'm sure you will. The world's your oyster, Faye.'

I put it down and sink into my usual position on the sofa, opposite him.

'I wish the world was my oyster,' I tell him.

'What's been going on?' he asks.

'Phillip's getting worse. He follows me everywhere. He even gets angsty if I am too long on the toilet now.'

Martin shakes his head, and crosses stonewashed-denim-covered legs. 'Maybe you need to make more fuss of him, reassure him that everything is OK.'

Tears begin to prick behind my eyes. 'I'm not sure I can. I feel so worn down, so trapped.' I pause. 'He still won't let me open any windows. His reaction is too extreme.'

Martin leans towards me, eyes riddled with concern. 'It sounds as if he could benefit from therapy too. Do you want me to talk to him?'

'I'm not sure that's a very good idea. He's very envious of you.'

A long, slow smile. My legs turn to jelly. 'Why?' Martin asks.

My heart stalls. 'Isn't it obvious? He thinks I'm attracted to you.'

A quiver of his eyebrows. 'Why would he think that?'

'No idea,' I say with a smile and a shrug of my shoulders.

Our eyes meet and we both laugh.

226

Phillip

You come out of your session with Martin looking invigorated and flushed, eyes shining enthusiastically. As soon as you get in the car your face closes.

'I don't want to go to the supermarket today,' you announce provocatively. Are you just trying to antagonise me, Faye?

'Let's just go home and talk then,' I say as I start the car engine.

We do need to talk about your attitude to Martin. You stood on the doorstep and put your hand on his arm again as you left, Faye.

'Why did your session run ten minutes over?' I ask as soon as we are standing in the privacy of our hallway.

You frown. 'We were in the middle of something.'

The word *something* punches me in the stomach. I know what happens when you get up to something.

'What exactly do you mean by that?' I demand.

'My sessions with Martin are confidential.'

The band inside my head snaps. 'Your session with Jonah was confidential until he sent me a moving picture.'

Your face becomes ashen. I cannot control myself. I pin you against the wall with my body, grab your wrists and force your arms above your head, heart racing in anger. 'I had to sort Jonah out. If anything like that happens again I'll sort the next one out too. It's in your own interest to learn to behave, Faye.'

'What do you mean, Phillip?'

'I told you. I know what happened between you.'

'No you don't.'

I put back my head and laugh, a harsh, angry, artificial laugh.
'Don't lie to me. I saw the film.'

'The photo was contrived, so was the film.'

'Don't try that. You will never get away with infidelity again.'

227

Faye

Phillip, your words rotate in my head: *I sorted Jonah out and I'll sort the next one out too.* I cannot sleep. I lie in bed remembering your anger. You lie asleep next to me, your face in repose, the face of the man I once knew and loved.

I sorted Jonah out.

What did you do?

The word trimipramine comes into my head. The tricyclic antidepressant stamped all over Jonah's autopsy report. Trimipramine that interacted with zopiclone and caused his death.

And now I am so wired I cannot make myself stay in bed, so I get up, creep downstairs and begin to pace up and down our small sitting room like a cage-crazed polar bear. The police were suspicious of you. They took your computer. I breathe deeply in and out to try and calm myself. They didn't find anything. But you are clever. Did you just cover your tracks with a scrambler? You know more than most people about things like that. You have always been a whizz with computers. The police didn't find anything, I reassure myself. Not a fig. Not a trace. My husband, you must be innocent. I wouldn't have married a man who would plan to kill another human being.

I am pacing around the sitting room, across the dining area. Walking past the table and a memory stirs. Two unmarked packages addressed to you, in brown jiffy bags, arriving when I was about to take Tamsin to school. So busy with the school run, and exercise, and Mimi. A detail so easy to forget, to ignore. I wish I could wind back the clock and touch those packages and open them. Would they tell me the truth? Tell me that my husband was a murderer?

Mind still working in overdrive, I force myself to pad upstairs and lie next to you, sleeping husband, who I pray is innocent. I fall into a restless sleep and know I am dreaming because I feel happy. And happiness doesn't seem real to me these days. Holding hands with Martin, running along Riverside on a soft summer day.

'Martin,' I say. 'Martin.'

I want to tell him something, but my mind is blank and the words won't come. We stop running. He turns towards me and begins to kiss me. His lips feel like gossamer. But something is wrong. He is shaking me.

'Stop it, Martin. Go away.'

I open my eyes. You are shaking me, Phillip. 'What's the matter, Faye?' you ask.

My body is riddled with fear, with panic. 'I was dreaming. That's all.'

'You said Martin's name.'

You are looking at me with such hatred. As if you are a murderer.

'I must have just said something that sounded a bit like that,' I say, scrabbling with my right arm to reach for my iPhone, which is charging at the side of my bed. Fingers trembling, I press camera. It's set on video so I know it will record. If something happens to me I want the world to know how.

'You said his name. What did I tell you, Faye?' I don't reply. 'I warned you. I killed Jonah. I poisoned him with trimipramine. I knew it interacted with the sleeping tablets zopiclone that he often overdosed on. The concoction he gave you wasn't enough to finish anyone off. He was such a plonker he calculated the wrong dose.' There is a pause. 'If you ever sleep with Martin he'll go the same way.'

My heart trembles with fear. 'Phillip, I love you. I'll never sleep with Martin.'

'I wish I could believe you, Faye.'

228

Phillip

Now I have told you what I did, you understand my power. Now I think you will behave. But I still need to watch you carefully, Faye.

229

Faye

Phillip thinks I am with Martin. He is waiting in the car outside. But with Martin's help I have given him the slip; left by the back entrance. I am rushing to the police station, heart racing, panic bubbling in my veins. Into the police station. A queue at the counter. I can't wait, so I push to the front.

'I need to speak to someone senior. Urgently. Right away.'

There is something so needy in my manner, in my laboured breath, my disarrayed state, that I am taken seriously and immediately escorted to an interview room. Within minutes DI Jones is here. I almost feel like hugging him with relief.

'How can I help you, Mrs Baker?'

'I need you to listen to something. I recorded it last night.'

I press the video I have recorded and hand him my iPhone. Your words are so sharp, so clear. They sear into me all over again. I'm living with a murderer. I will never recover from this.

'OK, Mrs Baker. Thank you. You have been very brave taking a recording and coming to see us. We'll need to keep your phone – you'll have to pretend you've lost it. We need to organise a party to come and formally arrest him and re-confiscate his computer. We've obviously not taken a close enough look. Can we get an unmarked car to give you a lift home?'

I feel my body trembling. I am in a cold sweat.

'No. If he sees me in a strange car he'll guess. He thinks I'm in my counselling session now. I need to get back.'

'Will he be at home this afternoon?'

I am trembling so much now that I can hardly speak. I have to push hard for my words to come out. 'Yes. He keeps an eye on me all the time. I'll stay at home so he will too.'

'We'll be around in about an hour.'

'You'll have to tell him I've done this, won't you?' I almost whisper.

'Yes.'

I try to keep calm. I try to breathe deep.

230

Phillip

Where are you, Faye? You are later than ever. I told you not to wear that short skirt and you disobeyed me. Your behaviour is getting worse. I slip out of the car and press down hard on Martin's doorbell. Time to get my wife back. She's mine, not his.

231

Faye

I burst through Martin's back door, out of breath from running.

'Did you do it?' he asks.

I nod my head.

'He's losing it. He's been ringing the bell continually. I'll wait to hear from you later; you'd better get straight out there now.'

Through the kitchen, through the hallway, opening the front door, trying to catch my breath. You are standing on the door-step, red-faced with anger, towering above me. My heart beats against my ribcage like a piston. I try to stretch my lips into a wide smile, but I don't think they move.

'Are you all right, Phillip? You seem very agitated.'

'You've overrun by half an hour,' you say as you grip my arm tightly and escort me towards the car.

'We were doing a relaxation session, pre-prepared, on a recording that took longer than Martin realised.'

'Why didn't you ring me to warn me?' you ask as you push me into the car.

'Please be gentle with me, Phillip.'

You turn the key in the ignition. 'Why didn't you ring me?' you repeat.

'In the middle of a relaxation session? Make a phone call? That's not really how it works.'

Silence coagulates around us as we drive round a few corners home.

Back home, I cannot bear to look at you. Two hours before we need to pick the girls up from school. You always come with me now. The police will be here before that. They promised not to do it in front of the children. These last few hours together are more than I can handle. So much fear. So much regret.

'I've got a headache,' I tell you. 'I'm going upstairs for a nap.'

232

Phillip

Tidying the kitchen, worrying about why you've got a headache when three police cars arrive. The doorbell rings. What has happened? Has there been a local incident? I open the door. DI Jones is standing on my doorstep, mouth in a line, a team of officers behind him.

'Can we come in?' he asks.

'Of course. How can I help?' I ask as he and his team follow me through the hallway into our sitting area.

He stands in front of me, face stony.

'I am arresting you for the murder of Jonah Mathews. You do not have to say anything, but it may harm your defence if you do not mention when questioned something which you later rely on in court. Anything you do say may be given in evidence. Do you understand?'

One of the officers is handling me roughly cuffing my hands behind my back. I am staring at DI Jones, open-mouthed.

'Do you understand?' he repeats.

'Of course I don't fucking understand. Where have you got this from?'

'Your wife. We have a recording of your confession on her phone.'

How could you do this? How could you betray me? Anger incubates inside me. It rises like a volcano, merging with the searing pain of your betrayal.

'So we have a warrant to re-confiscate your electronic devices, which will be more carefully investigated this time, and to search your home,' DI Jones continues.

Judas, Faye. Judas. There is a thin line between love and hate. I feel my emotion, sharp edged and slicing, slicing through that line. If I cannot be with you, no one will. I will kill you and your second lover, as soon as I get out. I've killed once for love. I'll kill for hate this time.

233

Faye

'Are you all right, Faye?' Martin asks gently, putting his arm around me as we sit on the sofa.

'Just about. I've almost stopped trembling. He was shouting as they took him. Shouting about how he's going to kill me when he gets out.'

'That won't do him any good. The police will have taken good note of that. He'll be banged up for ever if they think he's going to attempt murder as soon as he gets out.'

'I hope so.' I shake my head. 'I never thought I'd say that about my husband. He was always so stable. So steady.' I pause. 'If only I hadn't made that mistake with Jonah our lives would all be so different now.'

'The way Jonah and Phillip have behaved was hardly your fault.'

'But I was the catalyst. The trigger.'

'Not intentionally.' There is a pause. 'How are the girls?'

'Fine. I just told them Phillip was away on a business trip.'

'You'll have to tell them. They might hear something at school.'

'I know. I just couldn't face it today. How do you tell a six-year-old and a four-year-old that their father is a murderer? The police found some more trimipramine hidden under our bed. They think he was contemplating doing it again.'

Martin bends towards me and kisses me. This is not a dream. His lips do feel like gossamer. After a while I force myself to pull away.

'After all that has happened, I need freedom,' I tell him.

'I know. And I need freedom too. I promise you I do not want to tie you down.'

I lean towards him and begin to kiss him again.

THE END

Acknowledgements

First, I would like to thank my agent Ger Nicholl, who believed in my writing and made everything possible in the first place. Next up, my fantastic editor Phoebe Morgan, who it is a great privilege to work with. The supportive team behind me at Avon-HarperCollins. My publicists Ruth Cairns and Sabah Khan. My friend Charles who once again acted as my police advisor. And all my chums, both within and outside my family, who give me much needed solace, friendship and fun. You know who you are, and how much I value you.

Last, but by no means least, my husband Richard, who deserves a special mention. He is my long suffering first reader, dropping everything to read whatever I ask, whenever I ask. And he listens to me endlessly droning on about my plots and ideas. As I draft these acknowledgements we are about to celebrate our thirty-fifth wedding anniversary. Long suffering indeed.

She's your twin sister . . .
she's your enemy.

The *Sunday Times* bestseller.
Available in all good
bookshops now.

He's not your husband.
He's hers.

The number 1 bestseller. Available in
all good bookshops now.